# CRUISE CONTROL

A MIAMI JONES FLORIDA MYSTERY

AJ STEWART

Jacaranda Drive Publishing

Los Angeles, California

www.jacarandadrive.com



Cover artwork by Streetlight Graphics

ISBN-10: 1-945741-14-7

ISBN-13: 978-1-945741-14-2

*For the young, and young at heart.*

*And Heather.*

# CHAPTER ONE

Ron sank back into my office sofa, looking relaxed in a pair of Nantucket red trousers and a blue shirt. The fine winter sun shone in through the window, the shadow from the palm outside playing across his sun-splotched face. I sat at my desk, chair leaned back, boat shoes up where a normal person might have had a computer.

"A cruise?" I said.

"That's right."

"You need a few days off to go on a cruise?"

"Exactly."

"Is this a sailing thing?"

"No, Miami. It's a cruise. On a big ship."

"So you're not crew."

"No. All good times, no responsibilities."

"Is the Lady Cassandra aware you're going on a cruise?"

"She's the whole reason I'm going."

"I didn't figure her for the cruise type."

"What's the cruise type look like?"

I shrugged. I had never been on a cruise ship so I couldn't really say, but my impression was that it had something to do with enjoying buffets, and Cassandra wasn't a buffet kind of gal. She was Palm Beach old money, the kind of person who preferred her food to come to her. I couldn't blame her for that. I rarely felt the need to tend the grill at Longboard Kelly's. Rarely.

"Why a cruise?"

"It's a Super Bowl thing."

"You and the Lady Cassandra are going on a Super Bowl-thing cruise?"

Ron smiled and sipped water from a bottle.

"Have I fallen down the rabbit hole?"

"No. It's not your usual football crowd. It's more about the movers and shakers of football. The owners, the network people. There's going to be art auctions and dinners with Hall of Famers, that sort of thing."

"I still don't see it as Cassandra's bag of marbles," I said. "So what gives?"

"A lot of her friends are going, the Palm Beach set."

"Still not seeing it."

Ron screwed the cap back on his water bottle and sat up from his reclined position.

"I'm going to propose."

"Propose what?"

Ron raised an eyebrow.

Then the penny dropped. For me. Everyone else on the planet had gotten there eons ago.

"Marriage?"

Ron nodded and grinned like a school boy.

I said nothing more. The word on the tip of my tongue was *seriously?* But I figured that wasn't the politic thing to say. It would sound like I thought Ron asking Cassandra to marry him was a bad idea, and nothing could have been further from the truth. Ron and Cassandra had found each other while he and I were working a case at Palm Beach's grand dame of hotels, The Breakers. They had both been around the block a time or two, and they were different, to be sure. Ron had an impish grin and a raconteur's charm, and Cassandra had the grace of Diana Spencer. They had made each other smile from the get-go. And I knew Ron. He didn't do alone very well. His wasn't a solo voyage. He had been married twice—once well, once poorly—and had also been in a long-term relationship with the most amazing sprite of a woman, who had passed from this earth far too early. Ron was a romantic, pure and simple.

The hesitation was all me. I wasn't sure why. On the face of it, I suspected I couldn't see the point. Ron and Cassandra were both of a certain age. Cassandra herself was a widow. They were happy as they were. They weren't going to have a family and send kids to school. They weren't going to buy a home—they lived in Cassandra's Palm Beach apartment overlooking the Atlantic Ocean. Marriage wasn't going to change anything. But Ron looked giddy at the idea and that was good enough for me.

"Congratulations."

Ron shrugged. "Not yet."

"And when is this all happening?"

"This coming weekend."

"This weekend?"

"Yes."

"It's not the Super Bowl this weekend. It's Pro Bowl weekend," I said.

"I guess a lot of the folks on the cruise will be at the Super Bowl next weekend, so they're doing it a week earlier."

"Nice work if you can get it. Go on a cruise and then hang around in Miami for a week."

"I guess if you owned a team it would be considered work."

"I guess. But there's something I don't get. Why are you asking me for time off?"

"Isn't that what people do?"

"I don't know what people do. But that's not what you and I do. Never has been. You need time, you take time."

"Thanks, Miami. But the thing is, there's a client."

"What client?"

"We're seeing him in about five minutes."

"We are?"

Ron nodded.

"How do you know?"

"Because he made an appointment."

"We do appointments? Like, here in the office?"

"When the occasion calls for it."

"Huh. I always thought our clients tracked us down at Longboard's."

"I grant you, that does happen a lot."

"But this client is coming into the office? Very professional. So who is he?"

"His name is Fred Connors. I guess he heard around the traps what I do, because he cornered me at a party last night. He said he had something delicate to investigate and asked if he could make an appointment to discuss it."

"Not an insurance thing? I don't do insurance things, Ron."

"I didn't get that impression."

The muted noise of distant downtown traffic eased through the open window, until finally we heard someone coming in through the front door and the mumbled dialog with our office manager, Lizzy. Then Lizzy stuck her head in and announced Mr. Connors.

The man who walked in was preceded by an aroma that I thought to be distinctly English, but I couldn't say why for sure. Ron and I both stood and the man's gaze swept across me and onto Ron, who nodded. They shook hands.

"Ron, thanks for seeing me."

"Of course, Fred." Ron turned to me. "This is Miami Jones."

The man offered me his hand. "Frederick Connors," he said.

He was right. In this world, there are Freds and there are Fredericks, and despite what Ron said, this guy was most definitely a Frederick. He was average height, about five-ten, and a little wider around the belt line than his physician probably advocated. His gray suit was the kind of expensive material that shone at certain angles, and he wore a pink, French-collared shirt with no tie, open at the neck, offering up a little tuft of black hair below his Adam's apple. His pocket square was cut from the same cloth as his shirt.

I offered him a seat. Ron took the other visitor's chair. I looked at Connors' face. He was a well-groomed guy. I often let my stubble grow, out of laziness more than style, but I never let it go to full beard. Besides getting too itchy, it seemed to require more maintenance than keeping no beard at all, unless you went for the lumberjack look, and that was no kind of look for the South Florida heat. But Frederick Connors clearly didn't mind the upkeep. His beard was black as coal and trimmed to perfection. There were no stray hairs, the edges as sharp as cut Astro-Turf. The hair on his head was thick and black, too, and contained some kind of product that would likely keep it in place during gale-force winds.

"Mr. Connors," I said. "Ron tells me you have something delicate you wish to discuss."

"Yes, Mr. Jones," he said. "Most delicate."

I thought I caught a hint of an accent, perhaps Middle Eastern in some way, but it was so refined that it might not have been there at all.

Connors hesitated and then glanced at Ron. "You are married to Lady Cassandra, yes?"

"Not married," said Ron. "Not right now."

"But you are together."

"Yes, sir."

Connors nodded to himself like he was reconsidering the entire thing.

"Is there a problem, Fred?" Ron asked.

"Lady Cassandra is an acquaintance of my wife."

"I'm sure," said Ron. "Cassandra seems to know everyone on the island. Who is your wife?"

"Ana."

"I'm not sure we're acquainted."

"She runs a jewelry store," said Connors. "*Anastasia's.*"

Ron nodded. "Oh, that Ana."

"That Ana?" I asked.

"Anastasia's is a Palm Beach institution," said Ron. "Anyone who is anyone in Palm Beach gets their jewelry from Anastasia's."

"That right?"

Ron saw I wasn't convinced. "It's on Worth Avenue."

I gave him my mildly impressed face. Worth Avenue was the ritzy shopping district in Palm Beach. I didn't get there very often. Ron gave up and looked back to Connors.

"What is your hesitation, Fred?" Ron asked.

"As you say, Ron, everyone knows everyone on the island."

Ron nodded again. "Would you prefer to speak in confidence alone with Miami? I'm happy to step out."

Connors frowned and shook his head. "No, sir."

Ron said, "I can assure you, Fred, that anything you say here, stays here. I have many clients on the island, and I do not discuss their matters with Cassandra or anyone else."

It was true. There was no such thing as PI–client privilege. We weren't lawyers. But there was a code of ethics, and there was common decency. Besides, spreading your clients' news all over town was the fast track to having no clients at all. Ron took his position of trust seriously. He would have been a good priest. Except for the drinking and the eye for the ladies. But people trusted him. He was discreet. Me, not so much. But I didn't know that many people in Palm Beach who I wanted to tell anything to anyway.

Connors took a deep breath and looked at me and then at Ron.

"My wife is having an affair."

I said nothing. Neither did Ron. It was a grave pronouncement and deserved some consideration. Ron swiveled around and grabbed a bottle of water from the bar fridge and handed it to Frederick. He took it but didn't open it.

"Tell me your story," I said.

"I don't know where to begin."

"At the end. Who is the guy she's seeing? Or woman?"

"It's a man," said Connors. "I don't know his name. I don't know who he is."

"Okay. When did this matter come to your attention?"

"I don't know. Maybe a few weeks ago."

"How?"

Connors made to take a deep breath but didn't. He was a measured guy. "You see a man once, you think nothing of it. You see him twice you think maybe he is a customer or a business associate. But I kept seeing him. Over and over. In places where I wouldn't see him if he were a customer or an associate."

"Such as?"

"First at the store. Then at the golf club. Then again at the store. I followed her one time. She was supposed to be at a lunch with the girls, at The Breakers."

"And he was there?"

"Yes. I suspect he had taken a room."

"I see."

"But the last time was at home."

"Your home?"

Connors nodded deliberately. "Yes. I was supposed to be up in Cocoa Beach, on business."

"What do you do, Mr. Connors?"

"I run a franchise business. A chain of fast-casual restaurant outlets."

Fast casual wasn't my idea of food. I didn't really know what it meant exactly, and I certainly leaned toward the casual side of things, but I knew I preferred to take my food slowly rather than fast. I preferred to do most things slowly. I reserved fast for freeway driving and pitching.

"So you weren't in Cocoa Beach?"

"I was. But I came back early."

"And you saw him, this Guy X?"

"Yes. He was leaving my house."

"You saw him in your house?"

"Yes. Well, not inside. But I was driving down the street and I saw him come out of our front gate. He looked around like he was up to something."

"What did you do?"

"I pulled over to the side of the road." He took a phone from his inside jacket pocket. "And I took this."

He turned the screen toward me. On it was a photograph. A mid-distance shot of a Palm Beach street. This was not some suburban subdivision. There were no sidewalks, no open lawns. High fences and hedges channeled the eye toward the man in the picture. It was no portrait, and he was a good distance away, but it was clear he had heavyset features and dark eyes. He didn't look a million miles away from Frederick Connors himself, if Connors shaved the beard. Perhaps that was the point. Perhaps his wife had an eye for a certain look.

I took a good look at the picture, trying to commit as much

of the face as I could to memory, and then leaned back in my chair.

"What is it you would like us to do, Mr. Connors?"

"Find out who he is. Confirm what they're doing."

"We could do that," I said. "But first let me ask you, have you spoken to your wife about this?"

"Asked her if she's having an affair? No, I want pictures before I do that. I need to consolidate my position."

"Meaning?"

"Meaning, if she is planning to run off with this man, I need to make sure I have evidence in case I need it."

I took a long slow breath. I wasn't a fan of the peeping Tom type of work. It didn't sit right. It wasn't so much that people didn't have a right to know, or that they didn't deserve the truth. It was more that I always felt like by the time someone wanted pictures of events, those events had already been preordained. The end was going to be ugly regardless.

I looked at Ron and he shrugged.

"Okay, Mr. Connors. We'll look into it for you. I'll just need all the relevant addresses—your home, your wife's work, any other places they are likely to meet."

"Oh, I know where they'll meet. And when."

"You do? Where?"

"This weekend. There's a cruise."

I glanced at Ron again. He wasn't shrugging or nodding. But his eyebrows were up near his hairline.

"A cruise, you say?"

"Yes. It's part of the whole Super Bowl circus."

"And your wife is going on this cruise?"

"That's right."

"And this man, Guy X."

"I don't know for sure. But it makes sense."

"Can I ask why you are not going on the cruise with your wife?"

"I don't cruise."

"I don't tango, but I still dance when my fiancée asks me."

"My wife didn't ask me. It's not a vacation. She's there in a professional capacity."

"Doing what?"

"They're having an auction. Jewelry, rings, art, that sort of thing. My wife has created some rings for the occasion."

"So it's work. It's still a cruise though, isn't it? She surely can't be working all the time. Couldn't you hang by the bar while she's doing her thing?"

"I don't cruise."

"You mentioned. What does that mean?"

"I don't like cruise ships. I don't like water. I don't swim."

"You don't have to swim, Mr. Connors. That's what the boat is for."

"I mean, I can't swim. Being on the water makes me, well, apprehensive."

I nodded. I could see that. I swim well, so boats don't faze me. But then again, I can't fly and I have traveled by aircraft more than once.

"I understand, Mr. Connors. You're right, it does provide ample opportunity. There's just one problem. They'll be on a cruise ship. I won't."

I considered briefly the idea of dropping Ron into the slot, but I didn't want to ruin his big moment with the Lady Cassandra. He'd gone so far as to ask for time off, for crying out loud.

"I can get you on the boat," Connors said.

"You can?"

"Yes. The rings that my wife is offering for auction. They're expensive. I can get you on board as security."

I thought about it. I wasn't overjoyed by the idea. My

fiancée, Danielle, had finished her stint at the FDLE Special Agent Academy and had gone out of state for a while. She was getting back within the hour, so I didn't fancy running off on some ship of fools with my telephoto lens.

"You said you have a fiancée," said Connors. "You're not married?"

"No," I said.

"Well, why don't you take her? It would be a double berth cabin anyway."

I glanced at Ron. He was grinning like a lunatic.

# CHAPTER TWO

"You boys better be back for the big game," said Muriel from behind the bar at Longboard Kelly's.

"Why, you got something planned?" asked Ron, sipping on his beer.

"Only the usual. We'll wheel out a couple TVs into the courtyard, Mick'll make some of his fish dip."

"Reason enough," I said. "This thing is just for a long weekend. We'll be back on Monday at some point."

"Back from where?" I heard from behind me.

I spun on my stool under the palapa as Danielle came striding across the courtyard. Business was brisk. Every table was full of folks enjoying drinks under beer-branded umbrellas. That was the season in South Florida for you. Folks descended on Florida like frat boys on a keg and pretended like they were locals for a few months, prior to bugging out before it got too hot. Danielle glided around the tables to me.

"Back from where?" she asked again, giving me a kiss. "Where are you off to?"

"How do you feel about a cruise?" I asked.

"A cruise? Like on a ship?"

"The very same."

"Sounds a bit dull."

"But that was when we weren't on it."

She smiled. "You do have quite the opinion of yourself today."

"It's like our back patio. Drinks, lounge chairs and a water view."

"Where's this coming from?"

"A new client. Thinks his wife is cheating on him."

"Grim."

"True enough."

She slid onto a stool and Muriel dropped a vodka tonic in front of her.

"You look like you need this," Muriel said.

Danielle gave a slow nod. "Thanks." She took a long drink.

"How was Arizona?" I asked.

"Kind of like Florida. Lots of people escaping somewhere cold."

"How's your dad?"

"He was good. You know. Not happy to see me there at first. But then he was good."

"I'm sure he was happy to see you, even if he wasn't happy to be seen."

"Something like that," she said, sipping her drink. "So you're off on a cruise to follow an adulterer?"

"Adulteress, I think they call them."

"Only if *they* were born before Eleanor Roosevelt."

"You want to come? Might be fun."

"Sounds like a hoot."

"We haven't had a vacation in a while."

"Jamaica," she said. "And that went well."

"Ron and Cassandra are going."

"Really?"

Ron smiled and stuck his beer glass to his mouth.

"It's a sort of football-themed thing," I said. "Famous ex-players, team owners, various hangers-on down here for the Super Bowl."

"Sounds like a frat party for the jet set."

"Exactly. And on a client's dime."

"Well, I don't have my office assignment yet."

"Still?"

"They delayed it because I asked for the time to go to Arizona. I should find out in the next few days."

"So an ocean voyage then?"

"You're not going to be lurking behind some woman the entire time, are you?"

"Only you."

Muriel replaced my beer. "How can you refuse an offer like that?"

"Sadly, I can't," Danielle said.

Ron finished his beer and slipped off his stool. "I best be getting home to the Lady Cassandra. I'll be seeing you two on board the mighty *Canaveral Star*."

We wished Ron a good evening and settled back into our drinks.

"So where's the ship going?" Danielle asked.

"The Bahamas. The cruise line has a private island, apparently. Who knew?"

Muriel wiped the bar in front of me. "Must be nice to be able to drop everything to go on a cruise."

"This is work." I winked. "Besides, I didn't have a lot else on. Just—"

"Problem?" Danielle asked.

I patted my pockets like an old man who had lost his glasses. "No problem. I was going to visit Lenny. I'd better let Lucas know I won't be there this week."

I slipped off my stool and wandered to the rear of the court-yard, next to the shark-bitten surfboard, where the cell phone reception was best.

"Lucas," I said when he picked up.

"Miami, how's tricks, mate?"

"Looking up. I got a case I need to work tomorrow, so I won't be able to make it down to see Lenny."

"Yeah, no problems, mate. I can't make it this week either. Gotta head offshore."

"Offshore?"

"Yeah, one of our well-to-do clients took his fancy motor cruiser over to Bimini, but it broke down on him."

"And he's stuck in Bimini?"

"Nah, he chartered a chopper to fly home, but his boat's still out there, so I gotta go out and fix her and bring her back."

"Well, I'll wave as I go past. We're going on a cruise."

"I thought you said you were workin'?"

"Oh, I am. Guy thinks his wife's having an affair and she'll be on the cruise."

"Wretched business."

"That it is."

"You going to Freeport?"

"Actually, I don't know where we're going. A private island, that's all I know."

"Yeah, the cruise lines have bought up a few cays out between the Berrys and Abaco. Probably one of those."

"Sounds about right. It's a Super Bowl thing."

"That circus? You should see down here. Banners and signs everywhere. You'd swear folks in Miami actually cared a damn about football."

"They care about the money."

"That they do. What boat are you on?"

"*Canaveral Star*, I believe."

"Oh, yeah. She's a new one. Supposed to be pretty nice. Least you won't have far to go to get on board."

"Couple hours," I said. "Less, if it were you driving."

"Nah, she's not out of Canaveral. She's out of the Port of Palm Beach."

"Palm Beach? I can practically see that place from my backyard and there's never anything but freighters."

"They're trying to make a boutique port for short cruises, weekend getaways, that sort of thing."

"Why call it *Canaveral Star* when it goes out of Palm Beach?"

"Some marketing genius at work."

"False advertising if you ask me. Thanks for the heads-up. That would have been a very annoying drive home."

"Not a problem. Enjoy the cruise. The weather's in your favor. Conditions look good. A light southerly for the next few days. A fella could kayak across the Gulf Stream if he were predisposed to such malarkey. Cruise ships don't really care either way."

"Perhaps we can go see Lenny next week?"

"Sounds good. I shouldn't be more than a day or two, depending if I need parts. I'll give you a ring. Sail safe."

"Right back at ya."

I ended the call and then sent a text to Ron to confirm that our ship was indeed leaving from Palm Beach, which he confirmed within seconds. It was an odd embarkation point, given the Pro Bowl was in Orlando and Port Canaveral was only about forty-five minutes away from there. Perhaps the Palm Beach jet set didn't like to schlep up I-95. Either way, it worked for me.

I wandered back to the bar. Danielle had finished her drink and sat watching the breeze blow across the umbrellas in the courtyard. I stood by my stool, looking at her. She was miles away. I wondered if she was thinking about Arizona, or maybe her imminent posting to a location yet to be named. Maybe she was thinking about the cruise. Then she snapped back and gave me the half smile that sets me off every time.

"Penny for your thoughts?" I asked.

"Not sure they're worth a penny."

"I'll pay whatever the asking price is."

She slipped off her stool. "Finish your drink. We need to get home and pack."

"It's a cruise. I'd say it's come as you are."

She smiled again. "Sometimes you really have no clue."

"I know. That's why I've got you."

# CHAPTER THREE

WE WOKE THE NEXT MORNING TO THE FAMILIAR ROUSING sound of hammers. The Intracoastal had swelled during a recent hurricane and surged up across our back lawn, running like the proverbial bulls through my rancher-style house. Most of the mini mansions on the water were back to normal within days, but many of the houses like mine that lay further into the island were still stuck in a state of disrepair. Perhaps not everyone knew a guy who knew guy, like I did.

I wandered out of the bedroom in my running shorts and found a guy nailing trim onto my kitchen cabinets.

"Morning, Paco," I said, stepping around him to get at the blender.

"Morning Mr. Miami. You like?" He paused to show off the crown molding that he had installed around the cabinet tops. The cabinets were white with a beadboard look, and the trim made the whole thing look like a million bucks. Which was about nine hundred and ninety-nine thousand more than it was before.

"You do great work, Paco. A true craftsman."

He gave me an aw-shucks kind of shrug and returned to his

work. It was fine work. The entire house looked like a magazine shoot. The orange Formica counters were gone, replaced by what I was informed was a tasteful quartz countertop, and the shag carpet in the lounge had been sent to the great seventies dumpster in the sky and replaced by a tile that looked like driftwood.

Before this, I'd never had any kind of renovation done, and I had no plans to go through it again. The whole process had been like a time warp. After the hurricane, my friend Sal Mondavi had connected me with a contractor who owed him a favor. Danny Rucci and his guys stormed in and demolished the interior within two days. At that point I thought the entire rebuild would take a week. Then the rough work got done—reframing, fixing the foundation and rebuilding the subfloor, drywalling and electric and plumbing. Then time slowed as we waited for flooring and cabinetry. When the flooring and cabinetry arrived time slowed further as we waited for the guys to return from the other jobs they had moved on to—and there was no shortage of those. When the flooring finally went in, Danielle and I were able to move back inside from the tent that we had been sleeping in. I missed the lapping of the Intracoastal waters but not the bugs.

Once the cabinets were finished and the final drywall was installed and all the holes were patched up and painted over, the whole thing looked close to done. Close, but no cigar. Then came the finish work. Finish work is the black hole of home renovation, a place where time seems to come to a complete standstill even though much work appears to be happening. It was that way for a reason. Even for skilled craftsmen, the finish work—the trim, the molding, the fixtures, the tiling and grouting —takes time. It's the stuff you'll see everyday, and it's the stuff that sticks out if it isn't done right. And after a hurricane, when work is plentiful and homeowners are practically throwing money at tradesmen, it is common for the finish work to be rushed and done poorly, so the men can move onto the next desperate chump.

But this was not the case for tradesmen who worked for friends of Sal Mondavi. Like most of us, Sal was both an angel and devil, more of both than anyone I knew. He had helped so many at-risk kids get on the straight and narrow—Danny Rucci included—he was practically a one-man Boys and Girls Club. But he was also a made man, connected to all the wrong people in New York. So it was possible that the tradesmen knew of Sal's generosity and his wrath, or maybe Danny Rucci knew it and would pass said wrath onto his guys if they did poor work for one of Sal's friends. On the other hand, maybe they were just the kinds of guys who took pride in their work. Either way, they were taking their sweet time. I thought Paco had moved in. A dab of spackle here, a dob of stain there. It had looked done for weeks, but in Paco's mind it was still the scribbled outline underneath the *Mona Lisa*. But it did look good.

"How much longer, you think?" I asked him after the noise of the blender died down.

Paco shrugged. "Coupla days."

I nodded and took a smoothie back into Danielle. She had a small bag open and was tossing up between swimsuits. She took a sip of the smoothie.

"Paco here?" she asked.

"Yeah."

"You ask him how long until he's done?"

"Yeah."

"A couple of days?"

"Yeah."

Danielle nodded and pulled a black dress from the wardrobe. It was an all-purpose kind of thing, suitable to wear over a bathing suit to the pool or to cocktails with the captain in the evening. If they did cocktails. I may have just picked that up from *The Love Boat*.

I threw some shorts and shirts in a bag and I was done. Danielle was making me wear long pants to the ship, so I was already good for those.

"You need a jacket," she said.

"I don't get cold."

"Not that kind of jacket. Don't you have a suit jacket or a blazer?"

"You know how many suits I own."

"I do. Two. One for weddings and funerals, and your tux. Pack your tux."

"This isn't the Orient Express."

She put her hand on my cheek. "I just like seeing you in it."

It wasn't a good reason but it was a reason I couldn't rebuke, so I folded the suit bag containing everything I needed for it—right down to the socks and shoes—on top of my overnight bag.

I put our luggage in the back of my Cadillac SUV. It looked more like a soccer mom's car than any kind of Caddy, but that seemed to be the way of the world. We were all desperate to be unique in a way that was completely homogenous.

When I got back inside Danielle had gone to stand on the back patio. The brick pavers were gone, replaced by sandstone that looked like it belonged at The Breakers and that I hadn't quite grown to love. The water was calm and the same color as the sky. Danielle had wrapped her arms around herself as she stared at the water, or something much further beyond. I put my hand on her shoulder.

"You okay?"

"Sure," she said.

"You don't have to come on this thing, you know."

"I know. But what else will I do? Sit here and listen to Paco hammering away? It'll do me good to get away."

"If you're sure."

Danielle shrugged. It wasn't a sign of being sure of anything, but then I wasn't expecting that.

"Well, let's go find out what's so good about a floating bar," I said, leading her back inside and out to the Caddy.

I didn't lock the door to the house. Paco was still working and would probably still be there when we got back.

## CHAPTER FOUR

The Port of Palm Beach was a circus. Crammed into the space between Route 1 and the Intracoastal on the mainland side, It wasn't a large facility, and though the cruise terminal looked nice, it felt like an afterthought. I knew the port well so I wasn't surprised by the rows and rows of orange and blue shipping containers that dominated the landscape. What did surprise me was how many people were waiting on the valet parking. I'm not really a valet kind of guy. I'm perfectly healthy, so I'm happy enough parking my own vehicle and walking to wherever I need to be. But there was no self-parking at the port, and the NFL types were like Palm Beach types in their aversion to parking their own rides, so the line of cars was like Black Friday at Walmart.

Upon discovering the daily rate for parking, I wished we'd taken a cab, but it was all on the client's dime so I wasn't about to waste too much energy on it. I figured things would look up once we reached the cruise terminal. Instead we got into another line to deposit our limited luggage. Though I was perfectly happy to carry my own duffel, apparently that was not the done thing.

We were supposed to have printed some kind of tags for our baggage so the crew knew where to deliver them. We hadn't, since twenty-four hours previous we had never even heard of the *Canaveral Star*. With more huffing and puffing than I thought the job warranted, a young guy in a shirt and tie that made him look like an airline pilot, printed out a couple tags and looped them through the handles on our bags.

After that, we joined another line that appeared to be heading in the general direction of the dock. There were a lot of well-dressed people. I recognized a couple of NFL team owners, a handful of former players, and some media personalities. They were all in suits or blazers. There were also a good number of folks in palm-tree-print shirts like me, and more than a few in tank tops and shorts. It was quite the eclectic crowd, and I was impressed by the egalitarian nature of the boarding process. I didn't see a first-class line, an express line or any other kind of line for the well heeled and well traveled. Perhaps everyone here fit that qualification so the express line became moot. But I liked the idea that we were all in it together. It seemed a very ship-like way to start a voyage.

What I did see was a lot of sky-blue-colored canvas travel bags. The kind of things they used to give out when I was a kid, when flying somewhere was a big, expensive deal, not Greyhound in the air. My father had one with the Pan Am logo on the side. He had carried his lunch to work in it for years. I wasn't sure if he did it to stop the academics at Yale from looking down on him for being a lowly janitor, but I was pretty certain he had never flown Pan Am or anyone else. But here everyone seemed to have one. They were too big to carry easily and too small to fit more than a woman's cardigan and a hardback novel, so I didn't see the point. But they all had them and I didn't.

I had the photo that Frederick Connors had taken of Guy X on my phone, and I had taken a good hard look at it to imprint the general impression of it on my memory. It wasn't a clear enough shot to define the guy's face well, so I searched the crowd for a sense of him. He was a dark-featured guy, maybe late thirties or early forties. Quite a bit younger than Frederick. As I ran my eye across the men, I dismissed anyone older or balder or fairer. There were a few dark-haired guys but none of them had the jawline or deep-set eyes I was looking for.

Our line inched forward until we reached a banner that was set up like the advertising backing behind an athlete when they were interviewed after a game. But instead of logos for sports apparel or deodorant, this banner featured the cruise line's branding. Danielle was directed to stand in front of it and a perky young girl with a large camera took her photo. She then shuffled Danielle onward and pulled me in with an energetic smile.

"Sir, stand right on the dot for me," she said, dropping in behind her camera.

I frowned. "Why?"

"Big smile!"

"Why?"

She popped back out from behind the camera. It was considerably bigger than her head.

"You don't want to look grumpy on your ship pass, do you? Now, big smile!"

She dropped back in behind the camera and I dropped the frown but didn't quite manage the big smile. Or any other kind of smile. The flash burst and the picture was taken and the camera girl ushered me away to keep the line moving. I joined Danielle at a table where another young woman was producing things that looked like hotel keycards. A little printer was pushing the plastic cards out. The girl at the table pulled out a card and looked at it.

"Ms. Castle," she said. "This is your ship pass. How would you like to fund it?"

"Fund it?" Danielle asked. "What do you mean?"

"The ship is cashless. All payments are made via your ship pass. It acts as both your ID and your payment for incidentals."

Danielle looked at me, which I thought was a good way to both avoid and answer the question at hand.

"I'll take care of it," I said to the girl. She nodded and then turned back to the little printer from which she pulled out another plastic keycard. She looked at it and then at me.

"Mr. Jones," she said.

"That's me."

I handed her my credit card. She took it, processed a transaction for an amount she didn't care to share, and then handed it back with a smile. Then she slipped the ship pass into a clear plastic pocket attached to an orange lanyard with *Canaveral Star* printed on it, and handed it to me. She then did the same for Danielle.

"Enjoy your cruise," she said as she turned to the next person in line.

Following the lead of the people in front of us, Danielle hung her lanyard around her neck. I wrapped mine around the card and put it in my pocket. I'm not a lanyard kind of guy, and I prefer not to wear ID around my neck. I generally don't want people to know who I am until I'm good and ready. We moved slowly toward the exit. I kept an eye out for Guy X but didn't see anyone who fit the bill.

Now that we were properly identified and branded, we were allowed to wind our way out of the terminal and onto the dock. The *Canaveral Star* sat moored beside us, and we got our first proper glimpse.

And it was huge. Ron had told me for a fact it wasn't large as far as cruise ships were concerned. The Port of Palm Beach was targeting the short-haul market—two-to-five-day trips around the nearby Bahamas—and leaving the longer tours to the bigger facility up at Port Canaveral. Ron had said the *Star* held up to two thousand passengers, and I believed it. I craned my neck to look up at the top, way above. It looked like a massive apartment building had been built out over the water. It was high and wide and solid. The notion of a prison crossed my mind, and I tried to brush it away. It really didn't seem to be the right way to start a vacation.

But I wasn't on vacation. My eyes drifted down from the upper decks to the gangway by which passengers were embarking. It was there I saw a familiar face.

Frederick Connors. My client—who didn't swim and didn't cruise as a result—was walking up the gangway. He glanced down across the dock and our eyes met. What he would have seen in my eyes was surprise. I saw no such thing, but then, he was expecting me to be there. He might have offered a soft nod, the sort of thing people who watch too many movies think spies do. Then his attention was taken by someone handing him a fruity drink as he stepped onto the ship.

"You okay?" asked Danielle. "You look a million miles away."

"Just saw my client."

"I didn't think he was going to be here."

"Me neither. What say we get on this tub and find a drink?"

"There are many reasons why I love you Miami Jones, and that is definitely one of them."

We did the slow shuffle onto the gangway and up onto the ship. We stepped into a large foyer that might have been stolen from a mid-level business hotel. We weren't anywhere near the top floor—or as they all seemed to prefer to call it—the deck. A man dressed in a white uniform offered us a choice of fruity blue drinks or champagne. Danielle always went with the fruity drinks. I never ate or drank anything blue, so I took some bubbles.

A crew member wearing Bermuda shorts and a shirt with little ships offered to help us locate our cabin. I wanted his shirt, but didn't see much point in finding our cabin. They had taken my bags so I had nothing to deposit and therefore no reason to go to our room. But it seemed to be the thing to do. He looked at Danielle's ID.

"Ah, deck three. Elevators straight through the foyer here, and you'll be toward the stern. Enjoy!"

I drained my champagne and handed him the flute. He gave me a look that suggested holding empty glassware wasn't part of his job description and I gave him a look that suggested it wasn't part of mine either. He lost. We moved in the general direction of the elevators. Then I stopped.

Frederick Connors was standing off to the side of the foyer, in the mouth of a corridor than ran along the side of the ship. He wore a blue blazer and a white shirt with a white pocket square, and was holding one of those blue travel bags. He watched me but he didn't motion me over. I went anyway.

"Mr. Connors," I said. "I wasn't expecting to see you."

"I wasn't expecting to be here, Mr. Jones."

"I thought you didn't cruise."

"I don't. I can assure you I don't like being here one iota."

"So why are you here?"

He glanced beside me at Danielle. "Hello," he said. "I'm Frederick Connors."

"Mr. Connors, this is my fiancée, Danielle Castle."

Danielle offered her hand and gave him a good grip the way law enforcement types do.

"Mr. Connors," she said.

"Enchanté," he replied. For a second I thought he might kiss her hand like she was Maid Marian or something. That would not have gone well for him so I was thankful he dropped her hand and turned to me.

"You didn't tell me your fiancée was such a beauty, Mr. Jones."

"No I didn't, Mr. Connors. So why are you here?"

"I guess I thought I should be here."

"I'm not so sure that's a great idea."

"I can't imagine why."

I could imagine a thousand reasons why, starting with the idea that he didn't like being on water let alone open ocean, and ending with the idea that if I discovered firm evidence of his wife's infidelity he might go postal and do something incredibly stupid.

"Mr. Connors, if you are here, do you really think that your wife will do anything? It makes it most unlikely."

"Mr. Jones, I disagree. I think it makes it more likely. And it decreases the time and place. It could only happen when she knows I am not around. Like if I take a massage, for example."

I took a breath. I didn't like it, but he was paying the bills.

"All right, Mr. Connors. But if I can't do my job because you've spooked the game, I will spend the rest of the cruise at the bar and send you the tab. Do I make myself clear?"

"I won't be in the way, Mr. Jones. I assure you. And I can introduce you to my wife. As the security personnel for her jewels."

Connors told me the auction was setting up in the second ballroom. I wondered how many ballrooms a ship needed. We agreed to meet there after we had settled in. Connors turned down the corridor toward the forward elevators. Danielle and I made our way to the elevators in the middle of the ship.

The cars were glass enclosures on either side of an atrium open to a skylight roof several floors above. The entire space felt like a high end mall on Christmas Eve, and not just because of the decor. The area was packed with waiting people. The four elevators were working overtime, but they couldn't keep up with the flow of people coming aboard.

Danielle elbowed me in the ribs and directed us away from the throng toward the empty stairs. I liked taking stairs. It's the taking of stairs over elevators that allows me to enjoy the hospitality of Longboard Kelly's as often as I do and still keep up with my extremely fit fiancée.

We paused at the stairs and looked up, and then at the plaque on the wall that told us we were on deck five.

"Did he say deck three?" I asked.

"He did," said Danielle.

So we went down. The stairs were wide and bright and open, so it didn't feel like we were descending into the bowels of the vessel. But then we hit deck four and noted that the open feeling of the atrium was gone. The ceilings were lower and corridors split left and right toward rooms. We kept going down.

Deck three was like we had descended into the belly of the beast. Although the walls and the carpet were bright and light in an attempt to perk things up, the low ceilings and mechanical hum made it feel like the entrance to the engine room. There was a maid's cart down at the far end of the corridor, which was the only suggestion that passengers were supposed to be down here. We checked the signage and Danielle's ID card and confirmed our cabin number. Then we set off toward the aft end of the ship.

Our cabin was the last in the corridor. Next stop was probably a life raft. Danielle used her card to open the door. I stepped in behind her and stopped. I stopped because there was nowhere left to go. The cabin was about the size of a janitor's closet. There were bunk beds tucked into the wall, with curtains to pull across for privacy. There was no other furniture. There wasn't room for any. A small television was fixed to the wall opposite the beds, and the far wall featured a mirror in the shape of a porthole.

Danielle pivoted to look at me.

"I suppose the idea is that we aren't supposed to hang out in the room."

"I'm just glad we packed light."

We stood in silence for a moment and I glanced into the bathroom. I figured I could use the commode and the shower at the same time, which was a nice touch if I were in a hurry. The hum had grown considerably louder.

"Is that the engine?" Danielle asked.

I shrugged. "Why do I get the feeling like we're underwater right now?"

Danielle shuddered involuntarily.

"Why don't we go find this ballroom?" I suggested.

"Lead the way, good sir."

## CHAPTER FIVE

WE WERE GOING TO GET IN OUR DAILY ALLOTMENT OF steps, that was for sure. We walked back to the middle of the ship and took the stairs back up to deck five. There we found a map displaying the general layout of the ship. It seemed that we were bunking on the lowest of the passenger decks. Decks five and six were filled with shopping, restaurants and bars, while the upper decks contained cabins that I assumed were more spacious than ours, as well as the outdoor areas for pools, ziplines and a golf driving range.

There were three ballrooms. I couldn't imagine why they would need to hold three balls at once, but I suspected that *ballroom* was just a pompous way to say multipurpose room. The biggest of the three was just aft of the atrium. The other two were forward.

The first we came to was the wrong ballroom. This one had been set up like the Football Hall of Fame in Canton, Ohio. Glass cases showed off trophies and rings and pennants, old programs from early Super Bowls, framed jerseys from Green Bay and New England and Pittsburgh. Already a smattering of people wandered through, with hushed reverence, like pilgrims visiting the Sistine Chapel.

I surveyed the room for Guy X. Though there were a handful of likely candidates, I dismissed them all for reasons of age or manner or companion. A group of young guys huddled together, whispering in a way they no doubt thought was furtive. I knew the look. I'd seen it in plenty of guys their age. Guys who thought they were untouchable and invincible. My mother would have taken one look at them and concluded that they were up to no good.

"What's this one?" asked Danielle.

I turned back to her. She was looking at silver trophy inside a glass cabinet. The trophy looked like a football sitting on a traffic cone.

"That's the Lombardi Trophy," I said. "It's awarded to the winner of the Super Bowl."

"So there's just one of them?"

"No, the winner keeps it. A new one is produced each year. Did you know they were produced by Tiffany & Co?"

"Tiffany's? Really?"

I nodded.

"So who won this one?"

"This was . . . huh."

"Huh?"

"No one won this one. It's this year's. It hasn't been awarded yet."

I glanced at the group of young guys across the room. There was some nodding going on, like a decision had been reached, and some of the group were goading one of their number to do something. I looked at them and then I looked at what they were looking at. Then I connected some dots. At the door to the ballroom, a serious-looking security guy was standing in place, watching the room. But he wasn't watching all the room. It wasn't possible. I drifted over to him.

"You got some trouble coming," I said.

He frowned. "Excuse me, sir?"

"Trouble. You see the right rear corner of the room? That group of young guys?"

"You know them, sir?"

"No, I don't know them. But I know the type. The guys are wearing Cleveland Browns gear."

"Not a crime, sir."

"We can debate that later. But you see that trophy they're eyeing up?"

The guard squinted like his vision was failing him.

"It's a Heisman Trophy," he said.

"Not any Heisman. It was won by BJ Baker at Southern Cal."

"How do you know it's Baker's Heisman? They all look the same."

"That trophy and I know each other well. You remember BJ Baker?"

"Not at college."

"What about after college? Do you know where he played professional football?"

The guard thought for a second. "Pittsburgh?"

"Right."

Then the penny dropped. Cleveland and Pittsburgh were close, geographically speaking, and not close in any other respect. The Pittsburgh Steelers might have considered any number of other teams to be their biggest rivals, but the Cleveland Browns fans reserved a special kind of hatred for Pittsburgh.

The guard lifted a walkie-talkie radio from his belt. "Central, we have a possible situation in ball three."

He began edging his way toward the right rear of the room. I dropped in behind him like a running back and followed him.

"We got some hotshots with beers, looking to mess with the exhibits," he said into his radio. I had to hand it to him. I hadn't noticed the beers, but they were certainly there.

One of the guys separated from the group. He had sandy blond hair and a cocky swagger and reminded me of me, back in the day, but not in a good way. He held a beer can in his hand and moved rapidly toward BJ Baker's Heisman Trophy.

The Heisman looked defiant, his hand thrust out to perform a stiff-arm and then continue on to the end zone. The blond guy pulled his can back and set himself to pitch his drink.

But he didn't. The guard stepped in front of him and the guy only got halfway through his action, pulling himself up short and almost falling into the guard in the process.

"I'm sorry, sir, we can't allow beverages in the exhibition hall," said the guard.

"What?" The blond guy knew he'd been caught in the act, but his brain was trying to process the fact that the guard wasn't going to take him to the floor or something worse. Two more security guards moved in quietly.

"Why don't we just move back to a bar area and finish our drinks quietly?" The guard ushered the guy toward the door without laying a hand on him. These three were pros and I had to hand it to them. What could have become a situation fizzled into nothing.

The other two guards nodded the guy's buddies toward the door.

"Thanks for the spot," the first guard said to me.

I nodded in return and noted the scowl on the face of the blond Cleveland Browns fan. He clearly wasn't impressed with me, and I wasn't even wearing any kind of team colors. But I had rained on his parade before he had even gotten his float out of the garage.

I left the guard and the young guys to their testosterone and returned to Danielle. She wore a big grin.

"What is it with you and that trophy?"

"It's like we're cosmically connected, isn't it?"

"Why is BJ Baker's Heisman here anyway?"

"They probably asked him to loan it to them for this Hall of Fame or whatever it is. He wouldn't miss a chance to showboat."

"Shall we find this other ballroom?"

I nodded and followed her out.

We found the other ballroom after getting lost twice. It felt about the same size as the ballroom we had just come from. At least that was my sense from the doorway. Unlike the Hall of Fame room, the security guard here wasn't letting in any old Harry or Sally.

"Vendors only," he said.

"I'm private security for a vendor."

The guard gave me a scowl and I could see one of those turf-war things coming on.

"I'm not here to tell you how to do your job," I said. "The client's just a little paranoid, you know?"

He didn't drop the scowl.

"Mr. Jones."

I turned to find Frederick Connors, still in his blue blazer, white pocket square still perfectly in place and blue travel bag over his shoulder. He looked past me at the security guard.

"Anastasia's," he said, holding up his ship pass ID.

The guard consulted a clipboard and then nodded. "Yes, sir."

"And these two are with us," Frederick said. I assumed he was referring to Danielle and me, but he might as well have been talking about his pet Chihuahuas.

I had to fish my ID out of my pocket. The guard checked us off and then stepped aside to let us in. The interior of this ballroom looked like an art gallery. There were lots of sculptures and display cases and paintings hanging from wire frames. But the lighting was all wrong. Instead of bland walls and white spotlights, these walls were dark and the lighting a cabaret mix of blue and green and red. If it were really an art gallery, it could only have been in Las Vegas. A podium with a lectern had been set up at the front of a few rows of chairs, I assumed to facilitate the auction.

Frederick led us over to an area that looked like a mini Tiffany & Co. showroom. A range of display cabinets sat waiting to be filled. I didn't see the point. I couldn't fathom why someone would go on a cruise to buy jewelry or a picture for their drawing room wall. But I figured there was a lot I had to learn about how and why rich people spent their money, not to mention what the hell a drawing room was for, other than for hanging all this art they were picking up on cruises.

Frederick found a glass cabinet that was labeled *Anastasia's*. It was a counter-height cabinet with lighting on the inside that made the white interior glow. It was particularly bright because it was empty.

"Where is your wife's jewelry?" I asked.

"She has it. She will be here shortly."

"Where is she?"

"In our suite."

"Alone?"

"Yes, Mr. Jones, alone."

"How do you know?"

"She was getting ready. She would not interrupt that for a liaison."

"How do you know?"

"I know my wife, Mr. Jones."

I let it go. I didn't see an upside in bringing up the fact that if he knew his wife so well I wouldn't be on a cruise ship talking to him. Instead, we waited and watched other vendors setting up their wares. Guys in white gloves hung paintings that looked old but could have been printed onto the canvas that morning for all I knew. One booth was setting up sports collectibles—action photos, autographed cards, signed helmets—which looked a little out of place given the rest of the merchandise, but was, in fact, the most relevant stuff I saw, given the cruise's theme. I kept an eye out for Guy X. He could have been a fellow vendor. It would certainly give him good reason to be around Frederick's wife.

I was processing that thought when she arrived. Danielle nudged me in the ribs and directed my attention to the woman floating across the ballroom. She wore a long dress and pearls and didn't seem to take steps, but rather slid across the room as if on a skateboard or a dolly. Her hair was tied up in a sophisticated arrangement—the word *bun* wouldn't do it justice—and she held her chin high, giving her tight face a perpetual look of condescension. She made me think of Russian nobility.

Danielle and I smiled as she reached us, but the expression was not returned. She glided behind the glass cabinets, pulling one of those suitcases on wheels. Not a big heavy thing. A tiny little one that would house a laptop and a sandwich and no more. The kind of thing that breaks a lot of ankles in airport concourses.

She stopped the baggage at her feet and then raised an eyebrow at her husband. It was some kind of unspoken communication, the kind of thing people who have been married a long time pick up on but which is lost to everyone else. At the sign, Frederick stepped around the cabinet and put down his natty blue travel bag. He dropped the telescopic handle on the little case and then lifted it on top of the glass cabinet. Then he stepped back.

For the first time, the woman glanced at me and Danielle. Not for long though. She returned her attention back to the case but she didn't open it.

"Who are these people, Frederick?"

Frederick bowed slightly as he spoke. "This is Mr. Jones and Ms. Castle. I have taken the liberty of engaging Mr. Jones as additional security for the rings."

"Additional security?"

"Yes, my dear."

"You decided to wait until we were in a secure room on a ship in the middle of the ocean to engage security?"

"Yes."

"Not when I was transporting the items from the boutique to this very room? Not when I was on my own?"

"It was a last-minute decision, my dear. I realized when my schedule opened up and I could join you that perhaps it might be prudent."

"Yes, well you know what I think of that. You'll be seasick before dinner." Now she looked at me again. "You're dismissed."

It wasn't the first time I had been dismissed from a case, but I couldn't recall ever being dismissed before I even got introduced to the client. Then I recalled she wasn't the client. She was the subject of the investigation.

"Ma'am, I've already been engaged," I said.

"And now you are relieved."

"What I mean is, I require a contingency payment to engage services. I am prepaid, if you like. So I can happily leave you to your business, but it wouldn't be proper not to inform you that whether I am here or not, the price is the same."

She reserved her look of disdain for her husband. It was a doozy. A guy once rammed my car full speed into a tree on purpose—and then smashed every window and panel with a hockey stick, and I still hadn't looked at him the way she looked at Frederick. Then she turned her gaze upon Danielle.

"And you are what? The floozy?"

Danielle didn't miss a beat. She was better with people than I was. She touched my hand out of sight below the cabinet to calm me. Not that I knew what I'd do. I sure wasn't about to take a swing at Mrs. Connors, and complaints from minions like me rarely dented the armor of her class.

"Mrs. Connors, my name is Special Agent Danielle Castle, Florida Department of Law Enforcement."

I had never heard her use the title before. She had only just earned it. It was so fresh, she didn't even yet know where she would be stationed. But it sounded good to my ear. She stood a little taller when she said it. I was impressed as hell. I was the only one.

"The FBI wasn't available?" The eyebrow cocked in disdain once more and she stared coolly at her husband.

"You and I will talk later."

# CHAPTER SIX

Anastasia unlocked the case. It was more secure than it appeared. It boasted two locks that were each sturdier than the average luggage lock, and the sides of the case appeared to be reinforced by something stiff and hard, maybe steel or carbon fiber, which might have explained why she hadn't lifted the case. From it, she produced a black box that was about fifteen inches long, ten inches wide, and a good four inches thick. It looked like the sort of thing the president might open up to fire the nuclear arsenal.

Anastasia Connors removed the top with the flourish of a French waiter. Inside, the box was plush black velvet, with little indents in it like the spaces chocolates occupy in one of those expensive candy boxes men give women when they are courting in the movies. Each indent was occupied by a ring. There were more than fifty of them, each one different from the others. These were not the elegant rings that Russian princesses wore on their petite fingers. These were big and ugly and brought to mind the word *bling*.

"Super Bowl rings," I said.

"Astute," Anastasia replied.

"You collect Super Bowl rings?" She didn't strike me as the type but people can surprise.

"No, Mr. Jones, I do not collect rings. I am a jeweler."

"You made these?" Danielle asked.

"Stating the obvious must be what you two have in common."

"They're fakes," I said. I knew it wouldn't go down well the moment the words tripped from my mouth.

"Excuse me?"

"Most Super Bowl rings are made by Jostens," I said.

Anastasia arched an eyebrow again but this time it wasn't the look one gives a ketchup stain on their favorite shirt.

"You know more than you appear to, Mr. Jones."

"Usually. So they are fakes."

The ketchup-stain look returned. "No, Mr. Jones, they are not fakes. They are reproductions."

"That sounds like a lot of extra letters to say the word fake."

"Fakes are illegal or inferior or both. My rings are officially licensed by the National Football League. They are exact replicas of the original rings from every Super Bowl, down to the carat. Exact and exquisite in every detail."

I had to admit the handiwork was impressive, but I wouldn't have used the word *exquisite*. Exquisite makes me think of Lamborghinis and wedding dresses and Grace Kelly. Super Bowl rings are big and loud and gaudy, much like the men they are made for. But seeing the entire collection was something. I noted the first one, designed for the Green Bay Packers back when Super Bowls were just plain old championship games. The rings were in chronological order, and as I looked through the set they got bigger and louder and the number of diamonds grew. Even on a big ring there was a limit to how many diamonds a jeweler could fit but it seemed that NFL champions were determined to push that limit. I looked for and found the

New England ring from Super Bowl LI, which I knew contained 283 diamonds, to celebrate the comeback from 28–3 down against the Falcons. It would have been useful at picnics to put your beer and hot dog on, or to reflect the light from the sun to destroy far away planets. I cast my eye back to one ring I had seen before. The 1974 Pittsburgh Steelers ring. Anastasia's version looked exactly like the one I had seen at the home of BJ Baker, the same guy whose Heisman was in the ship's Hall of Fame. The ghost of BJ Baker seemed to be hanging over my voyage like the flu.

Anastasia slipped another box out of her case and opened it. Another complete set of rings were nestled inside.

"Two sets?" I asked.

"Correct. Two of each ring, from the first game through to last year."

"And people buy these?"

"This is a football-themed cruise, is it not?"

A tailgate at the Florida–Georgia game in Jacksonville was football themed. This was something else entirely.

Anastasia pulled a third item from her case. This one was a leather folio, zipped closed.

"Here comes Arnold now," she said.

I turned to see a small, balding man in a bow tie striding across the room toward us. He looked like an accountant, but not the kind of accountant who does the books in Palm Beach. He was an H&R Block kind of guy. Someone who would do my taxes. His shirt looked expensive, but it had a sheen to it that suggested this was his only one. He carried the ubiquitous sky blue cruise ship travel bag. He looked Anastasia in the eye but didn't smile. Instead, he took her hand and bowed. Maybe she was Russian aristocracy.

"Anastasia, always a pleasure."

"Arnold," she replied.

Arnold shook Frederick's hand and then he glanced at me and Danielle. Mostly Danielle.

"Security," said Anastasia.

"Ah," he said. "Shall we?"

The little guy pulled out a jeweler's monocle and attached it to his eye like some sort of bionic enhancement. I had seen Sal Mondavi use a less sophisticated version of the same thing to check jewelry that was pawned in his shop. Arnold's version looked like it might have had night vision. He slipped on a white glove and then picked up the first ring. Green Bay.

He inspected it all over, paying particular attention to the diamonds. He put more effort into it than I put into buying shoes. When he was done he replaced the ring carefully and took the second one, Green Bay again.

Arnold repeated the process with each and every ring, and then he moved on to the second case and repeated the dose. I used the time to looked around for Guy X. I didn't see him, so I started thinking about the map of the ship and where the bars were.

When Arnold was done with the last ring he replaced it as carefully as he had the first and then removed his monocle.

"Exquisite," he said to Anastasia. She didn't smile. She just nodded as if such a statement of fact warranted no pride. Arnold made no comment about the gaudy nature of the jewelry, but then I guessed if he commented on all the ugly stuff that rich people wore and bought and lived in, he'd never shut up.

"I have set the reserve at thirty thousand for each ring," Arnold said.

"Dollars?" I spat.

"Of course we deal in dollars," he said. "But I have no doubt many of the pieces will fetch much higher. We have a most discerning guest list for the auction on Saturday night."

I always enjoyed the way people became discerning when they were loaded with cash.

"May I have the certificates of authenticity?" Arnold asked.

Anastasia handed over the zipped folio.

"You have a safe at your disposal under your display area," said Arnold. "I assure you the pieces will be quite safe there until we open the gallery tomorrow morning." He glanced at me as if to reinforce the point that I was superfluous. "Now, if you'll accompany me to sign the necessary documents, we'll have you finished in a moment so you can prepare for the opening ceremony and cocktails."

I wasn't sure what preparing for cocktails required other than finding a bar, but Anastasia already looked ready to attend a coronation. She slipped the lids back on both boxes of rings and then bent down below the display case. I stepped around Frederick to take a look. This wasn't any hotel room safe. It was considerably larger and appeared to be both drilled into the floor and very heavy.

Anastasia glanced up at me. "Do you mind?"

I smiled and stepped away to let her set the code for the safe. Once she was done, she stood and brushed her dress.

"Frederick," she said.

"Of course, my dear."

Anastasia headed across the room with Arnold, and Frederick moved in behind the counter. I had a few things I wanted to ask him: about Anastasia, about his marriage, about the type of man who would have an affair with a woman like that. But I couldn't think of a remotely diplomatic way to ask any of them, so I kept my mouth shut.

"I didn't realize these rings were worth so much."

"Yes. At reserve, a little more than three million for the collection."

I made my impressed face.

"Have you seen him?" Frederick asked.

"Guy X?"

"Yes."

"I'm not sure I'd know him if I did. Your picture didn't give a lot of definition."

"He might be here." He took the first closed box of rings and crouched down to slip them inside the safe. I turned back to the room.

"It's possible," I said. "But I'd say the best chance is to watch your wife."

"Perhaps you're right." He took the second box. I kept my eye on Anastasia, talking with Arnold the auctioneer. He was having her sign something. Arnold certainly wasn't Guy X. I watched Anastasia to see if she was looking for anyone, or if anyone else in the room was paying particular attention to her. I saw nothing. Which was what I expected to see.

"There's a problem," I said, turning back to Frederick. He stood but left the safe open. "You going to lock that?"

"No. Anastasia will want to do that. What problem do you see?"

"You."

He frowned. "How am I the problem?"

"You're here. I understand the compulsion to get in between your wife and some other man, but your wife seems like a very considered person."

"Meaning?"

"Meaning she doesn't seem one for rash or careless moves. And now that you're on board, hooking up with Guy X would be risky."

"Some people like that risk."

"Your wife doesn't strike me as one of those people, Mr. Connors."

He considered this. "No, you are right. She is not. Except

that you have to acknowledge that an affair is itself inherently risky."

"Life is risk," I said. "Getting up in the morning, driving to work, swimming in the ocean, shopping on Worth Avenue. All have an attached risk. You might get in an accident if you go out, a plane might land on your house if you don't. Life is about risk mitigation. And the prudent move for her now is to do nothing."

"Unless I'm not around."

"We're on a ship. Where could you go?"

"My wife is right. I don't feel great, Mr. Jones. I feel every little tremble in the ship, every little bit of motion."

"The ocean's flat. I checked. Besides, we haven't left the dock yet."

"I'm telling you what I feel, Mr. Jones. It is likely that I will stay in our suite."

"Incapacitated," I said. "So your wife can go wherever she pleases."

He nodded. "As long as I have your assurance that you will keep an eye on her."

"That's why you hired me, Mr. Connors."

He gave no reply but watched over my shoulder. I felt Anastasia return before I heard her.

"We should prepare for the opening," she said as she moved behind the cabinet.

"I think I might retire to the suite, my dear. Do you mind?"

"I told you so," she said. "You know you don't do well on water."

"Perhaps I overestimated myself."

"Perhaps you did."

Anastasia pushed the door to the safe closed and locked it. Then she looked at me.

"I assume you will stay here and stand guard?"

"I think the room is safe enough," I said.

"As do I. Which makes me wonder what we are paying you for."

"Reassurance."

She gave me a look like she had just bitten her tongue and then stepped out from the counter. Frederick picked up his travel bag so that he looked like everyone else and offered his wife his arm. She looped her arm through his, which felt like an oddly romantic gesture, and they walked away.

## CHAPTER SEVEN

We didn't go back to our suite to change for the opening. I didn't have anything much different to change into short of a tux—and that seemed like overkill—and our sardine can of a room didn't exactly call out to us as a place to be.

I'm a private investigator. I'm good at finding things. So I found a bar. It was an indoor/outdoor kind of place, but that was where the similarities with Longboard Kelly's began and ended. They served all manner of fruity drinks and no stools cluttered up the bar area. We took our drinks and found a high table where we could look over the shipping containers on the dock. We didn't feel the ship cast off, but the containers began moving away from us, signaling the start of our Caribbean voyage. A loudspeaker announced that the welcome ceremony would be taking place in an hour in the Dolphin Amphitheater, followed by the opening reception and the opening of the buffet. I figured those two events would separate the sleeves from the sleeveless on board.

"What do you make of Anastasia?" I asked Danielle.

"Very old school."

"That's generous."

"I'm having trouble picturing her having an affair."

I shuddered. "I was trying to avoid doing that."

"I'm serious. What kind of a man would that be?"

"The same kind that she married, but a little different."

"What does that mean?"

"I don't know. I've never had an affair. But I figure there must be things about your partner that are attractive to you and you would look for in anyone, and there are things you've grown tired of and want to change."

"What do you want to change about me?" she asked. She grinned so I knew she thought she had me.

"Nothing."

"You have to say that."

"I do. Because it's the truth."

"No, it's not. No one's perfect."

"I didn't say you were perfect. I just said I wouldn't change anything about you."

I finished my beer and slipped out of my chair.

"Let's go find this opening ceremony, whatever the hell that is."

"Why?"

"Anastasia will be there. Maybe Guy X will be too."

We didn't consult the map. Instead we just followed all the other salmon. The Dolphin Amphitheater was at the stern of the ship, a semicircular, open-air theater with a stage at the bottom that opened up to a view of the Florida coast we were leaving behind. Just as we got to the top of the seating area I noticed Ron and Cassandra at the bottom. We skipped down the steps toward them and Ron gave me a nod. Cassandra offered her cheek for a kiss. She was big on cheek kisses. She was very European like that. Cassandra was dressed for the opening ceremony, or cocktails, or the opera for that matter. Ron wore a linen suit that I was instantly envious of. It was evening and most of the suits around us were dark or tuxedos. Ron liked to swim against the tide.

"So?" I whispered to Ron.

He shook his head.

"How's your suite?" Cassandra asked Danielle.

"Cozy," she replied.

The tapping of a microphone brought everyone's attention to the stage. Cassandra and Ron sat down at the front, and Danielle and I moved to the side as a man in a garish shirt and long white shorts asked everyone to find a seat and then began trying to whip the crowd into a frenzy. He asked the audience if they were ready for a good time and got a handful of mumbled affirmations, to which he responded with an *I can't hear you!* The response, if anything, was more muted the second time around. I couldn't help but feel he had misjudged his audience on this particular voyage. Palm Beach types don't tend to get worked into a frenzy, except on bad stock market days.

He didn't let it get to him, though. He continued in the same excited voice and told us that we were in for a once-in-a-lifetime cruise, a celebration of all things football. Again the response was limited to a few hollers from the sleeveless crowd. Then he announced that following the opening welcome there would be a ticketed reception in the Castaway Casino—a name that didn't engender a lot of confidence in the success of the voyage—and an open event featuring free music in all three buffet restaurants. Then, without further ado, he asked us to give it up for Captain Sterling.

I felt the response might have been something more if he had asked us to put our hands together, or even just welcome the captain. This was not a *give it up* crowd. But like his warm-up man, the captain didn't let it get to him. He was, however, a good few decibels lower in volume and energy. The audience seemed to appreciate this. Like aircraft pilots, people like their ship captains to be calm and considered individuals. Crazy and zany was generally not a great look for them.

"Hello, and welcome on board our new flagship vessel, *Canaveral Star*. My name is Captain Sterling."

This got the biggest applause of all—I suspect because it didn't include any confusing directions. Watching the audience, I also got the feeling that a few of the older patrons might have misheard his name as Stubing, the captain from *The Love Boat*, and no one had a bad voyage under that guy.

Captain Sterling was the very embodiment of a ship's captain. He was tall and thin and looked to be in his fifties, with gray at his temples and a spring in his step. He looked resplendent in his all-white uniform and hat, which he removed before launching into his speech. He welcomed us and hoped we would enjoy ourselves, or words to that effect. I wasn't paying a lot of attention. Instead, I was looking over the audience, specifically for Anastasia Conners. The captain went on about how many restaurants and bars were on board, and then gave us an outline of our sail, out and around the Bahamas with a day stop on the cruise line's own private island paradise.

I found Anastasia sitting a few rows from the front. She had actually changed into a burgundy gown, which made me wonder if our bags had yet made it to our bunks in the engine room. As the captain finished welcoming all the owners, current and past players and dignitaries—which I took to mean the rest of us—I scanned the audience around Anastasia for a sign of Guy X. Then the captain welcomed an honored guest to open the special voyage. One of Palm Beach's favorite sons, a football hero through and through.

I knew who it was before I turned around and before the captain said his name.

"BJ Baker."

The captain clapped and the audience followed and BJ

Baker stepped up onto the stage from the opposite side to where I stood. I glanced at Danielle, who smiled.

Baker strode up to the mic with all the vim and vigor of a thirty-year-old man, which wasn't bad for a guy who had been on the planet for thirty years twice around and then some. His firm frame and square jaw showed him to be the athlete that he was back in the day. He was a fine specimen of a man and an altogether unpleasant human being.

BJ took the stage and welcomed football fans and non-fans alike. Unlike the warm-up guy, BJ knew his crowd. He spoke about the proud tradition Florida had of hosting more Super Bowls than any other state. He put in a little jab about California wishing it had hosted.

He kept rambling on and I left him to it. I again turned my attention to the audience. After all, this was my best chance to spot a large chunk of the passengers all in one place. It wasn't everyone, not by a long shot. Plenty of folks didn't give a dime and two nickels about BJ Baker or his speech. The bars were already doing a roaring trade, and I was willing to bet the spa was as well. But there were enough people to make it worthwhile. Especially with Frederick in his room and Anastasia in the audience. Guy X might be close by. I started again from Anastasia's position and swept my eye up and down the rows toward the front.

Then I saw him. Not Guy X. I should be so lucky. On the other side of the seating I saw the half-drunk blond guy from the Hall of Fame. He was still with his buddies, and he still wore his Cleveland Browns uniform. And he still had a major grudge against BJ Baker. I had gotten security onto him before he had been able to do anything to BJ's Heisman Trophy. Now he had a better target. The man himself. I could see he had traded in his can for a nearly full plastic cup of beer, which splashed as he moved along the side of the seating, toward the stage. It was pretty obvious what his plan was. BJ hadn't played for Pittsburgh in forty years, and this guy looked like he had been born a good two decades after BJ's playing days were over. It made me wonder what those Cleveland guys would do if you really did something to upset them. This was a grudge of Olympic proportions.

And I wanted to let him do it.

I really had no problem with someone planting a full cup of beer on BJ Baker. I would go as far as to say it would have made my day. I watched the guy move toward the front of the seating and I looked around for any security who might stop him. There were none. I glanced at BJ. He was in full rant, a captive audience in his grasp.

Behind him, Captain Sterling was looking at the blond guy with the beer. He knew what was happening. But he was trapped between an iceberg and a hard place. He wanted to yell out, to stop the guy, or to jump up and push BJ Baker out of the way, to take one for the team. But he was paralyzed by the idea of causing a commotion, of starting the cruise on the very wrong foot. Paralyzed by the infinitesimal chance that the blond guy wasn't actually going to do what every fiber in the captain told him the guy was going to do.

Then the captain looked for help. For the security guards I couldn't see. He couldn't spot them either, or at least not close enough to do anything. I knew because his eyes settled on me. I don't know why. I was dressed like all the other second-class passengers, in vacation attire rather than any kind of suit. There was nothing about me that suggested I even knew what was transpiring. Except that he knew I knew, and his face was like that of a man who had just lost his balance on the edge of a cliff. He was going over, that was for certain, and he needed someone to save him, for he was beyond saving himself.

I couldn't let him start the whole cruise off like that. I took off in a half crouch, down below the line of the stage. I was visible to pretty much everyone, but figured it would be better to stay low. Perhaps I was just a guy who needed the bathroom. I dashed across and halfway there I glanced up. BJ was mid-vowel, his mouth shaped like he was saying "oooooo." It felt like slow motion as he looked down at the movement below him and caught my eye, and as time slowed, his brain raced through his mental Rolodex, and I saw it stop on J for Jones, and then his face changed from charm to death wish and then back again, as he realized he was still in front of his captive audience. I didn't see what happened after that. The blond guy reached a point where we were the same distance from the stage and he wound back his arm, cocking it, ready to pitch.

I was low, so I pushed up and hit the guy slightly from behind. His throwing arm was right back and starting forward, so I grabbed it and used his momentum to drive it into his back. His beer exploded against his spine and drenched his Browns shirt and his jeans. I kept going. I drove him away from the stage, away from the crowd.

Then I saw another guy. This one was dressed in white like the captain. He was serious looking and seemed to be heading toward the blond guy, but on realizing what I was doing broke left and met me at a door off to the side of the stage.

It was a personnel door, crew only. The guy in uniform tapped a keycard to a box on the wall and pulled the door open. I drove the blond guy right through it. The crew guy followed me into a bland, cream-colored corridor. I pushed the Cleveland guy up against the wall and he made his first noises since I tackled him. There were a lot of choice words. His swear jar was going to be full to overflowing.

"I'm ship security," said the man in uniform.

"I figured," I said, and I let him take hold of the guy. As I moved back, two more uniformed crew stepped into the corridor.

The security guy said, "Sir, are we going to have a problem?"

"No, man," said Cleveland. "I'm just standing there, minding my own business—"

"Sir, have you been drinking?"

"It's a cruise, pal."

One of the other crew members said, "It's the guy from the disturbance in ball three."

"Sir, we're going to take a little walk, okay?" said the security guy. "I'm going to let you go now."

As he was let go the blond guy turned around to look at me. He hadn't seemed to like me before in the Hall of Fame. He seemed even less enamored with me now. He flexed his arm and felt his wet backside.

"You'll be lucky if I don't sue. And who's going to pay for my beer?"

"I'm sure BJ will buy you one," I said.

The blond guy launched himself at me. I didn't step back, but he didn't reach me. The two crewmen stepped in and put him back against the wall.

"Let's go and dry out for a while, sir," said one of them, and together they frogmarched him away.

I was left standing with the security guy. I waited for him to give me a hard time for cutting in on his turf. He offered his hand.

"Mahoney," he said. "Chief Security Officer."

We shook hands. "Miami Jones."

"Thanks for your help out there."

"No sweat."

"I'm sure Mr. Baker will be most grateful."

"I highly doubt that."

The door to the amphitheater burst open, and on cue, BJ Baker charged in like a wounded bull. Even his nostrils flared. He paid no mind to Mahoney. He only had eyes for me.

"I'm gonna tear you a new one, Jones, you ingrate."

I looked at Mahoney and smiled.

"See?"

# CHAPTER EIGHT

BJ Baker came at me.

Mahoney, the security chief, stepped between us. "Mr. Baker, Mr. Jones just averted an incident."

"Jones is the incident."

"Nice to see you, BJ," I said. I may have said it with a big grin on my face.

"No one gets to interrupt me on stage, especially you, Jones."

BJ liked being the thunder and he didn't like anyone stealing it from him. He was, in the most pure sense, a limelight hog. I supposed a lot of media people were. They had to be, in a way. Having your face plastered all over screens across the country made you famous, and more than that, it gave people a false sense of familiarity. If you appeared in people's living rooms every week, you must be friends, right? As a result, these people had to either hide from their public or embrace it. BJ embraced it. He had been a big personality during college at USC, and he was a bigger personality during his stint in the NFL. In the decades since he had played, his personality had not receded any. And he still loved being the center of attention.

"Sir, there was a drunk patron," said Mahoney, "and Mr. Jones prevented him from throwing something at you."

"Probably one of Jones's buddies. You do drink your sad life away at a dive bar, don't you, Jones?"

I figured Mick would be okay with the tag of dive bar for his beloved Longboard's. It would keep the tourists away. But Mahoney turned to me.

"Do you know that man?" he asked.

"The Browns guy? No, I don't know him. Only saw him once before, in your Hall of Fame."

"You were the one who called in the disturbance in ballroom three?" said Mahoney.

"I was." I looked at BJ. "Before he went after you, he was going to try to damage your Heisman. That's twice I've had to save that thing. You really ought to keep better care of it."

"Why I oughtta—"

BJ didn't get to finish, which just wound him up even more, as the door was pulled open again and Captain Sterling stepped into the bland corridor. It was like the kitchen at a party, everyone wanted to be in there even though it was the least comfortable place to be.

"Mr. Baker, I'm glad you're okay," said the captain. He offered his hand to me. "Captain Sterling."

Mahoney said, "Captain, this is Mr. Jones."

"Miami," I said.

"Well, Mr. Jones, we owe you debt of thanks."

"A debt of thanks?" BJ Baker bellowed.

"Yes," said Sterling. "Mr. Jones stopped a man from throwing his beer at you, Mr. Baker." He turned to his head of security. "I didn't realize that people would be so passionate about their teams. We need to be more vigilant, Army."

"Yes, sir. I agree," said Mahoney.

"Don't let this guy fool you," spat BJ. "He's all kinds of trouble."

"I can't speak to that, sir," said Sterling. "But I did see the whole thing, and Mr. Jones dealt with the situation without alarming the passengers, and that is my primary concern." The captain turned to me. "You clearly know what you are doing, Mr. Jones."

"I'm on board as backup security for one of your auction vendors. This is kind of what I do."

"Ha!" said BJ.

"Well, sir, I thank you," said the captain. "I trust you will also have time to enjoy the facilities on board."

"That's the plan."

"I'd like to send a thank you basket to your suite. You're on which deck?"

"Three," I said. "It's a cute little fixer-upper next to the engine room."

"Deck three?" The captain shook his head. "No, that won't do. Army, didn't the morning briefing say the Palmentieri party had canceled?"

Mahoney nodded. "Yes, sir. Their child has chickenpox or something like that."

"They were to be in the Bermuda Suite?"

"I believe so, sir."

"Let's arrange to move Mr. Jones to the Bermuda Suite then, with our thanks."

"Yes, sir."

Veins were bulging in BJ's temples. "You're *upgrading* him?"

"The least we can do," said Captain Sterling.

"I sure hope it's not a better room than mine."

"You have the finest suite on the ship, Mr. Baker."

BJ's blood pressure seemed to drop a point or two. Sterling

sure knew how to handle these entitled types.

"Well, you better make sure nothing happens to my Heisman or my ring," said BJ.

"It is our highest priority, Mr. Baker. Right, Army?"

"One hundred percent, sir," said Mahoney.

BJ puffed out his granite chest and turned away, pushing through the doors and back out to the deck. I assumed that he had nothing further to say.

"Mr. Jones, I must get back to it. My thanks again."

"Anytime, Captain."

"Army."

"Sir."

Sterling marched away down the corridor. I was left standing with Mahoney. He really was a serious-looking guy, square of shoulder and he stood to attention even when relaxed. I stood in silence, waiting for him to tell me to keep out of his business. He knew that he and his team should have averted the situation with BJ. Guys like him didn't like being shown up.

"You're security?" he asked.

"I'm a PI, but we do a little bit of that kind of work."

"Do you mind telling me who you're working for?"

"Anastasia and Frederick Connors."

"The jeweler. That'll be handy."

"How so?"

"Your new suite is in the same passageway as the Connors."

I figured that would be handy, but not for reasons Mahoney knew anything about.

"Are you alone on board?" he asked.

"No, my fiancée is outside, probably wondering what the hell is going on."

"Is she a PI, too?"

"No. She's a special agent with the FDLE."

"She here professionally?"

"All vacation."

"We'll go collect her. I'll get someone to organize your new suite. But first I need to make a stop. If you don't mind coming with me."

He didn't say it like it was a question.

# CHAPTER NINE

DANIELLE HAD TAKEN A SEAT IN THE FRONT ROW OF THE amphitheater despite the welcoming address being over and most everyone else having left for cocktails or the buffet. I introduced her to Mahoney and then the chief security officer took us back into the corridor to the side of the amphitheater. We walked along a ways and then took an elevator down. We got off and followed another corridor toward the middle of the ship. Now we were on a much wider corridor that seemed to go on forever. The floor was blue linoleum and the walls were more bland cream. Mahoney kept walking.

"This is the main crew thoroughfare," he said. "We call it I-95, like the freeway. It runs from bow to stern and allows us to access any area of the ship without having to go through public areas."

I-95 was a good name for it. The corridor carried a lot of traffic. Crew moved about in both directions, trolleys of ingredients made their way from cool rooms to restaurants, and one area was lined with luggage.

"Mustering point," Mahoney said. "Housekeeping lines up

all the baggage you left at check-in and then delivers it from here to your individual decks."

"Decks? Not to the rooms?" Danielle asked.

"No. Baggage is left by the elevators nearest to your cabin. Except for the suites." He looked at Danielle. "Don't worry, I'll have your baggage moved to your suite for you."

Mahoney stopped by another elevator and we waited.

"Why did the captain call you Army?" I asked.

Mahoney smiled. "Why do you think?"

"You served."

He nodded.

"But I'm sure a lot of ex-military guys get into security."

"I'm sure they do. But most of the ones on cruise ships are former navy or coast guard."

But you were in the army?"

He nodded again. The elevator arrived and we got in.

"How long?"

"Twenty-two years."

"Rank?"

"Lieutenant colonel."

"Why don't they call you Lieutenant Colonel?"

"I'm not in the army anymore. And there are no lieutenant colonels in the navy."

Danielle asked, "How does an army officer end up on a cruise ship?"

The elevator stopped and the door opened.

"Long story," he said.

We stepped out onto a small carpeted landing. To the side, I could see windows and, beyond that, blue sky. We weren't in the bowels of the boat anymore.

"Forward of this point is the bridge," Mahoney said. "Aft is the security control room."

He headed for a door simply marked *security*.

"So what do we call you, Lieutenant Colonel?" I asked.

He stopped before the door. "Army is just fine with me."

The security office looked like any number of similar offices I had seen in hotels and casinos. A miniature version of Houston control. Lots of flatscreen monitors and computer terminals, displaying images from all over the ship—decks, corridors, bars, restaurants. The pool area looked busier than I had thought it would be.

"Could I have your ship IDs?" asked Army.

Danielle pulled hers over her head and I removed mine from my pocket. Then Army spoke to a woman in whites seated at a terminal.

"Rhonda, can you please reassign Mr. Jones and Ms. Castle to the Bermuda Suite and get housekeeping to collect their baggage from deck three?"

"Of course, sir."

"Did we take care of our errant guest?" he asked.

"Taking a break in his cabin, sir. Kirkland is posted. You want to rotate?"

"No, give him a few hours and a warning. Then keep your eye on him."

"Aye, sir."

"Our friend from Cleveland?" I asked.

Army nodded.

"You sent him to his room with no dinner?"

"More or less. That's first port of call. Give them a chance to cool off. A warning usually does the trick."

"And if it doesn't?"

"We confine to cabin."

"Can't he just walk out?"

"We post a guard. Plus, if we need to, we can reverse the locks so they only open from the outside."

"That's a neat trick," said Danielle. I didn't like the way she said it, or the way she looked at me after.

"You don't have a brig on board?" I asked.

He shook his head. "Ship's not big enough to warrant it. Some of the monsters out of Port Canaveral do. For serious crime or extremely unruly passengers—and the ones who don't take the warning—we have extra crew quarters below if we need to house someone. If people get too troublesome they get dropped at the next port of call, but that doesn't work for us since we're only stopping at our private island."

I looked over the security monitors. "How many cameras do you have on board?"

"Almost nine hundred."

"Nine hundred! Holy smokes. Is there anything you can't see?"

"Not much. A few dead areas because of the design, and of course we can't see into cabins."

"I'm glad to hear it."

"How do you monitor that many cameras?" asked Danielle.

"We can't. And most of the time we don't need to. But we can pull up vision within seconds of getting a report in from any on-deck security or crew, and we record it all so it can be viewed later if necessary."

"You get a lot of crime?"

Army shook his head. "Not really. Drunk and disorderly like our Cleveland friend, that's the biggest one. Most of our incidents are alcohol related. But there's the occasional assault or theft. That's why we record all the feeds even when we can't watch them all."

We looked around the room. It was an impressive operation. But I still had a question.

"Why did you bring us here?"

"I want you to understand that we have things in hand."

"Because I got to the guy first?"

"And I know you were the one who picked up on him in ballroom three. We should have caught that one."

I looked at him. I liked him. He was a serious man doing a serious job. He wasn't busting my chops for getting involved. Instead he was embarrassed that I'd had to. One more time and I call it a pattern, but for now I was happy to accept his mea culpa.

"You would have got there, if I hadn't," I said.We both knew that wasn't true but no one felt the need to correct it. The woman at the terminal handed Army two new ship pass IDs, and he gave them to us.

"Your new bunks," he said. "Let me show you where."

Army walked us back to the elevator. We went down but this time it was a short trip. When we got out we were at the forward end of a much smaller corridor. The carpet was turquoise and the walls whitewashed panels. It looked beachy. Army took us down two doors and then stepped aside so Danielle could do the honors.

"So you know, there are six suites on this passageway. Your clients, the Connors? They're two doors down from you. The passenger elevator is at the aft end of the passageway. It will bring you out around midships on any of the main decks."

"Appreciate it," I said.

"Enjoy the cruise," he said. "I hope we don't speak again."

He strode back toward the crew elevator.

I heard Danielle say, "Um, MJ?"

"Yes, my dear," I said, mocking my client, Frederick.

"Get in here."

I stepped through and let the door close behind me. I was in a living room. It was more spacious than our living room at home. There was a large sofa and a flatscreen television mounted to the wall. At one end there was a bar with leather stools and chrome accents, and at the other end a door hung ajar. Danielle stepped past the sofa and out onto a balcony.

We were up on the highest passenger deck. It was a long way down to the water. But the water was calm and deep blue, and the sky was the color of the travel bags I saw all over the ship. I wasn't sure if we were still in US waters or had entered Bahamian territory, but it was all the same. And it wasn't New England in the snow. It was February in the Caribbean.

I put my arm around Danielle and we watched the water splashing away from the hull as the ship carved its way through the ocean. The air was warm and fresh and the falling sun lit the sky a kaleidoscope of colors that sat near blue on the color wheel. I could have stood there until dark, but Danielle slipped out from my arm and went back to explore the massive suite. I was considering setting up a hammock and sleeping on the balcony.

"MJ?" I heard Danielle call from inside.

"Yeah?"

"Get in here."

Again I did as I was told. Danielle was highly trained with all manner of weapons, so compliance was usually a good strategy. I stepped inside. I didn't see her. The bar was inviting but empty. The sofa sat unused. The door at the end of the room was open.

"You want to find a drink, something to eat?" I asked as I walked across the living space. There was no reply.

I forgot about drinks. I forgot about dinner. The bedroom was a decent size but the bed took up most of it.

"That's a big bed," I said.

"It is. A California king."

"California? That's the whole West Coast."

I stood in place. For a moment I didn't want to move. I just took in the massive bed and Danielle lying in the middle of it.

She was on her side, one leg across the other, propped up on her elbow. She wasn't wearing a stitch of clothing.

"MJ?"

"Yeah?"

She gave me the half smile.

"Get over here."

———

# CHAPTER TEN

I COULD HAVE HAPPILY STAYED IN OUR SUITE ALL EVENING, but my always conscientious fiancée reminded me that I had a client to consider. We both dressed well. Danielle was a traffic stopper in her black dress. I looked like an old surfer at a wedding in my tuxedo. But Danielle liked it, so all other opinions could go walk the plank.

We were in our better-than-Sunday best because we were headed for the top end of town. The movers and shakers, the team owners and Hall of Famers, the Palm Beach set, they were all going to be at the reception in the Castaway Casino. We took the elevator down and found we were only steps away from it.

My late friend and mentor Lenny Cox had always said that there was no room he couldn't get into in Palm Beach if he was wearing a tux. I figured the theory was good for cruise ships too. The big guy in the suit at the casino entrance didn't agree.

"I'm sorry, sir, ma'am, but it's an invite-only event. There are open receptions in each of the buffets."

"Yeah, unfortunately we're expected in this one," I said.

"Then you'll need a ticket, sir."

He must have gotten a buzz in his earpiece because he

excused himself. I wasn't about to cause a scene, so I surveyed the surrounding area for somewhere we could sit and wait. I had a feeling that if Anastasia was in the casino there was a decent chance that Frederick hadn't gotten a ticket. He wasn't supposed to be on the cruise, and apparently taking a suite didn't come with one. So it was a great chance for her to meet up with Guy X. But we would have to wait outside and see if they came out together.

"There's a boutique over there," said Danielle.

"You don't see anything with a bar attached, do you?"

"Afraid not."

"Excuse me, sir? Mr. Jones?"

I turned back to the security guy at the door. My ship pass was back in my pocket so I wasn't sure how he knew my name.

"Yeah?"

"You can go in, sir."

"In the casino?"

"Yes, sir."

"What's the catch?"

"No catch, sir. Chief Mahoney says you can go in."

"Mahoney? How does he know—"

I stopped myself and turned around and looked at the ceiling. Opposite the casino entrance, on the other side of the corridor, was a video camera.

"He's watching?"

"Yes, sir." The guard held his arm out to usher us in. "Enjoy your evening."

The room looked like one of those casino nights that high schools hold as fundraisers. It wasn't big enough to be Reno, let alone Vegas, and the tables all seemed to be squeezed down at one end so a dance floor could be created at the other. No one was dancing. Cocktail tables had been set up along the periphery, and there was a door out to a large balcony or a small deck. I didn't know what distinguished one from the other.

A waiter offered us champagne. It would have been rude to refuse, and I realized why it was a ticketed event. My under-standing was that alcohol sales were a major money-spinner for the cruise lines, so giving it away had to come at a price. We looked around the room. There were a lot of tuxedos and a lot of gowns. It was a fine-looking group.

No finer than Ron Bennett. I was never completely sure if he was my sidekick or if I was his, but like air, he was always around when I needed him. He ambled over to us in his tux, his arm wrapped around the Lady Cassandra. She wore a long white dress and a silk shawl the color of the Caribbean Sea. They both looked happy. Cassandra kept her smile subtle and understated, just like her. Ron's sun-blotched face was grinning from ear to ear.

"Fancy meeting you here," he said.

"Lenny always said a tux could get you into any room," I replied.

"He was right more often than he was wrong."

I nodded. "You both look resplendent."

"You scrub up very well yourself, Mr. Jones," Cassandra said.

"So what have you two been up to?" Danielle asked, ever the investigator.

"Well, let's see." Cassandra tapped her chin. "Since we cast off from Florida? We checked into our suite, watched BJ's speech, then we went for walk, didn't we?" She looked at Ron and he nodded.

"We did."

"Oh, and of course, Ronnie asked me to marry him."

"That's fantastic," said Danielle, embracing Cassandra. Ron's face somehow got more flushed as he offered me his hand, but this wasn't a shaking moment. I gave him the big hug he deserved. I admired him. He was a romantic, in the old-fashioned sense of the word. And the old romantics, they put their hearts out there, on the line, more often than the rest of us. It meant they probably got hurt more often but at that moment I couldn't help but suspect that maybe the upside was more significant as well.

I hugged Cassandra and proposed a toast. We drank to their happiness, which they already had, and their longevity, which was never a given and so always worthy of raising a glass to. I found myself smiling, reflecting their faces. There was something about weddings and babies.

"Have you thought about the wedding?" Danielle asked.

"Nothing too big," said Cassandra. "We've both done that. I wouldn't care if it was just the two of us."

I was thinking about who exactly weddings were for when I saw Anastasia. She was in her burgundy gown and had put on a tiara I hadn't noticed back at the amphitheater. I figured for a jeweler it was product placement. She was chatting to a couple that I recognized from somewhere. It took a moment and some time travel but I got there in the end. They had been a famous ice dancing couple, a good few moons ago. They wore a few more wrinkles and he had a little less hair but they still looked trim and fit. They were hanging on a tale that Anastasia was telling. At least, I think they were hanging on her words. They may have drifted into comas. Anastasia spoke with a rhythmic motion to her head but she kept her body still and her hands by her side. She was about as animated as a cereal box.

I looked all around the vicinity for Guy X. There were a few dark-featured men but none had the look I had in my mind's eye. I started to wonder if I had the wrong picture in my head, the way movie stars never look the same in real life. Not that I had met that many movie stars. But I looked around the room and saw a decent number of recognizable faces. I saw a Hall of Fame quarterback from Denver and a coach from Chicago. A couple of owners of teams that never seemed to do any good. They all looked a little different in real life. Perhaps we all did.

We chatted for a while and Ron watched me watch the room. He raised an eyebrow and I shook my head. After a while they went back to mingle with friends. I didn't know anyone there except Danielle and BJ Baker, and I was already with one of them, and the other I didn't much care to see. So we took another drink and watched some folks play roulette. I didn't see the point. It was purely chance, no skill involved. It was tedious to play and more tedious to watch, but those around the table were reacting to the bouncing ball like they had some kind of control over it. Chance was part of life. Sometimes a pitch hit the bat in the middle, and the ball flew from the stadium and you lost, and sometimes the exact same pitch just missed the edge for a game-winning strike. But more often than not, good pitches won games and bad pitches lost them.

I caught the flash of a familiar white uniform as the captain headed for us. He thanked me again and I introduced him to Danielle.

"I trust your cabin is satisfactory," he said.

"Can I move in?" Danielle smiled.

"For the duration of the cruise, consider it your home."

"Thank you."

The captain grinned at me. "I understand you played football at University of Miami."

"I was on a football scholarship. Played might be overstating things a bit. I played more baseball."

"Dual athlete."

"Once upon a time. Can I ask how you know that?"

"I'm in the information business, Mr. Jones."

"Where does steering the ship come into it?"

"I have officers for that." He looked at our drinks. "Can I offer you a refill?"

"Why not?"

"Let me introduce you to some people."

Captain Sterling was wrong. He wasn't in the information business, although information was key to his role. His real business was the people business. He was charming and engaging. All the intel in the world did nothing for you if you had the demeanor of Henry Kissinger. But Sterling knew how to wield his information. He was like a politician. He knew everyone, their significant others, their team allegiances and their drink preferences. I started to wonder if he had someone whispering into his ear. That thought stopped me in my tracks. The notion that he had an earpiece just like the security guy at the door wasn't completely outside the realm of possibility.

Sterling introduced us to a group who turned out to be largely team owners. The interesting thing about them was this: They didn't talk about football. This was Pro Bowl weekend, one week until the Super Bowl. And that was the footballiest day of the football season and they didn't mention the game at all. Not the upcoming game, not the players, not the history of it all. On the one hand, it was reasonable. I owned a car and I didn't talk about cars much, except with my mechanic. But then I never went on car-themed cruises the week of the Daytona 500. If I had, I could conceive of chatting about cars to someone.

They were engaging people despite, or perhaps, because of it. They asked me what I did for a living, and I told them I was a contract killer. It always gets an uncomfortable giggle with the upper crust. They're never really sure if I'm kidding, and I'm never really sure if they actually know a contract killer and think I should be more discreet about it. Danielle told them she was with the FDLE, which she had to explain as being like the Florida version of the FBI.

"I've never heard of it," said one woman. "And I winter here every year."

"Do you carry a gun?" asked another.

"Most of the time, yes." Danielle smiled.

They seemed quite impressed with that.

"Mr. Jones," said a man with wire-frame glasses who owned a team on the left side of the Rockies. "Weren't you the one who did that work for BJ Baker?"

"Yes, sir. That was me."

"I heard he was very impressed."

"I heard different," I said.

The man nodded. "He can be quite the handful, BJ. But I have a matter that might be the sort of thing you can help with. Do you have a card?"

The fact was I did have a card. My office manager, Lizzy, had insisted that we get them done up. She was really thinking about Ron. He met a lot of people who had matters that were the sorts of things we could help with. He had probably given a card to Frederick Connors.

I pulled a card out of my wallet. It was curved to the shape of my butt but the man in the glasses didn't seem to care. He tucked it away in his breast pocket.

"I'll be in touch."

"Okay."

The man turned to one of the other owners. "Now who wants to try their luck on the craps table?"

They all nodded like that was an excellent idea. The man looked at me and Danielle. "Ms. Castle, Mr. Jones?"

"We'll leave you to it."

His wife frowned. "Are you sure you won't join us?"

I nodded and whispered, "I have a body to get rid of."

Her eyes went wide and she said, "How exciting."

We took our leave and grabbed seats at a bar away from the

gambling tables. Two big guys were already at the bar. These guys weren't big in the sense that most people think of it. They were enormous, built like retired super heroes. They were in regular suits, not tuxedos, and the material for their suits must have been measured by the acre.

I nodded to them as I sat and ordered two drinks.

"Enjoying the cruise?" asked the one closest to me.

"I could do without the suit," I said.

"I hear ya." He had a neck like a California redwood and it didn't look at home in a buttoned-up shirt and tie. "But at least the beer's free."

"Amen to that," I said. "I'm Miami Jones."

"D'Vante Morrison."

We shook hands. I'm a reasonably big guy. I'm a tick over six foot and have pitcher's shoulders, and I have the hands to match. But my hand disappeared inside D'Vante's. He could have pitched a bowling ball. His palms were like old leather. I introduced Danielle and he introduced his drinking partner, Adrian Pascal. I looked them over but I didn't recognize them.

"You gentlemen play?" I asked.

D'Vante nodded. "Once upon a time."

"Pro?"

D'Vante nodded and then asked, "You?"

"College."

"What school?"

"Miami," I said.

"Hence the name."

"Right."

Adrian spoke in a deep voice that reminded me of Harry Belafonte. "So what brings you to this thing?"

"Work, I suppose."

"You front office?"

"No. I guess you could say I work security."

"Security? At the bar?"

I nodded and sipped my beer.

"Nice gig."

"I like it. So you guys are all part of the pomp and ceremony?"

"Us?" D'Vante shook his head. "No, sir. We just here to make up the numbers, I guess."

"It must be a nice chance to catch up with old teammates, though."

Adrian shook his head. D'Vante said, "It is. Not that there's many of us left."

He said it the way a veteran spoke of GI pals from a long-forgotten war. I took a good look at both of them. They couldn't have been more than fifty. But they looked aged. Like that factory-beaten furniture that appears as if it came across on the *Mayflower* but really came on a container ship from Guangzhou last summer. The men's faces were hard and lined and it aged them some, but it was their eyes that aged them most of all. They had no sparkle. The color had seeped out and left them flat and dull.

"You're not that old," I said with a smile I didn't feel.

"There's old and there's old, you know?"

I nodded.

"Adrian here is gonna be inducted into the Hall of Fame next week, you know that?" D'Vante said. Adrian sipped on his beer as if he was embarrassed by the accolade.

"Congratulations," I said. "What position?"

"Offensive tackle," he said.

"What about you, D'Vante?"

"Tight end. And don't let my man tell you that tackle story. He played every position in the Gang of Six."

As he said it, a synapse fired in my brain and I connected the dots. Suddenly, I remembered them. In the early nineties they had been on one of the best offensive lines in football. For a couple years they were known as the Gang of Six, which I recalled being a strange moniker given that the standard offensive line in football only has five players in it. But there were six of them, and they could mix and match and move their positions depending on what plays the coach wanted to run. They were big and powerful and fast. They were fearsome. Looking at the big men before me, it felt like such a long time ago.

"Gang of Six," I said. "I remember you."

The men smiled gently but said nothing.

"You guys were ferocious."

"Yes, sir," said D'Vante.

"Well, congratulations on the Hall of Fame," I said to Adrian. He watched me but didn't answer or pick up his drink. D'Vante took up his own drink and tapped the glass of his buddy, who then nodded and picked his up.

"To the Hall of Fame," I toasted.

"To Clete," said Adrian.

D'Vante nodded. "Clete," he said softly.

"Clete?" Danielle asked.

"Clete James," said D'Vante. "He was one of us. He recently passed."

"I'm sorry," said Danielle.

"We all pass some time."

"We do," I said. "But let's delay it as long as we can, hey?"

"When you old, you old," said Adrian.

"You're really not that old," Danielle said.

"Football years is like dog years," said D'Vante. "You age seven for every year you play."

I was going to say something clever when I saw two women approaching with purpose, like school principals or Mormons. D'Vante turned to see what had caught my eye.

"We in trouble now," he said.

One of the women stopped by him and said, "I thought we might find you here."

"Just enjoying the hospitality," said D'Vante.

"You know Adrian here needs his rest."

The second woman had put her hands on Adrian's shoulders. He tilted his head in response, like a puppy.

D'Vante slipped off his stool. "It was nice talking with you folks."

"And you," I said. "I hope you enjoy the cruise."

As Adrian passed, I offered him the best for his Hall of Fame induction. He nodded and may have smiled. The woman behind him, who I assumed was his wife, smiled for sure.

"Thank you," she said. She looked dressed to kill but resigned to the fact that she wasn't hitting the town tonight.

We watched them walk away and then Danielle turned to me.

"He needs his rest? It's dinner time."

"It's Florida. Dinner time could be four in the afternoon."

"You'd love that, wouldn't you?"

"I would love—"

I didn't get to finish my thought because all hell broke loose in the casino.

# CHAPTER ELEVEN

THIS WAS NOT A WILD WEST KIND OF CROWD. THIS WAS the kind of crowd that believed in following the rules, mostly because they wrote the rules. But they were also a competitive bunch. Former players might have stopped playing the game, but they hadn't left their competitive natures back in the locker room when they hung up their cleats. And the people who owned the teams were generally rich business types who used cash reserves rather than points on the board as their way of keeping score.

So whatever way it had happened, no one was going to take being called a cheat lying down. But that was what had transpired. Someone at a card table accused another player of being a cheat, of slipping a card into the deck or some such. I didn't think such a thing was possible, but this wasn't Vegas. Tempers frayed and chairs got knocked over and punches were thrown. We watched the disturbance ripple across the room, and then all of a sudden security people were everywhere.

We stayed at the bar and watched things play out. Danielle remarked how proud she was that I hadn't gotten involved. I wasn't afraid of getting dirty if the situation warranted, but I preferred keeping my fights to issues that involved me, and this most definitely didn't. We saw Army come into the room and talk to a few of his guys, and then a couple of people were escorted out. The room didn't return to its previous mellow state. There was a jacked energy in the air. The kind of buzz I recalled when I used to take the field.

Army saw us at the bar and strode over.

"The cowboys getting out of hand?" I asked.

"I underestimated these people," he said. "Is it a full moon tonight?"

"Not sure the moon's even up yet."

"In that case, we're in for a long night."

"You look like you've got it under control."

"Here we do. I always have extra bodies in the casino. Gambling has a habit of bringing out the devil in folks. But elsewhere . . ."

"What happened elsewhere?"

"We just had another disturbance in the Hall of Fame room."

"The museum? Tell me it wasn't BJ's Heisman."

"No. A fight, we think."

"You don't know?"

"There was a lot of he said/he said by the time I got there with my guys. But we'll figure it out when we check the video."

"Cameras everywhere," I said.

"Excuse me, Mr. Mahoney." We turned to see the auctioneer, Arnold. He was still wearing a bow tie but he looked less like an accountant now, since the tie was accompanied by a tuxedo. His head glistened with a sheen of perspiration.

"Yes, sir?"

"I was just informed there was a melee in the Hall of Fame room."

"A melee?"

"A disturbance. And another in here."

"Yes, sir. But both situations are under control now."

"Yes, I'm sure. My concern is more with regard to the auction room."

"What about it, sir?"

He leaned in like he was about to share state secrets.

"Is it secure, Mr. Mahoney? I see a lot of personnel in here, and I assume more reported to the disturbance in the other room. So who is watching the auction items, Mr. Mahoney? There are some very valuable pieces, and the vendors are concerned."

"Sir, that room is not open to the public. It is locked and under guard."

"And those guards were not called away to these disturbances?"

"No, sir, they were not. There are two entrances to ballroom two and we have personnel on both, to be relieved on a rotating basis until the room opens again tomorrow for you and your vendors to prepare for public exhibition."

"You'll forgive me if I prefer to verify that? The vendors are concerned."

"I can show you the video feed, if you like. Or I'll be happy to take you down to ballroom two and you can see the guards yourself."

Army was clearly adept at handling the well-heeled clientele. I had imagined the ship would be more of a party vessel with its short weekend tours, and perhaps this trip was an anomaly. But either way, Army moved between the socioeconomic groups with ease. Just as well for him, as I noticed a line forming behind Arnold, with more concerned faces. The closest these folks usually got to violence was watching it on the field on Sundays, and even then, you didn't hear the impact of three-hundred pound body on three-hundred pound body from behind the glass of the corporate boxes.

Arnold turned to the worried faces and gave them a translation of what Army had just said. It was all under control, nothing to be concerned with. He would personally oversee security for the auction room. Though, I was pretty confident he didn't plan on sitting outside the door all night. One of the vendors—a guy I thought I recalled hanging a tropical Gauguin for auction—asked if he could follow along, just to be sure. Then another said if the first guy was going, then he was going too. Then it became a quorum. Arnold turned to Army.

"Let's all go for a walk, folks," Army said.

Army nodded to us and turned to lead the group away.

"Shouldn't you be going with them?"

I found Anastasia Connors standing before me.

"Since you are security, so-called."

I gave her a big grin. "Of course," I said. "We were just letting the vendors walk ahead."

She gave me a look that suggested she didn't believe me.

I winked at Danielle and she slipped off her stool.

"Field trip," she said.

We let the group of vendors, including Anastasia, form a line behind Army. We looked like a shore tour off to visit a rum distillery, or those swimming pigs in the Exumas. Danielle and I took up the rear. About a dozen of us trooped over to the elevator. The ballroom being used for the auction was one deck down from the casino. Danielle and I took the stairs and waited for the elevator to meet us. Army gave another nod as he led the group out and we again dropped in behind.

The corridor opened up into a lobby, and we found a man standing outside a closed door, like the Secret Service guys who wait while the president does his business inside. The man was at attention. I wondered if someone had given him the heads-up that we were on our way down.

"Chief," he said to Army, like they actually were in the army.

"Smith," said Army. "Anything happening?"

"All quiet, sir."

"Door locked?"

Smith didn't answer. He stepped aside and let Army test the door for himself. It was locked. Army turned to the watching faces.

"Ladies and gentlemen, as I said. The room is locked and guarded. The other door is around the corner and you will find it guarded in the same manner."

One of the group broke off to check. He stopped, looked and then nodded, before returning to us.

Anastasia looked at me.

"It's all good," I said.

"No thanks to you," she said.

"Can we get in?" asked the man with the Gauguin.

"No, sir. Your keycard won't work until the morning."

"I'd like to check my pieces."

"Me, also," said another man.

"I think we'd all like that," said Anastasia.

I watched Army closely. He was good. I would have let out an exasperated sigh. But he didn't. He knew that letting them in for five minutes to check their toys was better than arguing about it for ten minutes and then letting them in.

Army used his keycard and then an actual old-fashioned key to unlock the door. He asked the vendors to line up and show their ship pass to his security guard so he could confirm their vendor status.

I looked into the room and saw darkness. Army stepped inside and turned on a handful of lights. It wasn't the same cabaret look from earlier. Now it was closer to emergency lighting and it gave the room a lot of dark corners, which made me think of the *Titanic*, and that wasn't a direction I wanted my brain to go.

The vendors each drifted over to their respective stands or stalls and checked their merchandise. Artwork was inspected and statuettes uncovered and drawers of posters were opened. Nothing looked amiss. The thought occurred to me that if I wanted to steal something from the room, now would be the time to do it. The lighting was poor and the vendors looked like the ghosts of long-dead dancers floating across the ballroom floor. Though, of course, my logic was flawed—if there ever was any logic to thinking about ghosts—because the ship was new and no such people had trod its shiny floors at all.

I doubled-checked the door and to see that the guard that Army had put in place was standing firm, not letting anyone in or out without ID. I wandered over to Danielle who was at Anastasia's station. Anastasia herself had taken some time to get down behind her cabinet to access her safe. Wearing a long gown didn't make that kind of thing easy. I heard her punch in the code, then there was a clunk, and then she pulled out one of the black boxes and placed it on the glass top of the cabinet. She repeated the process with the second box. Then she slowly stood and brushed off her gown.

She took the first box and slipped off the cover. There was no spotlighting to highlight the gems inside, but the rings were all present and accounted for. Army was marching slowly around the room, watching. He made his way around to us and glanced at the rings. I thought they would catch his interest. He looked like a football fan to my eye.

"Everything in order, ma'am?" he asked Anastasia.

She nodded curtly. "Yes."

Army glanced at the rings again. "A fine collection. But you might consider putting them in chronological order."

"They are in order," she replied.

"With respect, ma'am, if they were in order, Green Bay would be the first, not New York."

We all looked at the rings. Army was right. The first ring in the collection belonged to the Jets, from Super Bowl III.

"Good eye," I said.

"Packers are my team," said Army.

That figured. In my experience, lots of solid, dependable types like Army turned out to be Green Bay fans. Perhaps it was the nature of the place itself—cold and harsh and unforgiving in the football season—or perhaps it was the nature of the ownership structure, being the only publicly owned NFL team. Were it in private hands, there was no doubt in my mind that in the media-obsessed world we lived in, the team would have been moved out of tiny Green Bay, Wisconsin, years ago. But the ownership structure all but ensured that couldn't happen, and solid folks like Army were drawn to that sense of permanence.

"I'm sure you're wrong," said Anastasia.

"He's not," I said. "Green Bay was first."

"That can't be. I put them in order myself."

"You may have done that, but earlier today when your rings were inspected by the auctioneer, Green Bay was first. I remembered it specifically, because they were in chronological order."

Danielle said, "Are you sure you remember all of them?"

"No. I couldn't tell you thirteen from fifteen, at least not without a lot of thought. But any real fan knows the last winner and the first winner. Those were the first two rings I looked at when the box was opened. And this morning those two were where they should be."

"Perhaps the auctioneer put them back in the wrong order?" asked Danielle.

"He didn't. He inspected them one at a time, leaving only one specific space in the box to put each one back. And anyway, I did the same thing after he valued them. Just before they were locked away. I looked at them again and was drawn back to the first and last. They were where they should be."

"Maybe you mistook the Jets for Green Bay."

I shot Danielle a look. "I'm from New England. We don't mistake the Jets for anything but the Jets."

Danielle shrugged. "What difference does it make anyway? They can be reordered."

Which is what I thought Anastasia was going to do. She picked up the Jets rings from Super Bowl III and looked at it and frowned. Then she looked up and around the room at the lighting and grumbled under her breath.

"I don't have my loupe," she said. "Where is Arnold?"

"He's around," said Army. "I'll find him."

"Is there a problem?" I asked.

Anastasia gave me a pinched look. "For you."

I said nothing to that.

Army returned with the auctioneer in tow.

"Your loupe," Anastasia said. "Now."

Arnold handed her his round magnifying glass which she snatched from his hand. She put the device to her eye and inspected the ring, then she held it out to Arnold.

"Look at this."

Arnold took the ring and the loupe and checked the ring over. Then he dropped the magnifying glass from his eye, put it back again and checked the ring once more.

"I don't understand," he said.

"You see it?" asked Anastasia.

"What is it?" asked Army.

Arnold held the ring up so we could see it.

"It appears to be some kind of zinc alloy with cubic zirconia stones."

"What does that mean?" I asked.

"It means this ring is a fake."

Arnold placed the ring back in the box and took the second one in line, belonging to the Kansas City Chiefs. He inspected it and then replaced it. He took the next ring, Baltimore Colts, and looked it over.

"They're all fakes," he whispered.

"Of course they are," I said. "Isn't that the point?"

"You stupid man," said Anastasia.

"No," said Arnold. "The other rings were reproductions, fully licensed. They were exact copies in every way. The gold, the diamonds, all the same as the originals. The gems alone were worth tens of thousands on each ring. These are cheap knockoffs."

"So the others were real fakes but these are fake fakes?"

"Yes."

"And the others were worth thousands?"

"I set the reserve on each ring at thirty thousand. Some would sell for double that."

"And what are these ones worth?"

"This ring," he said, looking at the Colts ring, "is worth maybe twenty bucks on eBay."

"How?" I said, my thoughts leaking out through my mouth.

"You," said Anastasia. "You were security. You're responsible."

I really wanted to tell her why I was actually there, but I knew Ron would think less of me for it, so I bit my tongue.

"I'm going to sue you for everything," she said.

"I don't have anything," I said. Then I thought of my newly renovated home. It was something, and it was something that meant something to me, although until that second I hadn't realized how much it meant to me.

"I'll have the shirt off your back."

"Perhaps we should check the other box?" said Army.

Arnold did so, with the same result. Fakes.

"Okay, let's take a step back," I said. "You inspected the rings earlier this afternoon?" I said to Arnold.

He nodded. "I did."

"And they were fine."

"Absolutely fine."

"And you couldn't have made a mistake?"

Now he gave me a look. Everyone was doing it. It was becoming a thing.

"I think I know the difference between a quality gemstone and a piece of plastic."

"Sure, I'm just asking," I said. "So you checked the rings and they went back in the boxes here."

"Yes. Then Mrs. Connors and I went to my desk to sign the auction agreement, and I took possession of the certificates of authenticity."

"The rings were left with you," said Anastasia, clearly making a point.

"They were," I said. "You put the lids back on both the boxes before you left. And your husband took the boxes and put them in the safe. He left the safe open."

"I locked it when I returned," she said.

"Yes, you did."

"Could the original fakes still be here?" Danielle asked.

"They are not fakes," said Anastasia. "Licensed reproductions, will you get it right?"

"I apologize, ma'am. But could the reproductions still be here?"

I made to get under the cabinet and search but Anastasia put a stop to that.

"Not you. Him." She pointed at Army, so he got down on his hands and knees and checked the area.

"Nothing," he said, standing. "I'll alert my staff and confirm nothing has left this room." He strode away to the door. When he came back he said, "My man confirms that no bags have been brought into the room and he will let none leave. Either way, you came straight here when the door opened. No other vendor could have gotten near without you seeing them."

"So how did two boxes of real rings turn into two boxes of fake rings?" I posed. "Inside a locked safe, which was itself inside a locked, guarded room, which was on a ship at sea."

"We need to check the video," said Army. He strode away again.

"There's some serious David Copperfield stuff going on here," I said.

Anastasia looked at me in disgust.

"Well," she said. "Go with him! Do your job! Or you'll be hoping David Copperfield can make *you* disappear."

## CHAPTER TWELVE

Army stayed until the vendors had confirmed that no other pieces had been stolen or replaced with fakes. Then he locked the room himself and left his guards in place. Danielle had offered to escort Anastasia back to her suite but Anastasia had suggested she wasn't going back to her suite, but when she did, it would likely be safer to do it alone. Danielle endured the jab without comment, but when Anastasia finally left, Danielle followed her regardless. Following someone solo on a cruise ship wasn't that easy to do, but Danielle was a pro, and hopefully she would wind up watching Anastasia in a dining room or bar or some other well-trafficked area.

I went with Army to the security room, which was buzzing. Video was being watched and fast-forwarded and rewound and watched all over.

"Who has ballroom two?" asked Army.

"I do, sir," said a guy at the end of the room.

"Talk to me."

We stood behind the guy, who paused the video he was watching.

"I have the video from the time ball two was closed to the

vendors for the night. I'm watching it through at speed for the first pass."

"And?"

"Nothing, sir. I'm not done yet, but so far no one goes in or out. Jeffries is on post first shift, and then Smith takes over. That's it."

"Keep at it. I need someone to go over the video for the other side of the room."

"I'm on it, sir," said a young woman in the next seat. She didn't pause her video or take her eyes from the screen. "No action at all."

"And inside the room?"

"You have video in the room?" I asked.

"Of course," said Army. "Three angles, if I recall correctly."

Another guy at a similar console directed our attention to the two screens on the wall. "Chief, I have the three cameras. With the way the room is set up, only two have an angle on the cabinet where the rings were held. And one of those is only partial. I'm focusing on the one on the left there, with the best view."

"Can you show me the rings arriving?"

"Yes, Chief." He tapped at his keyboard and brought up a long shot from behind the auctioneer's lectern. On the far right, I saw the booth where Anastasia would set up. The glass cabinet was empty. Then Frederick, Danielle and I walked into shot. We stopped by the cabinet and then waited. And waited.

"What was happening here?" asked Army.

"Nothing. We were waiting for his wife to arrive."

"They didn't come together?"

"No. Apparently she was still getting ready in the suite."

"What did you talk about while you waited?"

"Nothing at all. He didn't seem all that chatty."

"And he didn't have the rings?"

"No. She had them."

"So why were you with him? Shouldn't security be with the valuables?"

"We were a last-minute engagement, by him. I hadn't yet met Mrs. Connors."

Army glanced at me. He wasn't completely buying my story. Which proved again that he was a sharp operator. I considered telling him my real reason for being on board but decided to hold that for later.

He turned back to the screen, and we watched Anastasia arrive with her little roller case. She took the boxes out and placed them on the glass-topped counter, before opening each one. Then Arnold the auctioneer came over and did his appraisal.

"So he checked the rings?" asked Army.

"Yes. Each one individually. He was quite thorough."

"And he gave them the okay?"

"He did. Exquisite was the word he used."

"I've never thought of a Super Bowl ring as exquisite."

"Me either."

On screen, Arnold and Anastasia walked away and then Frederick took the closed boxes and put them in the safe.

"So what happened here?"

"The auctioneer asked Anastasia to sign some documents related to the auction. And he took the certificates of authenticity. Anastasia closed the boxes and her husband put them in the safe."

"You saw him do this?"

"I did."

"And then?"

"What you see on the video is what I saw. He didn't lock the safe, though. He said she would want to do that."

We watched Anastasia return and drop behind the cabinet to lock the safe.

"Did you watch her lock it?"

"No. She didn't want me seeing the code she used. But she closed it, and I heard the electronic lock."

"But you didn't test it to see if it was locked properly."

"No."

He nodded to himself.

"But she pulled on the handle to make sure it was closed. It was."

We watched Frederick offer his arm to his wife. They walked away and security ushered the vendors out. Danielle and I stayed in place for a moment, watching them go, then we left as well.

"That's it?" asked Army.

"That's it, Chief."

"Anyone go near the cabinet after that?"

"No one. I'm going to check the video after the room is locked."

"And did anyone go in or out that should not have?"

A woman at a table to the side of the room swiveled around. "Only two names didn't have proper vendor authorization, sir. Jones and Castle."

Army looked at me.

"Like I say, it was a last minute engagement. I guess Mr. Connors hadn't set that up."

"Right," he said.

He looked me in the eyes. I knew the look. He was summing me up. I'd been summed up plenty of times before. My fiancée did it often. But his look didn't reassure me. He had doubts. Millions of dollars in jewels had gone missing aboard his ship. That sort of thing didn't make for good PR. And I suspected his job in such circumstances was first and foremost to protect the interests of the cruise line. But I also knew he was a straight shooter. He'd take a theft like that personally. On his watch, that kind of thing. So he'd want to figure out what the hell had happened. And so far he only had two people anywhere near the stolen items whose stories didn't add up.

Danielle Castle and Miami Jones.

I ran it through. What would I think in his position? If I had taken the rings, how would I get away with it? By messing with any investigation. And how would I do that? By getting in on said investigation. But how? I thought about how I had gotten here. The incident in the Hall of Fame, and then the incident at BJ Baker's speech. Both events I could have set up. Save the captain some embarrassment and get in his good graces. Get on the inside of things. That's how I would have done it, if I wanted to set things up. That's what I'd be thinking if I were Army. And if I were Army, I wouldn't let me anywhere near the investigation now. Which might not matter to me, since I really wasn't security at all. But then again, it might matter if I ever needed Army's help to track Guy X. There were a lot of cameras on board, and only one of me. I could really use his help.

"We need to talk," I said.

"You're damn right," he said, directing me out of the room.

# CHAPTER THIRTEEN

Army's office was a locker-sized room next to security control. There was space against the wall for a desk and a single chair. He gave me the chair and he leaned against the desk so that he was looking down at me. Classic interrogation position.

"I was hired by Frederick Connors," I said.

"That much we know."

"Only I'm not security."

"That much we also know."

"This needs to stay between us."

"You need to clean up your story. What stays between us, I will decide later."

"Fair enough. Frederick Connors thinks his wife is having an affair."

He frowned. "An affair?"

"Yes."

"Mrs. Connors?"

"Yes."

"With who?"

"I don't know."

"You don't know?"

"Mr. Connors has seen a guy hanging around, coming out of his house. He doesn't know the guy's name. We're calling him Guy X."

"Guy X?"

"Yes."

"Guy X? This what you came up with? You read a lot of spy novels?"

"What would you call him?"

"I have no idea. Keep talking."

"Mr. Connors was not supposed to be on this cruise. He suspected that his wife would meet up with this Guy X while on board, and he hired me to confirm it."

"So why is he here?"

"I guess he decided to be here in case it was true, or maybe in case it wasn't."

"Wouldn't him being here scupper their plans to get together?"

"That's what I said. But he insisted he would stay mostly in his cabin."

"Why would his wife buy that?"

"He doesn't like cruises. He gets seasick. That's where he is this evening. In his cabin."

"He gets seasick?"

"Yes. He says he can't swim."

"And you're supposed to follow his wife."

"Right."

"You're not doing much of that."

"We were watching her at the cocktail thing in the casino."

"You find this Guy X?"

"Haven't seen any trace of him yet."

"They could be together now."

"Danielle is following her."

So your story is that this theft is just a coincidence."

"No. That's not my story at all."

"It's not?"

"No. Coincidences happen, sure. But this one's a doozy."

"So you have a theory?"

"Fragments of theories. Nothing solid."

"You want to share?"

"Guy X."

"What about him?"

"He's behind it. Maybe it's part of the affair. Maybe he and Mrs. Connors are in it together. Maybe he's using her to get to the rings."

"But you don't even know if he exists."

"No."

"And right now we know who the likeliest customer is."

"It's me. But come on. Do you think I'd be that sloppy? Surely I would get the proper credentials to be in the room. Why draw suspicion to myself?"

"Why indeed."

"And it doesn't answer the real question."

"Which is?"

"How did the rings go missing? I was there, sure. But I never physically touched them. Mrs. Connors locked them up tight and your video shows no one else going in the room."

"That's what you'd want me to think."

"Sure. So go do your job. Don't listen to me. Look at the videos. Follow the trail."

"And what do you think I'll find?"

I raised my eyebrows.

"The invisible Guy X?" he asked.

"Or someone else, I really don't know. But I know it's not me. So you do your job, maybe you find my guy."

"And you want in on the investigation?"

"No. Not if you don't trust me, and not if you can't use me. Put your cameras on Mrs. Connors. I bet she leads you to Guy X. If they do, just let me know."

He looked me over again. He knew I knew he was doing it and he didn't care one bit.

"It's a big ship. Where do think she is now?"

"Danielle will know."

"Can you call her?"

"Cellphones work out here?"

"Reception's patchy but the vessel has ship-to-shore via satellite."

"I don't think she has her phone. I know I left mine in the cabin."

"So much for that, then."

The phone on Army's deck rang. He picked it up.

"Chief of Security."

He listened and then said, "That so? Put her through."

He turned his eyes to me.

"Ms. Castle, what can I do for you?"

He listened again. He made no expression and gave nothing away. I wouldn't play him in poker. He'd have taken the shirt from my back before Anastasia Connors could get her mitts on it.

"Thank you, Ms. Castle. If you'll stay there I'll have one of my people come and bring you up to the security office. Mr. Jones is here with us."

He hung up and told me to stay put, and then walked out of the office. He wasn't gone long.

"I've got one of my team watching the feed from your suite's passageway."

"My suite? Why?"

"Because you're two doors down from your client, remember? Ms. Castle called from the house phone to let you know that Mrs. Connors had returned to her suite after all, and Ms. Castle found out that she couldn't watch it, since there really isn't anywhere for someone to wait up there without looking suspicious."

"She's good like that."

"I can see who the brains behind the operation is."

"Me too. Every day."

A moment later there was a knock at the door and a uniformed crew member opened up for Danielle. She stepped inside the small space. She smelled far better than the disinfectant that had dominated before her arrival.

"Cozy," she said.

"Ms. Castle, I won't go through everything because I'm sure Mr. Jones will update you. But as you requested, I have put a watch on your passageway. We'll know if either Mrs. Connors or Mr. Connors leave their suite."

"Thanks," she said. "Any movement on the rings?"

Army glanced at me and then at Danielle. "Not much. We'll comb the video and see what we see. But you're FDLE, right?"

"Yes, sir."

"So how do you solve a closed-room caper like this?"

"Eliminate the suspects, eliminate the possibilities."

"What possibilities?"

"The rings were in a safe, in a locked room, on a ship. So three options: one, they were never in the room; two, they were in the room and were taken out somehow; and three, they're still in the room."

"Makes sense. But option one, we know they were there."

"We suspect it."

"You were there, you saw them."

"I saw something. But I don't know anything about these rings. What I saw could have come from a Cracker Jack box for all I know."

"They were verified by the auctioneer."

"Right, which is a check against point one. But the auctioneer could have been lying."

Army nodded and I just watched. Danielle was on a roll.

"All right. Point two?"

"Point three first. They're still in the room. This is the easiest to check. You could go through that room with a fine-tooth comb. You could pat down everyone who leaves. And for sure you're going to keep videoing everything in and around that room. So if they're still there, getting them out is risky."

"I agree."

"Me too," I said.

Army shook his head at me. "So, point two."

"The most likely. If the auctioneer lied, then so did Mrs. Connors, which means they're both in on it. And I think that would be easy to prove. The auctioneer isn't going to do that for free. She would have to pay him. So we look at his financials. Too easy to find a trail."

"Crooks do make mistakes."

"They do. That's how they usually get caught, so nothing is ruled out. All these options should be explored."

"Beyond my resources," said Army.

"Not beyond mine," said Danielle.

"All right, let's keep that in our pocket. Let's assume the auctioneer was truthful. Then what?"

Danielle shrugged. "Then someone took rings from a locked box in a locked room, on a ship."

"That doesn't help."

"But it does. They're still on the ship. You can't just jump in a getaway car to escape a cruise ship."

"They have to get the rings off," I said. Both Army and Danielle looked at me like I had just appeared from thin air.

"Where do we make landfall?" she asked.

Army said, "Other than when we get back to Palm Beach, the only stop is tomorrow, on Paradise Cay."

"Maybe that's it," I said.

"But even that doesn't help them much," Army said. "It's a private island owned by the cruise line. They'd still be stuck on an island."

We were looking at each other, searching for some kind of solution, when Army's phone rang again. He picked it up and listened and then said we'd be right there.

"Mrs. Connors just left her suite."

# CHAPTER FOURTEEN

ARMY LED US BACK INTO THE SECURITY CONTROL ROOM, where one of his team had put the video from our deck onto a screen on the wall. Anastasia had changed out of her gown into a purple long sleeved blouse and white pants. I got the feeling that was her version of dressing down, but even so she would have fit in at a lot of weddings in gear like that. She walked as she had before, head high, an air of certainty about her, although she looked less like a Russian aristocrat and more like the Greenwich, Connecticut, kind of money that lunches after a long session of retail therapy at Bloomingdale's.

She headed aft to the elevator and waited for it to arrive. We waited to see where she was going. When the elevator came she got in and disappeared from view. The woman in front of the screen tapped her console and brought up another camera angle that showed Anastasia in the elevator. She checked her look in the mirror at the rear and then stood tall. When the elevator stopped, we waited for her to get out. She didn't. Someone else got in. A man. Our camera angle gave us a prime shot of his bald patch. The elevator stopped again and the man held the door open as Anastasia stepped out.

"Five," said the woman operating the console. She tapped again and brought up a camera angle across the open lobby area adjacent to the elevators. The balding man was walking toward the camera's position. Anastasia headed the other way, along a corridor.

"What's down there?" I asked.

"Retail, the spa," said Army. "Not much."

"It's Guy X," I said.

"Where?" asked Army.

"She's meeting him. I need to get down there."

Army snapped up a small walkie-talkie and spoke to the woman operating the video. "Tell me where she goes."

Army led us back out to the elevator. We didn't have to wait. The car was waiting for us. Army swiped his card and hit the button for deck five. We descended in silence. When the door opened Army called in.

"Do you have a location?"

"She went to the lobby near the spa."

Army led us to the port side and then cut up the corridor toward the bow of the ship. We entered what looked like an airport concourse. Lots of brightly lit stores selling spirits, cigarettes, the latest fashions. We stopped just beyond a store selling electronic gadgets and Army called in again.

"Where?" he said.

There was a pause at the other end. "One moment, sir."

"Come on."

"Sorry, sir. I've lost her. She was in the spa lobby and then I changed cameras and she was gone. I see you now."

"We're not looking for me," Army said, but he didn't say it into the walkie-talkie. He looked at me and Danielle.

"I'll take port, you take starboard."

He broke left and we made our way right. In front of us was the entrance to the spa. It smelled like lilies and the interior was all soft lighting and pale Scandinavian wood. Danielle ducked inside as I headed for the corridor that ran alongside it. The corridor came to an abrupt end at a door that was marked *crew only*. I stood for a moment and looked it over. It didn't seem to be alarmed or locked. It had a big push bar across it. Danielle arrived at my hip.

"She's not in the spa."

I heard the sound of several sets of feet behind me but didn't investigate. I pushed through the door and we found ourselves outside. The moon wasn't full after all, but it did throw plenty of light across the ship's forward-most deck. It was plain and utilitarian, probably a green non-slip paint covering the surface, ropes coiled in the bow. In the middle of the deck was a hot tub. It was dark and dormant and I couldn't fathom why it was there. Then the door open again behind us, and Danielle and I both turned to Army.

But it wasn't Army.

"You got me in trouble," said the blond guy in the Cleveland Browns jersey. Not only had he not bothered to change for dinner, it appeared that dinner had been of a liquid variety. He stumbled as though we were rolling in a fifty-foot swell, rather than floating on the dead-flat Bahama Banks. I took note of his three buddies. They had less to say but seemed equally well lubricated. They fanned out into a line.

"It's time to party," he said.

"Really?" I said. "That's what you're going with? *It's time to party?*"

"You got something better?"

"Everything is better than that. A barbaric yawp would be better than that. You've had hours to come up with a pithy remark and all you've come up with is a bad Schwarzenegger retread."

I wanted this goose thinking. Clearly it wasn't a strong

point, and while he was doing it, I was looking around the deck for some kind of weapon. I wasn't concerned about getting beaten up by four drunk frat boys. Danielle could take three of them and I was good for the last one. But random punches sometimes landed and I wasn't eager to wear one. What I did want was to get rid of them. Army was just as likely to be right behind them, and he was already a little suspicious of our relationship. I didn't think it would improve much if he found us out on a crew-only deck. I scanned again for a weapon. I didn't find one.

I found Frederick Connors.

He was standing on the other side of the deck with his hand in the air. While I tried to figure out what he was doing, Danielle stepped forward.

"Boys, I am a special agent with the Florida Department of Law Enforcement. I think it might be best if you head back to your cabins before things get out of hand."

I watched Frederick step around in a circle. For moment I thought he must have been throwing up over the side of the deck, but I realized he holding up a cell phone, trying to get a signal. I'm not sure what kind of cell tower he thought he would find out in the middle of the ocean, but I suspected logging onto the ship's satellite system would have produced a better result. I was going to call to him when Cleveland doofus number one spoke up.

"You gonna hide behind a chick?"

I glanced at him. I wanted to remember what his face looked like before Danielle disfigured it. I took a second look and decided that Danielle would only have to take down one of her three, because two others were already backing off. I glanced at Frederick to make sure he was staying put. I'd catch up with old Frederick shortly.

And then I saw Guy X.

Like the photograph I had memorized, the lighting on the bow deck wasn't great and in a strange way that helped. I saw the outlines, the shape of his head, and the shadow of his deepset eyes. I forgot all about Cleveland. I turned toward Guy X just as he stepped out from the shadow of the decks above and moved along the edge toward Frederick. For a second, I thought a fight might break out on both sides of me. That would make Army really happy. But Guy X didn't raise his arms to suckerpunch Frederick. He did the opposite. He went down. He wrapped his arms around Frederick's legs. And he tipped Frederick off the deck.

For a second I was dumbstruck. I couldn't quite comprehend what I had just seen. Then it all clicked into place. The wife's new boyfriend getting rid of the husband. It felt so cliché. Throwing the husband off a cruise ship into the ocean.

*The ocean.*

Frederick hated cruise ships. He hated the ocean. Because he couldn't swim. I didn't think anymore. I broke into a sprint. I saw Guy X cut back into the shadows, and Cleveland yelled out "chicken." I didn't pay either of them any mind. I pumped as hard as I could and sped across the deck, past the hot tub. I'm not an Olympic sprinter. Few baseball pitchers are. But I run on City Beach pretty regularly, so I got there quick enough. I didn't see Guy X. I didn't look for him. I just hit the gunwale hard and vaulted over the edge.

# CHAPTER FIFTEEN

THE FIRST THOUGHT I HAD AS I LAUNCHED INTO THE NIGHT was that I would probably die from the impact. Such thoughts are all about timing, and would have been useful while I was sprinting across the deck. Once in midair, not so much.

My second thought, however, was a memory. I recalled that as we had boarded earlier that day I had looked up at the sheer size of the ship and noted that the lowest outdoor point appeared to be the forward deck, with the other decks towering above. I had the notion that the distance from the forward deck to the water was the height of about two or three high-dive platforms. I had no premonition that I would need this information or I would have probably refused to get on the boat. But knowing that as I did, I figured I might just make it after all. I had jumped off a high-dive platform before. It was accurately named. It was damned high. Two or three times that was madness, and if I had climbed a ladder to get there I would have left Frederick Connors to drown. Damn him for living in Florida and not being able to swim.

The breeze felt warm as I dropped, and I made myself long and thin like a six foot one pencil and braced for impact.

The water was cold. Not Bering Strait cold. Not even California cold. But it took my breath away, although that may have been due to the impact. I shot down and down, and for a moment I thought I might hit bottom. Then I slowed and stopped and found myself in stasis, floating like a lab experiment in formaldehyde, deep under the ocean surface.

First thing I did was lose my jacket that had become tangled around my head. I thrashed it off and pushed away from it and swam for the surface. The water stung my eyes so I couldn't see a thing and I had no idea how deep I was, but I kept kicking and stroking, hoping that buoyancy had pointed me in the right direction. My lungs burned and I felt bile rising in my throat. I came to the conclusion that I was going to gag and take on water and then my lungs were going to fill and I would be done.

I didn't believe the first gasp of air. I gulped a second greedily, as if someone might take it from me. Then a wash of water was shoved down my throat and I reconsidered if I had reached the surface at all. I coughed and spluttered and spat. Then I opened my eyes. A great steel hull loomed above, pulsing through the water and sending waves crashing across me.

The downside was that I had jumped from the front of the ship. That meant I was going to bear the full impact of the wake. The upside was it pushed me away from the vessel. I rode the wake away from the hull and as I watched the ship power on through the water, I pulled off the tie that was choking at my throat. I ripped the top button from my shirt and took a couple breaths, and then I set about doing what I was down there to do.

The lights from the decks above only shone out so far, so my search was based more on sound and dumb luck. I looked for a man thrashing in the water and hoped that Frederick hadn't already given up and sunk. I didn't spot anything in the breaking wake. I called his name but heard nothing. Then I got the idea that like leaves tossed in a river, given we had hit the water at the same place, we would follow the same approximate path away from the ship. It wasn't an exact theory but it gave me something to work with. I began stroking in the direction the ship was leaving. Frederick had hit the water around seven or eight seconds before I had. He would be behind me, if he wasn't below me.

By the time the wake of the ship leveled out, I was just about done. The ship was gone. I could see the amphitheater at the stern mocking me as it drifted off into the night. I kept my eye on the water and called Frederick's name again and again but my calls got increasingly weak.

I thought what I hit was a shark. I nearly had a coronary. I flapped like I was a drowning man myself and turned and saw the body floating right by me. Frederick Connors was facing the sky, like a kid in a pool, floating on a summer's night, taking in the stars. But Frederick's eyes were closed. I pulled him to me and slapped his face.

"Fred!" I yelled. "Fred!"

I coughed up some water but got no such response from Frederick. Perhaps he didn't respond to Fred. But I figured he would have cut me some slack, given the circumstances. I pulled him around in the water so I could slip in underneath him and rest his head on my shoulder. Then I checked his air passage for obstructions. There were none. He was just full of water.

CPR was going to be tough. For starters, I didn't have a lot air myself. But my bigger issue was having nothing to push against. I decided to try the mouth-to-mouth first. I came out from under him and tipped his head on my shoulder like I was going to give his furry face a passionate kiss. I pinched his nose, pulled his chin down, put my mouth to his, and blew hard. I took another gulp of air and went in again. I knew I wasn't going to be able to keep it up for long. I could tread water all night if I had to, but I couldn't do it while puffing everything I had into

Frederick. I gave it another minute or two. I wasn't sure how long it was. Time was as fluid as the ocean around me.

I cursed the stupid man and why he got on a damned ship in the first place. And I cursed myself and why I hadn't seen Guy X earlier and why I hadn't picked up on what he was about to do. I spat salt water and told Frederick to hold on. I told him I'd give it one last try. I breathed in as deep as I could, and I pulled him in and I blew hard. I blew until I was about to pass out, and then I fell away from him, spent.

Frederick spat water into my face. Then he tried to sit up and fell below the water again. I dived in under him and dragged him back up. I got in behind him again and wrapped my arm around his shoulder so he couldn't hurt me. Then he threw up. I pushed his head to the side so he didn't swallow it, and hoped that sharks weren't fans of human vomit.

Then he started thrashing. The panic was setting in. I held him tight so he couldn't get hold of me and drag me down with him.

"Fred," I yelled. "It's okay. It's Miami. I've got you."

He didn't seem to buy it. He kept splashing water like he was trying to attract all the ocean beasties.

"Fred, I've got you. You're floating. I've got you."

It took him a while to get it, but eventually he stopped flapping. Still, I could feel his tension.

"Who, what?"

"It's okay, Fred, I've got you."

"I fell off. I fell off."

"It's okay, Fred."

"The water. The ocean."

"It's okay, Fred. I've got you."

"Where's the ship!"

Now he started panicking again. Flailing his arms, trying to kick so he could get on his stomach and grab me. I wasn't going to let that happen. The moment he turned was the moment we both went to meet my long-lost relative Davy Jones. So I strained hard against his panic and held him tight. Keeping us both above water was hard work, and I knew if he didn't quit it soon then I would run out of energy and I would have to let him go.

"Fred, it's okay. It's Miami Jones. I've got you. Now stop kicking or I'm going to break your arm."

"Miami?"

"Yes."

"The ship."

"Yes, you came off the ship. But I've got you."

"I don't swim."

"Don't worry. I'm a great swimmer. I swam the English Channel."

"You did?"

I hadn't even been to England, let alone swum there. It just came to me as a big body of water that someone could actually swim. Swimming the Atlantic seemed unbelievable.

"Yes," I lied. "Now relax. You're going to wear us both out."

"Where's the ship?"

"It's stopping."

"Where is it?"

I turned in the water so he could see the lights of the ship. I had to admit, they looked a long way away. And I had no knowledge that it was stopping. I assumed Danielle would sound the alarm or yell *man overboard!* or whatever, but I imagined a big boat like that took a whole lot of stopping.

"It's going away," said Frederick.

"No, it's not. It takes a while to stop, that's all. They'll be back soon."

"You promise?"

"I do. They know we went over. So just relax. We can float here for a while. This is the Bahamas, after all."

I didn't tell him that although the water was warm—probably around seventy-two degrees—it was a long way short of the ninety-eight point six that our bodies preferred. We could develop hypothermia. Not fast, not like in the Arctic. Not *Titanic* fast. But it could happen.

But it wouldn't. I would run out of energy from keeping two bodies afloat before hypothermia became a problem. I hoped Danielle was fast in raising the alarm. I hoped the ship stopped quicker than it looked like it would. I hoped the Marlins would make the playoffs. I hoped the sun wouldn't explode in a supernova, taking the measly Earth with it. I started to enjoy the taste of salt water and the burning sensation it made in my throat. It was a new normal. The ship didn't come back.

I heard the engine but made nothing of it. It was just noise. It could have been some guy mowing his lawn, or a small plane taking off from somewhere. I thought I saw a flash of light, like a lighthouse, and I wondered if we had floated into Jupiter Inlet. I felt confident about making the shore from the Loxahatchee River. Then the sound of the lawn mower stopped, and I heard my mother.

"Miami," she said. "Miami Jones."

Which was strange because my mother didn't often use my last name when calling me, and because I hadn't been called Miami by anyone until I was at University of Miami. And my mother had been dead four years by then. So why was she calling me Miami?

Water broke across my face, and I spluttered and heard the call again.

"Miami!"

I felt good. I probably shouldn't have. I was probably closer to dead than I realized. But the moment I realized that my mother wasn't calling was the moment I realized I was safe. Because I knew that voice. I knew that it was a voice that had never failed to save me from myself. It was the voice of an angel, sent down from wherever angels hang out while waiting to save lost souls like me. It washed over me like the water, and told me that everything was okay.

I wrapped my arm around Frederick and called out.

"Here!" I said.

I didn't sound very loud to me. I wasn't sure I heard it myself. I called again but my throat had nothing left. No sound. So I started kicking. I wasn't trying to swim anywhere. I just wanted to make noise.

"You hear that?"

"There, that way."

A beam of light shot across my face.

"There!"

I heard the lawn mower again and realized it was a boat, and I saw the bulbous form of a rescue tender pull up alongside me. A pair of hands dropped down and pulled Frederick away from me. They lifted him up into the boat and then came back for me. I was dragged from the water and across the gunwale of the tender and dumped onto the deck of the boat. Frederick lay beside me, eyes closed.

"No, there's a pulse, and he's breathing."

"He's breathing?"

"I think he's just passed out."

Then Danielle dropped in beside me.

"Say something," she said.

I hacked a dry cough.

"I knew you'd come."

I saw her lips quiver, and a teardrop fell from her eye onto my cheek.

## CHAPTER SIXTEEN

I was dying for a beer. My throat was so dry I thought I'd eaten the Sahara. But the woman in the infirmary made me drink water and offered me a lozenge. I lay on a gurney with Danielle on one side and Frederick Connors in a gurney on the other. He was lying back all quiet and contemplative. He was pale and his manicured beard looked like sea debris, but he looked alive.

The door to the infirmary flew open and Army rushed in. He looked at me and then at Frederick.

"Mr. Connors, are you all right?"

"Alive," Frederick whispered.

Army looked at me. "There is something seriously wrong with you."

"It says that on my medical record."

"You jumped off a cruise ship."

"You make it sound more than it was."

"What it *was* was insane and reckless."

I nodded. It was. The man spoke the truth.

"And one of the most selfless acts I've ever seen."

"Not that selfless. He's my client. If he dies I won't get paid."

Army shook his head. "Oh, boy. You really are something. Listen, next time you see someone fall overboard—"

"He didn't fall."

"He didn't?"

"No."

"Then how did he end up in the ocean?"

"He was pushed."

Army grimaced. He knew what that meant. Someone falling overboard was their own stupid fault and a minor PR and legal headache. Someone being pushed was a major PR and liability nightmare.

"I was pushed?" I barely heard Frederick say.

"Yep."

"By who?" he asked.

I looked at Army.

He shook his head. "Don't say it."

"Guy X," I said.

"Dang. You saw this?"

"I did. You should have him on video. He was on the forward deck. I think he followed Fred there."

"It's Frederick," said Frederick.

I smiled. Some people were Freds and some people were Fredericks.

"We'll get into it," said Army. "We're still looking over the video from before." He turned to the doctor or nurse or whatever she was. "Will you keep them here?"

"No reason," she said. "I'm sure they'll both be more comfortable in their own cabins."

Army said, "Mr. Connors, I'll have a wheelchair here in a moment to take you back to your suite. If you want anything,

anything at all, just pick up the phone and cabin services will provide whatever you require, compliments of the cruise line."

Then Army turned to me. "Miami?"

"You just try wheeling me out of here."

"That's what I figured."

"But the *anything you want phone thing* sounds cool."

"Absolutely. Just name it."

"I'd kill for a beer."

"They'll be in your suite when you get there. But on the way, would you mind?"

I didn't mind. One of the crew brought me a tracksuit that fit just right but looked like something women wear in New York City. They bagged my tux, or what was left of it and promised to clean and deliver it back to my suite.

After I was dressed, Army led me and Danielle back to the security control office. I had spent more time there than I had in our palatial suite.

"Porter," said Army. "Bring up the video."

A crew member at the video console tapped her keyboard. "This is Mrs. Connors leaving her suite," she said. "Then she goes down to deck five."

"We saw this," I said.

"Then she crosses over to the port-side passageway and makes her way to the spa foyer."

We watched the screen as Anastasia entered the foyer area in front of the spa, and then the angle changed and another camera showed her duck into what looked like the spa.

"I checked the spa," Danielle said. "The staff said no one had come in."

"She didn't go into the spa proper. That door leads into a bathroom facility that can also be accessed via the spa."

"She went all that way to use the toilet?" I asked.

"I can't say what she did in there, but a few minutes later, here she is."

We saw Anastasia walk out of the bathroom and retrace her steps out of the foyer.

"Where does she go?"

"I can show you, but basically she just returns to her suite."

"That's weird," Danielle said.

Army said, "Okay, let's move on to the forward deck. I want any vision of Mr. Connors going overboard."

"Let's see." Porter pulled up a shot of the forward deck. It looked across toward the starboard side. "Fast forward to the time," she said. She did that, and we saw me walked out onto the deck with Danielle behind. Then our little friends from Cleveland appeared. I looked at Army. He looked at me.

"Really? You don't know them?" he said.

"On my word."

We saw the brief interaction with the boys from Ohio and then I turned and ran across the deck and under the view of the camera.

"We need the view from the other side," said Army.

She brought the new angle up. It showed a man with his hand in the air, trying to get cell phone coverage on the high seas.

"His phone should just connect to the ship's satellite system," said Porter.

Then there was movement in the shadows.

"There," I said.

A man moved along the gunwale.

"He's not looking at the camera," said Danielle.

The man bent down, grabbed Frederick's legs, and tossed him over the edge.

"Certainly not an accident," said Porter. Army grunted.

Then the man slipped back into the shadows and the video showed me run into frame and vault over the side.

"That was you?" asked Porter as she paused the video.

"Yeah," I said.

"Awesome. You saved that dude's life."

I shrugged.

Army said, "Can we see the guy who did it leaving?"

Porter tapped away and brought up another angle inside the port-side corridor or passageway or whatever they called it. We saw Army step out of the bar. He moved back to the spa foyer, and then stepped back to the port-side corridor.

"The guy should be right in front of you," said Danielle.

"I didn't see anyone come through that door," said Army.

And no one did come through. Army spun in place when Danielle came rushing out of the starboard corridor. He met her in front of the spa. She was clearly telling him what I had just done. He shook his head, which I thought was a reasonable response, and then Danielle led him back down the corridor and out onto the deck.

"Watch that other door," said Army.

We watched. We saw nothing. Guy X didn't come out.

"Did he stay on the deck?" I asked.

"Couldn't have," said Army. "We went right over to that side of the deck to look at where you went over. Then I called it in."

"And we logged the GPS coordinates so we knew where they went over," said Porter.

"I was right there," said Army. "I would have seen him. There's shadow there, but there's nowhere to hide. Nowhere to go—" He looked at his crew member behind the console.

She said, "The crew passageway." She began tapping again.

"There's an unmarked hatch on that side, for crew use only," said Army. "It leads down to the crew deck and I-95."

"Is there a camera there?" I asked,

Porter kept tapping. "There is. On the inside of the hatch, looking down the stairs." She stopped tapping and a new image appeared on screen. It was green in color, like the stairs weren't well lit. We saw nothing for a moment, then a flare of white at the bottom of the shot.

"That's the door opening," she said.

Then the picture went black. Not snow or fuzz like the connection had been severed. It just went black.

"What happened?" asked Army.

"I don't know, Chief. The feed seems to be running but there's no picture."

"Maybe he covered the camera with something," Danielle said.

"Another camera?" I asked.

More tapping. "If he went all the way down to I-95 there's cameras. But those stairs also cut into the prep kitchens behind a couple of the bars. No cameras in the kitchens, but there are in the bars. But once he's in there, he might be hard to spot." She slid her chair to another keyboard and started tapping again.

"We've lost him?" I asked, somewhat rhetorically.

"We'll find him. What do you have, Porter?" asked Army.

"That hatch. It's not an emergency exit like the access you came through to get on that deck. It's crew only. It's keycard access."

"So you can find out who opened the door?" I asked.

"Yes," she said. "Here. The log says the door was opened by Angel Rodriguez."

"Who is Angel Rodriguez?" asked Army.

"Looks like he works food prep for the lounge and the sports bar."

"That's our man," said Army. "Let's find him."

More tapping. "Um, Chief?"

"Yes?"

"There's a problem."

"Which is?"

"Angel Rodriguez isn't on board."

"What do you mean, he isn't on board?"

"Just that. He's rostered off for this voyage. He's not on the boat."

"But his card is," said Army. "Someone's using his card."

"You don't void them?" I asked.

"Not every voyage, not for crew. If he was fired or he quit, sure, his card would be voided. But not for a weekend off."

"You know what that means," I said.

Army looked at me. "Not necessarily."

"You've got to consider it."

"I'm considering it."

"Considering what?" Danielle asked.

"It's an inside job," I said. "Someone's helping Guy X. Or he's crew himself."

"Not necessarily," Army said again.

"And that makes me very suspicious about the missing rings."

"You think that could be an inside job?" asked Danielle.

"How do you get into a locked room? With a key."

"There's video," said Army. "No one in or out."

"Video can be altered," I said. I'd seen it done.

"Not this," said Porter. "It's time stamped and encoded. We use it for legal proceedings if anything happens on board. It's tamperproof."

I said nothing about nothing being tamperproof. Everything could be got at. But I accepted the point that it would be hard to do, and all the more difficult at sea.

"Thanks, Porter," said Army. "Keep at it. If we can't see him leaving, maybe you can find him arriving."

"I'm on it, Chief."

"Miami, I'm sure you're tired. But before you go, could you look at something else?"

Army sat me at a desk to the side with a laptop on it. I looked at photos of every passenger who had been issued a ship pass. Then I looked at all the crew. I was borderline comatose by the end.

"I saw about fifty possibles, two hundred if you cast the net a little wider. I'd know him if I saw him live, but on a photo I just can't tell."

"Worth a shot," said Army. "You should get some rest."

Danielle led me to the door. Then Army asked me to stop. He stepped over and handed me something. It was orange and looked like a chunky cell phone or walkie-talkie.

"It's a satellite comms unit. You can text us and we can text you from anywhere on the planet, and anywhere on board via wifi. We'll keep an eye on your passageway and buzz you if Mrs. Connors leaves her suite."

"Thanks," I said, and turned to follow Danielle out.

"And Miami, that comms unit," said Army. "It's also an emergency locator beacon. Water activated. Just in case you get any more ideas about jumping off my ship."

"Thanks, Army, but that was a once-in-a-lifetime trip."

## CHAPTER SEVENTEEN

Seeing Frederick going overboard on the video made me think about the isolation of a ship on the high seas. I had certainly felt a long way from anything when floating in the ocean. And thinking of myself in the water made me think of land, which made me long to reach some. My limited recollection of the layout of the Bahamas told me we were on the Bahama Banks somewhere south of Grand Bahama. Army had said we were headed for the cruise line's private island, Paradise Cay, which was part of the Berry Island chain. To the south was Andros Island. But where the ship was floating now was in the middle of a great big bathtub. Which made me wonder about the rings.

If they were gone, then they weren't really *gone*. They had to be on the ship. And if they *were* on the ship, then they had to get off, but the only place we were stopping was Paradise Cay, which itself was a tiny island in a chain of tiny islands in the middle of the ocean. Once there, there was nowhere to go. Which made the logic of the missing rings baffle me. Why would someone steal jewelry on a ship if they couldn't then get away?

The answer was simple. They wouldn't. There was no point.

And finding their way into a locked room on a ship did not smell of a crime of opportunity. It was all kinds of *Ocean's Eleven*. It had been planned. I couldn't see it any other way. But once the thief got the rings out of the locked room, and off the ship in the middle of the ocean, then where? Onto a private island? I couldn't see anywhere else to go. Between us and Florida there was nothing. Nothing but some tiny dots of land that didn't appear on most globes. The Biminis.

Which made me think of Lucas. He was there on North Bimini, probably sipping on a cool beer in a bar in Alice Town. He knew the Bahamas. He knew every fishing spot and escape route in the region. Fortunately Danielle had Lucas's numbers, both his cell phone and his satellite phone, which was the one Danielle called whenever I went missing in action down in Miami, or thereabouts. I asked her if I could borrow her phone and connected to the ship's satellite system.

"Don't take too long," Danielle said. "It's like ten dollars a minute."

"Billable." I smiled and I wandered to the window to look over the ocean. It was dark and all I saw was my reflection in the glass. I turned away from it.

The call connected. "Yeah?"

"Lucas?"

"Yeah."

"It's Miami."

"Mate, how's it going?"

"It's been an adventure."

"Always is with you."

I had to agree. I told him about the rings, how they had gone missing, and how I couldn't see how the thieves would get them off. I didn't mention jumping off the boat. I figured that was a conversation for a time when I wasn't charging the client ten bucks a minute.

"Where are you going?"

"We stop at a private island tomorrow. Paradise Cay. You know it?"

"I do. It used to be paradise."

"What is it now?"

"Disneyland."

"So could someone get the rings off the cay?"

"Depends on the security. That's officially the Bahamas, so they might have passport control."

"Might?"

"It's a private island, so the government might waive full passport control in return for a landing fee. But even then, it's an island."

"Right. So if they got the stuff off the ship and onto the island, then what? A getaway boat?"

"Possible, but the business side of the island is where the deep dock is. They dredged it out so the cruise ships can dock right on the island. But you couldn't get a boat in there without being seen, and the only boats with permission will be the cruise line's."

"Is there an airstrip?"

"Nah. It's all vegetation on the interior. Nowhere to land. Hang on."

"What?"

"There's no buildings on the east side of the cay. All the action is on the west side. But there is a beach. You could get a speedboat in there."

"And there's no one there to see?"

"No buildings at all, as I remember it."

"Maybe that's it."

"Who do think has the rings?" he asked.

"I have no idea. I don't even know for sure they've left the room. But they have to leave the ship eventually, so this is my best bet."

"You could hide over there and see if anyone comes."

"I could, but the ring thing technically isn't why I was hired."

"Oh, right. The sheila having the affair."

"Exactly. I should be keeping my eye out for this mystery guy."

"No worries. If you want, I can pop over there in the morning and hang off the island, watch it for you."

"I thought you were fixing a boat in Bimini?"

"Done. Just a clogged fuel line. Some people seriously shouldn't own boats. So I'm done."

"I can't ask you come all this way."

"Not that far, mate. I can be there in a couple of hours. I'll leave before dawn and be there before all you lot get off your barge."

"You don't have to work?"

"I'm fixing a client's boat in Bimini, remember? You can bill your client for my fuel, bait and beer. I'll get a spot of fishing in."

"If you're sure."

"I'm sure."

"All right, thanks. I've got a communication locator device thing they gave me on the ship. It can send text messages. If I can figure it out, I'll send you a message so you have the number. Just let me know when you get there tomorrow."

"Will do."

We said we would touch base the following day and then I took out the communication device Army had given me. It had a screen and some buttons on it. The screen didn't respond to touch, so I tried the buttons. They seemed to do the trick. I found a message screen and typed in a quick message to Lucas and hit send. I wasn't sure whether my message would float off into the ether or land somewhere useful, but I returned the device to my pocket and Danielle's phone to her.

Then I had a thought. I went back to the security control room and knocked. Army opened the door.

"Do we go through passport control tomorrow?" I asked.

"We were just talking about that," said Army. "No, is the answer. The government of the Bahamas doesn't require it since it's a private island. We pay a landing fee for each passenger. But we do check everyone off and on with their ship passes. We don't want to leave anyone behind. We do have the option to set up a metal detector and search bags. We're going to do that."

"Don't people get spooked?" asked Danielle.

"We tell them it's a government requirement. Bureaucracy generally placates people. I was thinking maybe you should set up on the dock and see if you recognize the guy who pushed Mr. Connors."

"Guy X. Yeah, I was thinking the same thing. What time can folks get off?"

"We'll be in dock by seven, but passengers can disembark from 8 a.m. on."

"I'll see you in the morning, then."

Danielle and I left them to it and took the elevator down to our deck. I wasn't in a stairs kind of mood. Danielle took my hand and led me down to our suite. She used her ship pass to open the door, and I was about to follow when I stopped and looked down the corridor.

"MJ?"

"I'm just going to check on Fred."

I wandered down to the Connors' suite and knocked on the door. There was no response and I looked at Danielle.

"Maybe they're asleep," she said.

"It's not that late."

"It's not that early, either. And he did have a pretty traumatic evening." She put her hand on my cheek. "And so did you."

The door opened and I found myself looking at Anastasia Connors. She was dressed in a tracksuit that was remarkably similar to the one I had on, except for the thousands of sequins.

"You," she said.

"Me," I said. It was witty repartee at its finest.

"Frederick is sleeping."

"Good."

She didn't seem that enthusiastic about letting us in. I wasn't planning on kicking off a room party.

"Is there something you wanted?" she asked.

"How are you?"

"Excuse me?"

"How are you? Are you okay?"

"Nothing happened to me."

"Your husband went overboard on a cruise ship. That's pretty traumatic for everyone. I just wanted to make sure you were okay."

She frowned at me. Her face said she was annoyed by the question, but her eyes said something else. They were searching for comprehension. I got the distinct impression that few people ever genuinely asked after her well-being. I supposed that was a result of her holier-than-thou countenance. It didn't really drive people to care much about her. She lifted her chin and regained her composure, to the limited extent she had lost it.

"I am fine, Mr. Jones."

I nodded and gave her a moment. I was curious to see if she said anything about me rescuing her husband. I certainly didn't do it for her thanks, or his. Or anyone else's. I wasn't really sure why I had jumped off the cruise ship, other than the fact that I knew I could swim and I knew that Frederick Connors could not. It was as simple as that. But Lenny always said you could tell a lot about someone based on whether they chose to say thank you or not, even for the little things.

She said nothing. Instead, she raised an eyebrow.

"Before I go, one quick question. Do you know why Frederick was out on the deck?"

"I have no idea."

"It's just, I thought he was staying in your cabin because he wasn't well."

"That was my impression, but when I got back from the auction room I assumed he was in bed, and I didn't want to disturb him."

"So you went out again?"

"How do you know that?"

I didn't want to tell her I had watched her on the security video. Even though everyone knew security video was there, they chose not to think about the watching eyes. Plus Army's crew was still watching, and I didn't want her second-guessing herself or her movements.

"The crew came to find you when Frederick went overboard."

"They did find me."

"The first time," I lied.

"Oh. Well, if you must know, I got a call."

"A call?"

"About the rings."

"Your rings? The stolen rings?"

"No, Mr. Jones, the *Lord of the Rings*."

I hadn't known she did humor. I hoped she was a good jeweler. Stand-up wasn't going to put pasta in her pot.

"Who called you?"

"I don't know."

"What did they say?"

"They said they had information about my rings."

"And?"

"And I should meet them."

"Meet them where?"

"In the ladies' bathroom beside the spa."

"It was a woman who called you?"

"No. It was a man."

"A man wanted to meet in the women's room?"

"I assumed a lady would be present."

"And you didn't think to mention this to security?"

"No, I didn't. Security seems to be a bit of an afterthought on this boat."

I nodded, ignoring the jab. "And what happened in the bathroom?"

"Nothing. I went, I waited, no one came. It was a waste of my time."

"Well, thank you, Mrs. Connors. I hope Fred's feeling better."

"It's Frederick, and I don't think he'll be better until he gets onto solid land."

"Listen, would you like to join us for dinner?"

The confounded face returned. "No, thank you. I must stay in with my husband."

I wished her a good night and we stepped away and the door closed behind us.

"That was weird," said Danielle.

"Which part?"

"All of it. But did you hear her? She must stay in with her husband?"

"So?"

"I wouldn't say it like that."

"How would you say it?"

"I *want* to stay with my husband."

I thought about the difference as we reached our suite. Small but important. Then I looked up as the door down the corridor opened again. Mrs. Connors stepped halfway out.

"Mr. Jones," she said.

"Yes, Mrs. Connors?"

"Thank you."

I nodded and she stepped back inside and closed her door. Danielle gave me a grin.

"People never cease to amaze me," I said.

"You're telling me. You want that beer now?" she asked, opening our door.

"I do. But you know what I want more?"

She gave me the half smile that lit me up. "We already did that, but I'm game."

"No, not that. Well, not this minute. I just want to be somewhere where there are people. You know? I don't need to talk to them. I just want them to be there."

Danielle nodded. "Okay. Let's find a bar."

## CHAPTER EIGHTEEN

We got to the bar by the pool but I didn't get my drink. Instead, I caught the eye of someone I vaguely recognized, walking toward us.

"You," she said. She looked me up and down and was a bit confused. I couldn't fault her for that. When we had seen each other last time I was in a tux, and now I was in a fashionista track suit.

"You were with Adrian and D'Vante in the casino," she said.

"Yes, ma'am. Miami Jones, and this is Danielle Castle."

"Have you seen Adrian?"

"Not since you left the casino. Is there a problem?"

"He's gone missing."

I suppressed a groan. I couldn't handle another man overboard.

Danielle took the baton. "Ma'am, what do you mean he's gone missing?"

"I took him back to our cabin and he went to sleep. I was watching TV and fell asleep myself, and when I woke he was gone."

"Could he have just gone for a walk?" I asked.

"You don't understand. Sometimes Adrian goes wandering and he doesn't remember where he's been."

"Okay, let's see what we can do," I said. "What was your name?"

"I'm sorry. Denise. Denise Pascal. I'm Adrian's wife."

"All right, Denise, let's see if we can find him." I led her over to the bar and pulled out the comms unit that Army had given me. I sent a message to the only number in it other than Lucas's.

A moment later the phone rang behind the bar. A bartender picked it up and then glanced at me.

"You Mr. Jones?"

I nodded and he handed me the phone.

"Army?" I said.

"No, sir. Chief Mahoney has gone back to quarters. This is Emma Porter. We met earlier."

"Sure, Porter. Thanks for calling back. I've got a passenger here who has lost her husband and he has a history of disappearing and not remembering, if you know what I mean." I was sure she did. I had no doubt they got plenty of drunks on cruise ships.

"Yes, sir, I get you."

"Any thoughts on tracking him down? Your cameras?"

"No, there's nine hundred of them. That's like a needle in a haystack. But I have a couple of tricks."

"I thought you might."

"We can see if he has used his ship pass to buy anything. That might shrink our target area."

"Good thinking. The passenger's name is Adrian Pascal. He was a football player."

"If you say so, sir. Let's have a look. Yes, I see him here. He paid for some drinks in the sports bar. Deck four. Do you need assistance?"

"No, thanks. We'll check it out, and I'll let you know."

"Aye, sir."

"Thanks, Porter. I'll let Army know he hires good people."

"Happy to help, sir."

We took the elevator down to deck four and then used the map to track down the sports bar. It was large, with big-screen televisions, and a lounge area with plush seating around small tables. It looked like a fine place to hang awhile.

It didn't take long to find Adrian. He was at the bar, sitting on a beer but staring into thin air. Danielle and I hung back. Denise approached him like a keeper approaches a lion, careful not to spook him, and then she moved in and rubbed his back as she spoke to him. He offered the resigned nod of a man being taken from his beverage, and then he got down from the stool. The bartender made to get his attention, I assumed to pay his tab, and I grabbed his eye and let him know that I would get it.

I watched Denise walk Adrian away. It looked like a woman helping her grandfather, not her husband.

"Didn't he already pay?" I asked the bartender.

"For the first one."

"How many did he have?"

The bartender shrugged. "In an hour? That's his second."

It was only half-gone. If he was getting drunk he was doing it in slow motion. I realized my ship pass was still in my trouser pocket which was in a laundry somewhere, so Danielle came to my rescue again and slid her card through the reader to pay the remainder of Adrian's tab.

We caught up with Denise and I offered Adrian an arm. I reminded him where we had met. He gave me a nod. We got in the elevator and helped them back to their cabin. It wasn't as nice as our suite but it was fine. No balcony but enough room for a bed and a sitting area and a television. Better than our original cabin. I helped Adrian lie down on the bed and Denise retrieved a bottle of tablets from her bag and gave him one with a sip of water.

She walked us to the door.

"Are you okay?" I asked.

"He'll be fine. He'll sleep now. He doesn't sleep well without the medication."

"Are *you* okay?" I repeated.

She looked at me like Anastasia had, as if no one ever asked her that.

"It is what it is."

"You want to let him sleep? There's a coffee shop down here. Grab a decaf with us."

"I shouldn't leave him."

"He had his sleeping tablet, right? Just a quick coffee. He can't go anywhere without us seeing."

She shrugged and half nodded and stepped out into the hall. The coffee shop was set up like a Parisian bakery, with al fresco tables overlooking the Champs-Élysées. Only, the Champs-Élysées was painted on the opposite wall. We each got a decaf coffee and sat in the fake outdoors.

"Thank you for your help," Denise said.

"Not a problem. Is Adrian okay?"

"How do you know him?" she asked.

"We don't. We met him and D'Vante at the casino. They told us there were players. Gang of Six."

"Yeah. Gang of Six." She didn't say it like she was proud of it.

"What happened to him?" Danielle asked.

Denise shook her head. "Football happened to him."

We said nothing and she continued.

"We met in college. He was playing and I was in cheer."

My surprise must have shown in my face, because Denise nodded.

"Yeah, we're the same age. But he looks like my daddy, doesn't he?"

I didn't say anything, despite thinking that and more.

"He was something. A gentle giant. He was fast and tough on the field, and off it, he was quiet and reserved. He liked to read. You think of this big man and he must be a tough guy, but Adrian wasn't that at all. First Christmas that he visited my family, he sat under the tree and played dolls with my five-year-old niece. Three hours they played. Three hours. Not once did he look for an excuse to get away. Big tough guy." She smiled at the memory and Danielle and I looked at each other.

"College was hard on him, but he got drafted. He got good. Gang of Six. Big, tough offensive line guys. Best of the best." She sipped at her coffee but didn't stop talking. She was getting something off her chest. "Then he started not being able to sleep. First after games, and then all the time. But there are pills for that, right? And then he'd forget things. We have two boys of our own. They were his world. He would read to them every night. Hardy Boys, Roald Dahl. Then he would start talking to them at the dinner table and just stop like he'd forgotten what their names were."

"We saw some doctors, they said they couldn't see anything wrong. He was All-Pro. He was too good to let go. So they kept sending him on the field. And then one day, he got chopped on the knee and he was done. I hated myself for thinking it but my prayers were answered. But after he stopped playing, it didn't get better. He was sort of listless without football. For a time he drank too much, but we got through that. And then he went missing for the first time." She sighed and made to sip her coffee but didn't.

"The sheriff found him about five miles from home sitting by the side of the road. His car was two miles away. He had no idea how he got there. So we go and see another doctor. Only this time, its not a league doctor. He does a CAT scan, all that. They don't find anything. But clearly there's something wrong. They gave him meds that turned him into a zombie. One time he sat in a chair in the den for three days. He got up to sleep and then walked right back to the chair. Never said anything. Scared the hell out of me."

"I'm so sorry," said Danielle, but it was like water off a duck's back. Denise looked beyond pity.

"How long did he play?" I asked.

"Pro? Seven years. Washed up at twenty-nine."

"Was it concussion?"

Denise shrugged. "Who knows? So you've heard of CTE?"

"Sure," I said. "Chronic Traumatic Encephalopathy. Too many concussions, right?"

"Yeah, too many. Now the doctors are saying sure, it's the big concussions, but maybe it's also the smaller impacts. Every single time his helmet hit something. Another helmet, a body, pads, the ground. All of it. But of course, they can't say for sure he's got CTE until he's dead."

"Really?" said Danielle.

Denise nodded. "They slice open your brain. That's how they tell you smashed your head into something too many times."

"Is it treatable?" Danielle asked.

Denise shook her head. "You can try and treat the symptoms, the depression, the mood swings. But it doesn't change the end result."

"End result?" I asked.

"You said you knew the Gang of Six?"

I nodded.

"You know how many of them are left?"

I shook my head.

"Two. Adrian and D'Vante. D's not as bad, but he's headed

the same way. I feel for Winnie. She knows what's coming, but she can't do a damned thing to stop it. That's the worst part. Watching the man you love turn into someone you don't know, and then someone you can't trust, and then someone you're afraid of. Some days I just wish it was done with. I know God will have his time with me for that, but I feel it. Gang of Six. One was a drunk driver, hit another car. The second had a brain aneurysm. The third took his own life at the end of a shotgun. And we just lost Clete James."

"D'Vante said they were toasting their old teammate."

She nodded. "They found Clete hanging from the rafters of his garage. Our boys are toasting their old friend knowing exactly what waits ahead for them."

"Isn't the NFL doing anything?" asked Danielle. "It doesn't seem right."

"What will they do? Stop playing football? Tell everyone to go home, take up checkers? You got billions of dollars at stake. Advertisers, owners, players. They're all getting rich off it. Sure, the players are the ones paying the price in the end, and the families they leave behind. But they didn't say no either. They played. Adrian earned more money in seven years of football than he would have earned in sixty years working at a real job. He felt it, the headaches, the pain, the memory loss. He knew. I knew. I could've stopped him. But I liked my house and I liked my boys going to good schools. You can blame the NFL. But you can blame the players and the families and the schools who promote lettermen as some kind of heroes. Blame the owners for profiting off it all, and blame the fans who cheer every big hit. Blame us all. We're all in on it."

She took a long drink of her coffee. It was probably cold. Mine was. I didn't want it anyway. I wanted to help her. I'm sure Danielle did too. And it tore me up. Because I couldn't. There was not a damned thing either of us could do for her.

Adrian was ill beyond repair and she would lose her husband and her boys would lose their father. If they hadn't already. And nobody could fix it.

We walked Denise back to her cabin. I asked her the question again.

"Are you okay?" I wasn't sure what her baseline was.

"Thank you both. It takes the load off for a while, talking about it."

"Do you have anyone to talk to?" Danielle asked.

Denise nodded. "I do. There are a lot more of us than you know. A lot more."

She opened the door and slipped quietly inside. We walked back to the central lobby and took the stairs. Danielle opened our door and I walked inside. I had almost drowned earlier that evening, but I had less energy now than I had ever known. And I never got my beer. I flopped onto the bed. Danielle crawled up around me and I gripped her tight.

I whispered, "I love you."

She was already asleep.

# CHAPTER NINETEEN

Ron always says the gentle rocking of a boat is better than any sleeping pill. I didn't feel much rocking on the *Canaveral Star*, but I could vouch for the fact that jumping off a ship and having to get rescued was equally effective. I fell into a deep dark hole of slumber and didn't wake until the dawn came in through the bedroom porthole. I was still in my tony tracksuit and Danielle was still in her black dress.

I got out of bed and ditched the tracksuit for my palm-tree-print shirt and khaki shorts. Danielle took a shower and I was looking for her ship pass so I could run down to the Champs-Élysées cafe for some coffee when there was a knock on the door.

I opened up to find two crew standing in the corridor. One was pushing a cart covered with a white tablecloth.

"Mr. Jones," he said. "Chief Mahoney thought you might like some breakfast."

I stepped aside and let him in. The smell instantly made me hungry, and I recalled I hadn't eaten in some time. The crew guy set the cart up as a table and then placed a dining chair on either side.

The second crew member was carrying a suit bag and one of the cruise line's sky-blue travel bags.

"Mr. Jones, your suit. Cleaned and pressed. Unfortunately your jacket was lost, I believe.

"It was."

"Chief Mahoney says feel free to visit the boutique and get fitted for a new tuxedo. Our tailors will have it ready for you this evening."

"I'm supposed to wear the penguin suit again?"

"For the auction." He then held up the blue travel bag. "Your effects," he said. "We dried out your wallet and contents. And your ship pass is in here. We didn't retrieve a phone, I'm afraid."

"It's here in the room."

"Very good. If there's anything else please just let us know."

The two crew retreated and I poured the coffee. Danielle came out of the bathroom.

"What is that smell? Coffee? Bacon?" She stopped when she saw the spread.

"You arranged this?" she asked.

"I'd like to take the credit, but no. Army."

"Is this the kind of service rich people get all the time?"

"I don't think they have to jump overboard for it, but yeah."

"We've got to get more money, MJ."

We sat and drank coffee and ate eggs and bacon and breakfast potatoes. I followed up with a bagel with cream cheese and lox and some Florida OJ. It beat my regular smoothie. After breakfast I ran through the shower and washed the last of the ocean off me. Then I grabbed Army's comms device and we headed out.

It was one of those Bahamian days. They were pretty similar to South Florida days. The sky was blue, and a hint of breeze kept the morning pleasant. The water was turquoise and clearer than any I had ever seen before. We were docked at a purpose-built dock that led onto an island. Paradise Cay. It looked like paradise, if you excused the whopping great ship parked by the beach. The dock led to a walkway along the water, like a promenade. Behind the palms that lined the promenade, I could make out buildings in tropical colors. The beach extended out from the other side of the dredged area into the distance. I could see loungers being set up on the sand, and my eye stopped on a tiki bar, complete with palapa shade.

Lucas was right. It was Disneyland. It wasn't real. But it was still paradise.

We stopped on the deck and looked over the dock. A gangway had been set up coming out of what looked like deck two, with a popup shade, like folks used at tailgates. There was a table and computer and a couple of big security-type guys. I figured under the shade, out of my view, was where Army had set up his metal detector.

I took out the comms device and sent a text to Lucas's sat phone to check if he had made it. The response came within thirty seconds:

*Gone fishin' :)*

Lucas was in place. I saw Army step down the gangway and onto the dock to speak with the big guys. Then he moved out into the sun and looked up at his boat and scanned the decks. I waved. He saw me and saluted. He gestured to ask if we were coming down and I gestured that I would watch from where I was. It was a good spot. I could see every face coming off the ship and at a distance that I was actually familiar with seeing Guy X. Plus, I was hidden out of the way. Standing on the dock watching everyone get off might spook Guy X somehow.

Further down the dock, staff and crew were already walking around, streaming out of a different hatch toward the bow of the ship. They appeared to be moving trolleys of food and drinks onto the island. That made sense. It was a small island. There probably wasn't a brewery hidden back there.

Passengers had lined up well before eight. It was like watching people get off an aircraft. There was always a mad rush to stand up and another mad rush to get off, and then a mad rush to get down to the baggage claim so they could stand closest to the carousel. Perhaps these folks were the frequent sailors, the ones who knew the best spots, the best lounge chairs, the best places to kick back, and they were ready to get on land and stake their claim.

On the stroke of eight, Army opened the line and it pulsed rather than surged forward. Everyone wore hats and sunglasses and carried their blue travel bags. It wasn't going to make identifying Guy X very easy. Bags were checked and people strode through the metal detector and then some speed-walked along the dock while others ambled. The beach began to fill, and other people disappeared behind the palm-lined promenade into the buildings I could see hints of.

By 10 a.m., the line had become a trickle. Most everyone who was getting off had done so. I hadn't seen anyone that made me think of Guy X and my back was getting stiff from leaning against the gunwale. Army appeared on the deck.

"Anything?" he asked.

I shook my head. "You?"

"We searched every bag and everyone has gone through the metal detector. Nothing."

"Is that the only metal detector?" I asked.

"Yes. Why?"

"What about the people who got off at the other end?" I pointed down the dock.

"They were crew."

"Right. And somehow Guy X seems to know the inner workings of the ship and its security."

"You really think he's crew?"

"I think he's either crew or he's being helped by crew."

Army said nothing. I could see his conflict. He didn't want to admit that crew could be involved, because that opened up all sorts of liability issues for the cruise line, but he couldn't dismiss the idea completely because he was a straight shooter. So he said nothing. That was the smart play.

I asked, "Do you bring everything with you to the island?"

"Stores, you mean? Yes, pretty much. We have supplies shipped in, especially diesel fuel and stuff like that. But we're a ship, so we might as well bring it."

"What about staff? Does anyone stay here on the island?"

"Most of the service staff will come off the ship. This isn't a day off for crew. But there is also a cleanup team that will follow up after we leave tonight. They get the place shipshape for our next vessel. They get shuttled back to Great Harbour Cay. I assume most of them live there."

"And then the island is left empty?"

"No. There is a skeleton team of caretakers who live here full time."

"Where?"

"There are staff accommodations on the interior of the island. Come down and I'll show you both."

We followed him down to deck two and across the I-95 corridor to where the gangway led off the ship. We checked through security and walked down the dock to the island. One side was full of rocks that didn't look inviting at all. The other side began the promenade. As we'd seen from the boat, palm trees lined the walkway along the beach, and on the land side we found a range of buildings. They were designed to look like Caribbean plantation buildings, painted in blues and pinks and yellows, and which boasted a range of stores that sold pretty much the same crap that was available on the ship. There was a buffet and a restaurant with a balcony overlooking the beach and the ship. I imagined it would be like eating at the Port of Palm Beach.

Army pointed to a gate between the restaurant and a store selling sunscreen and cheaply made, but not cheaply priced, sunglasses. Beyond the gate was a path.

"That's the service area. The track runs behind all the stores, and then into the interior where the staff quarters, storehouses and utilities are."

"I don't see anything," I said.

"That's the point. The trees hide it all. It's supposed to be a deserted island paradise."

"With mojitos. So how far back are the buildings?"

"Maybe five hundred yards."

"And the other side of the island?"

"If you cut through the middle? Maybe another five hundred yards."

"Can passengers go over there?"

"No. There's no guest access through the gate, and it's not really possible to get around the island via the shore."

"It's not?" asked Danielle.

"No. You have the main beach here. Then further down there's a breakwater and beyond that the adults-only beach. Then there's a rocky outcrop like on the other side of the dock. You could swim around it, I suppose, but you couldn't walk it very easily."

I looked across the beach. People were lying back on loungers and beach towels. A group played volleyball. Some folks swam in the clear water. I turned my eye to the tiki bar. It called to me. I wasn't the first person it had called. I saw Ron Bennett's silver mane at the bar, so I wandered over.

"It's early, even for you," I said.

Ron smiled. "It's five o'clock in Kiev."

"If you say so."

"But sadly it's just orange juice."

"Lady Cassandra got you on the short leash?"

"Actually, I was waiting for you. In case you needed me."

"We're keeping you away from this one, remember?"

"I'm open today."

"Where is your lovely fiancée?" I asked.

"She's having a spa day with some friends. Not much of a beachgoer."

I shrugged. I didn't understand why people who didn't love the beach lived anywhere in South Florida, let alone in a place called Palm Beach.

"You find Guy X?"

"Sort of," I said. I explained what had happened to Frederick and how I had ended up in the water with him.

"I take it you're okay," he said.

"Still intact. But we haven't seen him get off the ship, so we're square one with that. Plus we have no idea about the rings. Security has searched everyone but no dice."

"You want me to watch the comings and goings on the ship?"

"You look pretty happy here, my friend."

"I could set up a lounge chair under an umbrella at that end of the beach and see everyone coming off the end of the dock."

I looked at Army.

"Can't hurt," he said. "I'll get guest services to set it up."

Ron slid off his stool.

"Thanks, Ron," I said.

"No problem," he said. "Just let me turn this orange juice into a mimosa and I'll get right there. What will you do?"

"I'm going to take a look around the island."

# CHAPTER TWENTY

Danielle and I took a walk. We wandered along the beach with the water lapping at our bare feet. The ocean was warmer than it had felt the previous evening but that might have had something to do with the visuals. The scene wasn't dark and foreboding now. It was glorious and sunny and inviting. All the reasons I lived in this part of the world. Swimmers were bobbing in the gentle waters. Another couple played Frisbee. There were fewer kids than we normally saw at the beach, but I figured a Super Bowl cruise wasn't the most kid-relevant event. We walked to the end of the beach, where large rocks concealed a concrete breakwater.

We made our way back up onto the promenade and around the breakwater that seemed to serve no other purpose than to separate the beach into two. On the far side of the beach was more of the same. More sand, more folks lying around, more shops selling trinkets and food and drinks. This was the adults-only beach. A place for the adults to get away from all the screaming kids. Instead of kids, there was a DJ whose large speakers blasted music that I didn't recognize. Instead of a tranquil scene, it sounded like a nightclub, a heavy beat and deep bass. It wasn't Jimmy Buffett. It wasn't even Kenny Chesney. It brought on the beginnings of a headache.

We picked up our pace along the promenade to get away from the music. Though it was still early, the bars were doing gangbusters on this section of the beach. We passed another bar that was playing steel drum music, which was at least a little more appropriate. Then we reached the end of the road.

The promenade stopped at a dead end of wild grasses and shrubs, and the beach turned into another rocky outcrop. I figured a motivated person could get through, but they would probably want the use of a machete. We turned and walked back, past the bars and the music that wasn't, and around the breakwater and back to the main beach.

We stopped by the gate Army had shown us earlier. It was locked and required a keycard. But this wasn't Disney World. Getting backstage there was close to impossible. Here, we retreated past the store with the sunglasses and down the side and pushed through the palm fronds to a small fence, which we stepped over, onto the service track behind the stores.

The back sides of the buildings weren't painted in the same bright colors. Instead, they were a military-looking gray. We followed the path as it broke inland, where there was a stretch of dirt track surrounded by palms and shrubs. Within two minutes we couldn't even hear the activity on the beach.

A couple minutes more saw us in front of another gray structure, giving off the signature hum of a utility building. We kept going until we found another couple of buildings in the same plantation style, though these were painted white, with rocking chairs on the verandas.

"Staff accommodations," Danielle said.

I nodded.

We kept going and came upon several electric carts like the greenskeepers used on golf courses. They were parked against the trees where the service track came to an end. Beyond the carts the track became one person wide path as it cut further into the vegetation. Danielle took the lead. We walked for another five minutes through a tunnel of trees and bushes and grasses, as the path became sand.

Then the path ended at another beach. It was long and glorious and covered in seaweed and kelp. Clearly not maintained like the beach on the other side. There were no people. There was no music. The only sound was of the breeze in the tall grasses. I saw Lucas's point about it having once been a paradise. I could have sat down in the sand with Danielle and watched nothing happen for the rest of the day.

But I didn't. I cast my eye out to the ocean. About five hundred yards offshore, I could make out the outline of a boat. It was low in the water and hard to spot, and it wasn't moving. I took out the comms device and typed in *we're on beach*. I waited for a response but didn't get one. We watched for a few minutes more, taking in deep breaths of fresh ocean air. I recalled something about the fact that negative ions from ocean waves make you feel happy. I couldn't argue. I felt pretty happy.

Danielle and I looked at each other and smiled and then started back toward the sand path. Then the comms device pinged.

"What does it say?" Danielle asked.

"Lucas is out there. He just caught a big wahoo."

"Of course."

The device dinged again.

"What now?"

I typed a response. "He asked if anything was happening. I said no."

The device pinged a third time. I nodded.

Danielle said again, "What?"

"He says to wait. The animals feed at sundown."

We left the beach and ambled back through the middle of the island. It was hot out of the breeze. We still didn't see any staff but assumed they were all working in the shops and bars. We returned through the gate to the promenade. Danielle took a bench on the promenade and watched the view while I wandered down the beach to where Ron acted as sentry. He was kicked back in his chair, the umbrella offering nice shade. A mimosa in a plastic cup was nestled in the cup holder on the chair arm. But despite appearances, Ron was vigilantly watching the comings and goings on the dock.

I stood in his shade. "Anything?"

He turned slightly back toward the promenade and pointed. Anastasia Connors drifted between the palms. She was in a long yellow summer dress and wore the kind of visor favored by lady tennis players and football coach Jon Gruden.

"Guy X?" I asked.

Not yet, but if she's here . . ."

"Keep at it, Kemosabe."

"Nothing'll get by me." He sipped his drink and I strode up the beach toward Anastasia. I dropped in behind her. She walked slowly but with purpose, like wherever she was going was important but not time sensitive. Then she spotted Danielle sitting on the bench.

"Ms. Castle," she said.

"Mrs. Connors," Danielle said, standing. I stopped behind Anastasia.

"Enjoying your day?" she said like she really, genuinely, didn't care about the answer but social convention demanded it be asked.

"It's beautiful," Danielle said.

"It's debauchery with skin cancer."

"Good morning, Mrs. Connors," I said.

She spun around like I had startled her.

"Where there's one there's the other," she said.

"How are you this morning?" I asked.

"I'm fine."

"How's Frederick? Not with you?"

"Frederick is remaining in our suite. He doesn't feel up to being out today."

I nodded. "I would have thought he would be eager to feel terra firma."

"He needs rest. I've ensured he's getting it. But my question to you is, what are you doing here?"

"What do you mean?"

"I would have thought that given you've lost the jewelry you were paid to protect you would be out looking for it, rather than spending the day at the beach."

"I am looking for it."

"Really."

"Yes, ma'am. This is where the people are."

"You think someone will be wearing one of my rings on the beach?"

"Stranger things have happened."

"My goodness, you are even worse at your job than I gave you credit for. You will be lucky to have any kind of business left after I'm finished with you."

"Mrs. Connors—"

"Don't *Mrs. Connors* me. Get your tail back on that ship and find my jewels."

I really wanted to set her straight. I wanted to tell her that not only was I not responsible for her rings going missing but it wasn't actually my job to find them. I wanted to let her have it. But I didn't. For once, like some kind of tropical miracle, I managed to stop my mouth going off before my brain had time to engage. She was on the island. Frederick was not. She had said that Frederick would rest comfortably on the ship. And how does a man who hates water and has recently almost drowned in the ocean rest comfortably on a ship? With serious pharmaceutical assistance, that's how. If I were a betting man and I had those three pieces of information, I would be laying my money on Guy X coming onto the island. And Guy X was what I was getting paid for. So I bit my lip.

I glanced at Danielle. She nodded. She knew. She gets me. Then I looked at Anastasia and gave her my best contrite schoolboy look.

"Yes, ma'am," I said, and I turned away and walked back toward the ship.

Except I didn't get to the ship. I left Anastasia to do whatever she was going to do, up to and including catching up with Guy X. Danielle would keep her eye on Mrs. Connors.

I wandered down the beach parallel to the boardwalk and came upon four young guys lying back on lounge chairs. There were lots of young guys on the beach. Most of the older men were in the restaurant or had stayed aboard the ship, so the crowd on the beach skewed young. So I was of a mind to pay them no attention. Except for one thing. They seemed to be paying close attention to me.

I glanced toward the water to see if there was some young girl who was the real object of their interest, but I found no such person. I looked back to confirm. I was sure. They were watching me. So I did what I do on such occasions.

I cut up the beach toward where the guys lay. I'm always curious when people are looking at me with the focus of a chess champion. Sometimes it's because I've left my fly open. Sometimes they recognize me from my ball-playing days. It happens. I wasn't that famous. More famous than the guy who runs the local used car outlet with the late-night television ads, less famous that the local weather girl. But on a ship full of sports-associated people, there were bound to be a few minor league baseball fans.

But these guys weren't baseball fans. Baseball fans slap each other's shoulders as I approach and say things like *it's him*. These guys didn't. They just watched. As I got closer, I noticed that each of them had a can of beer pushed into the sand beside them. As I got closer still I realized why they were looking at me. And it wasn't my fly. They knew me. And I knew them.

It was the Cleveland Browns boys. The times I had run into them before—in the Hall of Fame, at BJ's speech and on the forward deck—they had been wearing their Browns jerseys and no ball caps. I hadn't recognized them this time because they wore ball caps and no shirts at all. They were each tanned somewhere on the spectrum between polar bear white and shrimp pink. I had no desire to get into anything with them again. I had a job to do. But now I had made a beeline for them, so I couldn't just turn away. That might provoke them.

So I kept going but changed my angle slightly so I would end up walking past at a respectful distance. Not that I respected them. I didn't. But young turks like them care about things like that. I was going to keep on walking when I looked at the first guy's face. He was the ring leader, the one who kept trying to throw his beer at both BJ Baker's Heisman and then later at BJ himself. I couldn't help notice that below his ball cap the guy had two black eyes. One was really nasty—truly black—like he'd run into a pole at speed. The other eye looked less bruised, more a purple or violet. He had a plaster tape on his nose.

"What happened to your face?" I asked before I thought not to.

"You're a funny guy."

"Sometimes, it's true. But seriously."

"What do you want, man?"

Then I noticed something. There was no bravado about them. Maybe they hadn't yet had their fill of beer. Bravado and beer are allies in the dumbass army. But what had been there on our two previous meetings was gone. The ringleader wasn't happy to see me but he wasn't going to do anything about it. His buddies weren't similarly marked up, so I figured the idiot had tripped on his own feet and face-planted the deck. Ship decks were unforgiving that way. Now he was semi-sober and sheepish about it.

"Just enjoying the beach. You guys?"

"It's all right."

"Well, stay out of trouble."

"Yeah, whatever. Run back to BJ, now."

I made to move away but stopped. I had a nagging question. One of those questions that won't keep you up at night, but can get in your craw a little all the same.

"Say, what is your beef with BJ Baker anyway?"

The guy made to snarl but clearly his face hurt when he did it.

"Being a scumbag isn't enough?"

"No, it's enough. And he certainly is a scumbag."

"Tough man dissing his boss when he's not around."

"Whose boss?"

"Yours."

"Sorry, kid. Wrong tree. I don't work for BJ Baker, and I doubt I ever will."

"So why'd you give us grief."

"I gave you grief?"

"You stopped me in the room, with his Heisman. And then you did it again at the speeches."

"I can assure you it had nothing to do with helping BJ. I stopped you because you were going to destroy property in the one instance, and commit assault in the second, and that really isn't cool."

"It isn't cool? Really."

"Really. So I ask again. What exactly is your problem with BJ? And don't say scumbag. Most people think he's a scumbag, but few of them try to throw a beer can at him."

"He is a scumbag. He's a lowlife and a backstabber and he doesn't think about anyone but the mighty BJ Baker himself."

I crouched down so I could see the guy better. His face was a mess.

"I know you Browns fans like to hold a grudge, but don't you think life would be a little more pleasant if you just let it go?"

"Let it go? You think this is about football?" he said. "Look, I don't like anything about Pittsburgh. But that guy's a special kind of maggot, you know what I mean?"

I knew.

"Why?"

The young guy looked at his buddies and then back at me. He moved slowly like his face was bothering him.

"You ever been to eastern Ohio? Youngstown?"

I shook my head. "No."

"It's a border town. About halfway between Pittsburgh and Cleveland, but on the Ohio side."

"Okay."

"But half the damned town roots for Pittsburgh. Can you believe it? Ohioans rooting for a Pennsylvania team?"

"It's a crazy world."

"You bet it is. You should see our Thanksgiving dinners. It's hell."

"I bet. Does BJ Baker enter this story anytime soon?"

"Yeah, I'm getting to that. My *grandad*, he's from Youngstown. My dad moved to Cleveland to find work. That's where I grew up."

"I saw the shirt."

"Yeah, so grandad, he's a Pittsburgh guy. Worked in a steel mill and everything back in the day. So guess who his favorite player is?"

"I'll take a stab. BJ Baker."

"Yeah, BJ Baker. So my grandad, he's sick, right? He's got this thing in his lungs. Mesoleafy-something."

"Mesothelioma," I said.

"Yeah, that's the one."

"I'm sorry."

"Yeah, so you know what it is, right? He ain't coming back from that. So they move him to Pittsburgh for tests or chemo or something. He's going downhill. Then, just before Christmas, he hears that during the football halftime they're going to do a cross to the hospital on the TV. And guess who's going to be there for it?"

"Still BJ Baker. Go on."

"So the nurses and doctors or whatever, they know my grandad's this massive fan of BJ's, right, so they choose him to be one of the patients that BJ visits with on TV. They always choose little kids and old people, don't they?"

"I guess. So what happened?"

"They wheel my grandad out, prop him up so he can do this thing, meet his hero. And what does BJ do?"

"I really have no idea at this point."

The kid shrugged. "He doesn't show. At all. Like, ever. Just doesn't turn up. So gramps waits out there in the lobby or wherever and BJ doesn't bother to show up. Doesn't call, doesn't send a letter, or whatever those old people do. Nothing. So they wheel my grandad back into his little sick room and say *sorry, pops, time to die.*"

"He died?"

"Not yet. But he will. Soon."

"So let me get this straight. You boys came all this way to cause trouble for BJ Baker because he slighted your grandad?"

"No, man. Dixie won this trip on the radio station. Didn't ya, Dix?"

A guy with brown hair and a very poor excuse for facial hair waved his hand at me.

"So you're not here because of BJ?"

"Nah. I just saw him, you know? After what he did to my grandad, I just saw red."

"He does bring out the best in people. I'm sorry about your grandad. But keep your nose clean, pardon the pun. It doesn't do him any good if you're in a jail in the Bahamas."

The kid nodded and I stood and stretched my back out. Then I told them to enjoy their day, and kept walking along the promenade toward the ship.

# CHAPTER TWENTY-ONE

Once again I didn't do as Anastasia had ordered me and return to the ship. I walked down the promenade until I reached the dock, and then I cut into the hut renting out the beach toys. I rented another chair, which I went and pitched next to Ron's. I gave Ron a bathroom break and he returned with two bottles of Kalik beer. He was a prince among men, of that I was certain.

We kicked back for the rest of the afternoon. We didn't see Guy X get off. We didn't see Anastasia get back on. Ron got burgers and beers for a mid-afternoon lunch. They weren't as good as Mick's, but the view made up for it, as did the notion that we were literally eating cheeseburgers in paradise.

We whiled away the hours watching a big ship do nothing. It was like staking out an apartment block, something we had done plenty of times before. But sitting on the beach with a beer and burger was a vast improvement.

"You think whoever took the rings will bring them off onto the island?" asked Ron.

"It seems like the best place. Back in Palm Beach the security will be much tighter."

"And Lucas is watching?"

"In between reeling in wahoo."

Ron said, "You know what I think?"

"No."

He didn't say anything.

"What do you think?" I asked him.

Nothing.

"Ron? What do you think?"

He turned to me and smiled.

"I think that's Guy X."

He nodded at a man coming down the dock. He wasn't tall, maybe five eight, with deep-set eyes and broad shoulders. He wore a ball cap with a flat peak and a garish yellow shirt that was supposed to look tropical but just came off as loud, and he was carrying the ubiquitous blue travel bag. It didn't suit him at all. He looked like a mob guy playing a regular guy on vacation.

"Ron, my man, your beer goggles really are superior. I'm going to follow him. Can you get up to the security there on the dock and find out who he is? He must have used his ID to get off the ship."

We waited until Guy X left the dock and hit the promenade, and then we went our separate ways. I ambled along the water line of the beach, staying just backward of where Guy X walked. Ron made a beeline for the dock. I looked around the beach for Anastasia but didn't see her. She wasn't the *sand between your toes* kind. She would likely be waiting somewhere up in the village, in a bar or on the promenade.

Guy X didn't go too far. He stopped at the tiki bar by the beach and took a stool at the end of the counter, facing away from the water. He dropped his bag and then removed his ball cap, revealing thick black hair. I saw him nod to the bartender, who brought him over a beer. I wanted to get closer but didn't dare. I didn't want to spook Anastasia.

I dropped back to the water's edge and pretended to be mooching around with nothing better to do. It wasn't easy, because most people dipping their toes in the water tended to keep their eyes on said water, rather than up the beach at where Guy X sat. I pulled off my deck shoes and splashed my toes in the ocean. I watched a group of shirtless young guys with beers, standing in waist high water. Then I splashed and turned and glanced along the beach, and then around and up at the promenade. Guy X was enjoying his beer. Anastasia wasn't there. I slowly turned back down the beach toward the ship and saw Ron striding along the water line to me.

He was huffing when he reached me.

"Don't do yourself an injury," I said.

"Walking on sand," he said. "It's tougher than it looked on *Baywatch*."

"What do you know?"

He handed me a piece of paper. I faced the water as I looked at it. Ron stood shoulder to shoulder with me, facing the other way. The paper was a printout of Guy X's passenger record. I looked at his picture. I had seen him before. It was definitely the man who had pushed Frederick Connors overboard. But there was a problem. I knew it was him, but I couldn't swear it in a court of law. Frederick had been pushed overboard at night, and what light there had been was shadowed by the decks above. My guts knew, but my eyes could not guarantee.

Guy X's eyes held a cool charm, like he could love you or kill you, it could go either way. With his dark features and black, combed-back hair, he looked more Atlantic City than Palm Beach. But I knew plenty of Atlantic City types who found their way down south to our little paradise. My friend Sal Mondavi was one of them. He knew most of the others. I wondered if he knew this guy.

His name was Francis Martelli. I would have put hard-earned on the fact that he went by Frankie. Some guys were Francis and some guys were Frankie. This guy was all Frankie. Which gave me another problem. I couldn't connect Anastasia with Frankie. With Francis, maybe. But Frankie, no way. I just didn't see them together. The Russian aristocrat and the Atlantic City shylock. It didn't fit.

But then, it rarely did. A scruffy former ballplayer turned PI had no business being with an FDLE Special Agent. A bankrupted former insurance guy had no business being with a lady of the Palm Beach set. There was no logic to these things. Not that I could find. I turned slowly and handed the paper back to Ron. He turned toward the water.

We did that dance for a half hour. One of us looking up at the bar, the other looking over the turquoise water. There was an unspoken understanding that it would have been better with beers in our hands. But we took our licks and did the thing that had to be done. We watched Guy X enjoy his beer. He took his time, like he had plenty of it. Like he was waiting on someone and was happy to wait.

But no one showed. No Anastasia, no one otherwise. I wondered if she had spotted us and was staying away. It was possible. But then she had no reason to suspect I was watching her. And I couldn't believe that if she saw me standing around on the beach she wouldn't take the opportunity to come and yell at me once more.

Eventually Guy X finished his beer. The sun was dropping toward the United States to the west of us, but no one looked in a hurry to leave the beach. Except Guy X. He finished his beer, nodded to the bartender, and then picked up his blue travel bag off the sand. He carried his cap in his hand and stepped up onto the promenade.

"He's leaving," I said.

Ron turned around.

Guy X—Francis—walked toward the buildings behind the promenade. I began to move up the beach.

"I'm going to follow," I said. "You head to the dock, just in case I lose him and he heads back there."

I didn't run but I wanted to. I got to the promenade and looked around. I saw Guy X near the restaurant with the balcony view, so I tapped my feet and slipped on my deck shoes and ambled toward him. As I approached, he slipped between the restaurant and the trinket store. There was nowhere to go in there. That was where the gate was.

Then I started running. Because I knew the gate required a crew keycard to open. And I recalled the crew hatch that Guy X had used after throwing Frederick overboard. He had Angel Rodriguez's crew keycard. I wondered if Army or Porter had voided it. On board they probably had. I wasn't sure it was the same system as on the island.

It wasn't. When I got to the gate it was closed and locked, and no Guy X in sight. I ran around to the other side of the store and jumped over the small fence and onto the service track where Danielle and I had come out earlier.

I saw the gaudy shirt disappear down the path that cut through the middle of the island. I ran along the track behind the stores and bars. I could hear the music and laughter. When I got to where the track cut into the island's interior, I stopped. There was no motion, no sign of the shirt or wide shoulders or the slick hair or the blue travel bag. I ran again, into the island's interior.

When I reached the utility building, I could no longer hear the music and laughter, just the buzz of the generators. No footsteps. I moved forward toward the plantation houses Danielle and I had seen. There was nothing to see. I decided to take the walking track to the back beach.

"Hey!" a voice called from behind.

I spun around. A man stood back near the utility building. He was lean and wore a green shirt and matching trousers, like a gardener's uniform.

"You can't be here," he said, striding toward me.

"I'm with security," I said. I didn't look like I was with security. I was in a palm tree print shirt and shorts.

"I don't think so," he said as he came to me.

"No, I mean I'm with Army—Chief Mahoney."

"I don't know who that is, but you can't be back here. It's staff only."

I glanced back toward the track to the beach and then at the man. It wasn't worth the effort. I had lost Guy X. But I now knew he existed. I had no idea what he had come this way for. Maybe he was meeting Anastasia in the plantation house while the staff were at work. Maybe he had cut back and was headed back to the boat.

"Okay," I said to the man. I took a step to leave, and he made to take my arm to escort me out.

"I'm leaving, friend, but you really don't want to put your hands on me."

I think my tone of voice sold him on the fact it was a bad idea, because he backed off and pointed in the direction of the main beach. I left him to his rhododendrons, or whatever the hell he was doing.

By the time I got back to the promenade there were the beginnings of a change in tide. Not so much in the water as the people. More of them were moving back to the ship and none appeared to be getting off. I walked along the promenade, past the tiki bar where folks were still enjoying beverages, to the dock, where I found Ron. He put his palms out to ask what happened.

"He went into the staff area," I said. "I lost him. I take it he didn't come back here yet?"

Ron shook his head. "Nope."

"You see Danielle?"

"Not yet."

We looked around. The line was forming as passengers checked back onto the ship. I recalled Army saying they check ID both off and on. They didn't want to leave anyone behind.

"He's going to have to check back in, right?"

Ron nodded.

I took off down the dock with Ron in tow. I wandered around the line of passengers to where one of the security crew was checking people aboard.

"Sir, you'll just need to join the line."

"I need to know when a passenger gets on board."

"Sir, if you get in line you can go and find them."

"Call Chief Mahoney, he'll tell you."

"Yes, sir. He'll tell me to tell you to get in line. I won't ask again."

He didn't ask again. He turned and scanned the next person in line, a squat woman with a pinched face who gave me a look of distaste. As the security guy scanned her ship pass her photo came up on the screen of the laptop they had set up. Same pinched features, slightly less distaste.

Ron was gone. I found him in line, people already behind him. I cut in and stood with him, people's distaste be damned. We slowly ebbed our way to the security checkpoint. Ron held up his ship pass that was around his neck. The security guy scanned him in and glanced at the screen.

"Sir," he said.

Then he looked at me. He showed no sign of recognition.

"Sir, your ship pass."

"Look at me. I'm in line. Now I need you to put a flag on this passenger's record." I handed him the printout that Ron had procured.

The guard looked at it and frowned. "Francis Martelli?"

"Yes."

"Why?"

I didn't want to mention that a man had gone overboard. I'm sure the ship had slowed when we went over the previous night in order to launch the rescue tender, but I was also sure that most of the passengers had no idea it had happened. Ron stepped back to us.

"Mr. Mob," he said to the security guy. "The perp."

The guy looked at Ron and then at the paper. Then he tapped the laptop keyboard.

"Mr. Mob?" I asked Ron.

Ron whispered in my ear. "It's ship code. MOB, as in man overboard."

I shrugged and took out the comms unit and held it up for the security guy. "Can you ping this when he gets back on board?"

"No," he said.

"No? Why not?"

"Because this says Mr. Martelli is already back on board."

# CHAPTER TWENTY-TWO

O~NCE WE WERE CHECKED IN, WE WERE IN, AND THEY~ weren't letting us back out, so Ron and I wandered up the gangway and onto the ship. We took the elevator back to the suite deck. Ron went to check on Cassandra, and I told him I'd be at the pool bar waiting for Danielle. I stopped in our suite and left a note for her and then headed down.

The pool area was busier than I'd thought it would be, given most people had spent the day at the beach and a good half of them were yet to get back on board. But it seemed plenty of people never even bothered to get off. I supposed in the end it was more of the same. Same beer, same buffet, same staff, same sunshine. Choose your water—salt or chlorine. One of the bars around the pool was closed, I figured because half the crew was staffing bars on the island, so the one bar that was open was busy.

I went and sat at the closed bar. Although I wouldn't have said no to a drink, I wasn't desperate. I just wanted away from the crowds. The sun was dropping and the mood of the boat was changing. People were moving from laid-back and lazy mode into party mode. As the thought passed through my mind, the music playing across the deck changed from contemporary country to seventies disco.

A throng of people caught my eye. They were a decent-sized group, maybe thirty people, but they all seemed to be hanging around the one person, like planets around a sun. It took me a moment to catch a glimpse of the person in the middle. I saw him from behind but that was all I needed. I knew the clean-cut head of hair and the square shoulders pushing at the seams of his blazer. It was BJ Baker doing what BJ Baker liked doing most. Holding court, and no doubt talking about his favorite subject: BJ Baker.

I watched him for a while. He really was a charming so-and-so. The people in his orbit hung on his every word. I could tell them some stories. BJ talked for a while and then he looked at his massive watch and declared the court over, and then took another few minutes to untangle himself from the galaxy he had created.

BJ smiled and waved and nodded his way around the pool. He kept away from the busiest area around the bar. Which took him right by me.

I gave him a big old country smile. He took it in the spirit it was intended.

"What the hell is wrong with you, Jones?"

"Top of the morning to ya?"

"You're not Irish."

"Neither are the words *Notre* or *Dame*, and it doesn't stop them."

"Jones, I'm very busy."

"Relax, BJ. You're on a cruise."

"You think I've got time to relax?"

"You're going to give yourself a coronary."

"You are going to give me a coronary."

I wished. "Speaking of coronaries, I just met a fan of yours."

"There are lots of my fans here."

"Yeah, but this fan has a special place in his heart reserved for you."

"You get used to being a hero, Jones. Not that you'd know."

"Yeah, a hero. That's what this guy said when you brushed off his grandfather."

"I don't know what you are talking about."

"You were going to do a cross to a hospital as part of the television coverage from Pittsburgh."

"I do a lot of those."

"Well, you didn't do this one. They rolled the old guy out on life support to wait for you—his hero, so-called—and you just didn't show up. A room full of sick oldies and kids. And the great BJ Baker didn't bother to come."

"I'm sure I had a reason."

"I'm sure every scumbag in the world who ever crapped on the little people had a reason. You probably had to polish your Heisman."

He looked at me. Safe to say it wasn't a look of love.

"You're a class act, Jones."

"If by that you mean I've never jilted a dying man in a hospital, you'd be right."

"So a hospital didn't get its five seconds of fame. So what? When did this travesty occur?"

"Just before Christmas."

"You mean the whiteout game? I had to leave before we got stuck for a week in Pittsburgh under ten feet of snow."

"As long as you got home okay, BJ. That's the main thing."

"Look, Jones. What can I tell you? I'm not responsible for the weather or airline delays or old men in hospitals. Life's tough."

"Yeah, it is. You're right. Life in Palm Beach is a grind, I get it. And guys who worked their backsides off in steel mills to give your old football team a place to play your little game should stop complaining about the cancer it stuck in their lungs and suck it up. Except they can't suck it up, 'cause their lungs just don't work. And of course, my bad, they didn't complain, 'cause guys like that never do. It's their grandsons doing the moaning for them." I shook my head. "And the old guy says you're his hero. Geez, did the guy never watch any quarterbacks play?"

BJ leaned in close to me. I had to give it to him. He was one intimidating piece of work, even on the wrong side of seventy. His nostrils flared like a bull again. He puffed out his chest and made to let me have it.

But then he didn't. He just turned and strode away at a rapid rate of knots. I didn't watch him go. I was done with him. I sat at my empty bar and waited for Danielle to come and save me.

Cassandra and Ron found me before Danielle did. Cassandra looked like my car after a good session at the car wash. She was radiant and relaxed and her skin shone like it had been covered in butter and the butter had soaked in. Her hair had been styled and her nails were polished like a trophy.

"You look like a million dollars," I said, and then wondered if she would take offense. Looking like a million bucks in Palm Beach was probably no kind of compliment at all. She smiled.

"You're too kind. But it's amazing what a good soaking and buffing can do to an old chassis."

She wasn't all Palm Beach. She was wearing a summer dress that I'm sure the fashion police would have argued shouldn't have worked on a woman her age. But it did. It worked because she ate healthily and stayed active, and because she didn't give a damn what the fashion police thought. She liked to look elegant but she clearly didn't do it for them. She did it for herself. And maybe a little bit for Ron.

I offered her a hand onto one of the bar stools and Ron took the next one along.

"Seen Danielle?" he asked.

"Not yet."

"How was the island?" Cassandra asked.

"It's nice," I said. "But it's no Longboard Kelly's."

She smiled again. "It's a beautiful planet but nowhere beats home."

I would have toasted that, but I didn't have a drink. Which was rectified when a bartender skipped in under the bar and took up station.

"I'll be opening up in just a moment," she said. "But can I get you something while I do?"

Ron and I both looked at Cassandra. "Three beers," she said.

"Domestic or imported?"

"Domestic," she said. "We're in the Bahamas still, aren't we?"

The bartender opened three bottles and poured them into plastic cups. We each took one.

"Cheers," said Cassandra.

"Cheers," said Ron.

I just nodded. I liked Cassandra a lot. But I kept finding myself putting her into pigeonholes because of where she lived. And she kept breaking out of my pigeonholes. I sipped the beer and glanced toward the island. I wondered where Danielle was. I wondered where Anastasia was. I wondered where Guy X, or Francis Martelli, was. I wondered how I was going to prove their relationship for Frederick. Maybe I wouldn't. Maybe he'd find out the old-fashioned way. Maybe they'd eventually tell him. Then I thought about him going overboard and I wondered if they ever would tell him, and I shivered at the idea that maybe Frederick's own wife wasn't just having an affair. Maybe she wanted him dead.

"Goose walk over your grave?" asked Cassandra.

"Too many thoughts, too small a head," I said.

"You don't give yourself enough credit."

I shrugged. Sometimes it was probably true. But there were plenty of times it wasn't true at all. Sometimes I gave myself way too much credit. Sometimes my confidence outmatched my ability. I brushed the thought away with a sip of beer.

"What's the plan for this evening?" I asked.

"It's auction night," Cassandra said. That reminded me of the rings. Maybe they were still on the ship, maybe they weren't. I had no idea. And with the sun dropping low in the sky, within an hour neither would Lucas. I thought about texting him and telling him to get back to land before he lost the light. Then I remembered who I was thinking about. Lucas could navigate by the stars, or the scent on the wind, or the way the magnetic poles affected the stiffness in his hands.

"You going to buy anything?" I asked.

Cassandra sipped her beer. "I doubt it. Football memorabilia is not really my thing."

"I saw a Gauguin in there," I said. Ron shot me a look from behind her.

"I'm more a Monet fan," she said. "And Ron likes Warhol."

Ron nodded. "Soup cans. Genius."

I couldn't tell if he was serious, so I smiled like an idiot and kept my mouth shut.

"We're going to the captain's dinner first. Are you doing that?" she asked.

"Not that I'm aware of. We'll see what Danielle wants to do, but I think a quiet night might be order."

"Of course," she said. "How self-absorbed I am. I can't believe you went overboard. Are you all right?"

"He didn't really *go* overboard," said Ron. "He jumped."

"To save someone. Frederick Connors. How is he?"

"I don't think he'll cruise again anytime soon," I said.

"And Anastasia," she said. "She must be mortified."

I looked at Ron and he at me. Mortified was a good word. I wondered how Cassandra would feel when she found out that Ron had hidden the affair from her.

"I must find her at the dinner, Ron. Ask her if she needs anything."

Ron nodded and said, "Here's trouble."

Trouble sauntered across the pool deck. It was my kind of trouble. Danielle strode toward us, oblivious to the heads she was turning.

"What are the odds of finding you all at a bar?" she said.

"Where have you been?" asked Cassandra.

"Checking out the boutiques."

"Find anything good?"

"Nothing I couldn't live without," she said, looking at me.

"Drink?" I asked.

"Sure. Vodka tonic." The way she said it set me on edge. Then I got it. She had been following Anastasia, and Cassandra didn't know. I ordered Danielle's drink and then looked at Ron over the bar. I was about to make a ham-fisted attempt at excuses when Ron slipped off his stool.

"Well, as much as I love smelling of salt water and beer, I'd best have a shower before this dinner."

He offered his hand to Cassandra and she took it, setting the remains of her beer on the bar.

"Thank you for the drink, kind sir," she said.

"Anytime."

"I'll see you later," she said to Danielle, as if they had more to discuss.

Ron shot me a wink and then headed away across the pool deck. The bartender put Danielle's drink down and she took the stool by me.

"So what happened?" I asked. "Where did Anastasia go?"

"She didn't go anywhere."

"She didn't go anywhere?"

"She looked at trinkets in the stores and then she sat on a daiquiri for an hour. Then she took a walk along the promenade and came back on board."

"That's it?"

"That's it. But I don't want to talk about her. I want to talk about you."

"Me? What did I do?"

"You followed him."

"Followed who?"

"The guy at the tiki bar," she said. "So tell." She sipped her drink and looked at me, waiting.

"How did you know that?"

"I saw you. You and Ron doing a slow motion tango on the beach. You guys are as subtle as a tax bill."

"You were watching me?"

"No. I happened to see you, and you were watching something, so I started watching what you were watching. The guy at the tiki bar."

"You were supposed to be watching Anastasia."

"I was. I can do two things at once."

"That's why you're the special agent and I'm good at opening pickle jars."

"Sure it is. And it's because I'm a woman and you're a man. So what happened? I saw you follow him."

I sipped my beer. Now I felt sheepish. She would have done a better job of following him and there would be no arguing otherwise.

"He went into the interior. Where we went earlier."

"Yes."

"He had a crew card for the gate."

"Of course."

"And he went to where the utility building and the planta-tion accommodations were."

"And?"

"And I lost him."

She frowned. "You lost him?"

I shrugged like it could have happened to anyone.

"Yeah. I got pulled up by an employee asking what I was doing there, and he got away."

"He got away?"

"Yeah."

"So you didn't see what he did with the bag."

"No. Wait. What bag?"

"The travel bag."

"What travel bag? What are you talking about?"

"What am I talking about?" she said. "What are you talking about? Why were you following him?"

"Because it was Guy X."

"That was Guy X?"

"Yes."

"The one having the affair?"

"Yes. Why are you talking about a bag?"

"You didn't see it, did you?"

"See what?"

"The drop."

"What drop?"

"The bag drop. That guy, your Guy X. He arrived with a blue travel bag."

"Sure. Everyone's got one. Even I've got one now."

"And he left the tiki bar with a blue bag."

"Yes, I know. I followed him."

"It wasn't the same bag, MJ. They switched bags at the bar."

# CHAPTER TWENTY-THREE

"How do you know they switched bags?"

"I was watching, MJ. You were watching Guy X in order to connect him with Anastasia. I didn't know it was Guy X. I thought you were watching him for some other reason. So I watched what he did, not who he met."

"And you think he swapped bags?"

She swatted me on the head. "I don't *think* it. I *know* it. He put his bag on the ground near the side of the bar. A little later, another bag was put next to his."

"By who?"

"The bartender."

"The inside man."

"You're quick when you want to be."

"You're making me feel bad about myself."

"Grow a pair, MJ."

"So he took the second bag when he left."

"Right."

"And I lost him."

"You did. It happens."

"That didn't make me feel better."

"Suck it up, MJ."

I took a long drink of my beer. "Well, I've got some news for you."

"Hit me."

"Ron got the guy's name from security."

"Nice. Do tell."

"Francis Martelli."

"Francis? He didn't look like a Francis. He's a Frankie, for sure."

"And that's why I love you."

"That's why?"

"One of a library of reasons. So when I went after him, Ron went to the dock to make sure he didn't double back."

"See, you guys are good at this stuff."

"And when I got back, we asked security to alert us when he got back onto the ship."

"Good thinking."

"And they said he was already checked back on board."

"Did he beat Ron there?"

"No chance. I followed him for a few minutes. Ron went straight across the beach to the dock."

"So how?"

I shrugged. Another thing I didn't know.

"This whole thing is weird," she said.

"Tell me about it."

We sipped our drinks and thought on it. I wasn't coming up with anything, but I didn't want to tell Danielle that.

"I've got nothing," she said. "I haven't eaten since breakfast. You?"

"Had a burger for lunch."

"You guys really know how to stakeout."

"I would've gotten you something but I know you all prefer donuts on a stakeout."

"You're a card."

"That's what they tell me."

"I need to think, and to think, I need to eat."

"Then let's test that *get whatever you want by phone* thing."

We returned to our suite. The last of the sun was sending spears across the sky as the final few passengers left the beach empty and alone. The beach didn't look sad about it. If anything it looked relieved. A cleanup crew was already marching in a line across the sand, picking up the beachgoers' debris. It never ceases to amaze me how much crap people can leave on a beach. When running along City Beach in the evenings, we always find litter. Cans, wrappers, plastic bags, fast-food containers. And there are trash cans at every entrance, just like trash cans line the beach on Paradise Cay. The name seemed ironic now.

People were buzzing. Either because they were already buzzed from day-drinking, or because they were feeling that natural instinct all animals felt as day turns to night. On the African savanna, dusk is rush hour. The day animals take their last drink at the waterhole before finding their sleeping quarters, and the night animals get up and take a drink at the waterhole before setting off for a night of roaming and hunting. A lot of activity. I had seen it on *Wild Kingdom* a long time ago. *Wild Kingdom* didn't lie. Lucas had said it best. *The animals feed at sundown.* Even the higher-level mammals.

Some people were settling in for a big night at the bar by the pool. Other were changing out of their beach gear to nab a good spot at the buffet. Cassandra and her gang were dressing up for the captain's dinner, which sounded like a fancy affair and not at all my cup of joe. The restaurants were preparing for the onslaught, and the bars were preparing for the post-dinner avalanche. The casino was ramping up. The night animals were at the waterhole.

We went to our suite. I had no intention of changing clothes for dinner or any other reason. Danielle decided my lunch choice had given her a hankering for a burger with bacon and cheese, with lots of fries. She was thin and athletic and looked like she wouldn't go near a fat-laced burger, and maybe the point was that she very rarely did. But when she did, she went all the way. I picked up the phone and asked if I could order something and was told that yes, Mr. Jones, you can have whatever you like, which was an offer I could have gotten used to. I ordered Danielle's grease trap and a plate of fries for myself. Although I'm still reasonably athletic, I'm not as thin as Danielle, and I do have a tendency to enjoy burgers more often than she does. But I had already eaten one on the beach, and wasn't that hungry, so I went with the fries and then as an afterthought ordered a chef's salad, a bottle of Sauvignon Blanc, and a bottle of water.

Dinner arrived as breakfast had, except this time, there was just one delivery guy. He wheeled the cart in but we told him we'd be happy to set it all up ourselves. There were plates and cutlery and a little vase with a single rose in it, which I smelled. It had no scent but I was impressed that it wasn't plastic. We took it all out onto the balcony and ate under muted lights.

I felt the slight shudder as I stuffed some fries in my mouth. It could have been an earthquake. I had felt a similar sensation when I played ball in Modesto, California. The kind of brief movement that makes you think you had a tiny dizzy spell. A teammate from the Bay Area had told me it was a little tremor, which I hadn't believed at first, until I felt the same thing again three times in a week. Either I had a neurological disorder or the tremors were real. I asked my teammate if the tremors were a sign that we were coming up on a big one, and he said that the little ones were like a release valve, and we should worry if we didn't feel them.

But I was on water, and after a moment, I felt the drift and realized that we had cast off. The ship was headed out to sea. I poured some wine and we looked at each other as we held our glasses up in silent toast, and then I looked to the dark ocean.

"What are you thinking?" Danielle asked.

"About Francis Martelli. Guy X. I thought he was meeting Anastasia."

"Uh-huh."

"You saw him do a bag drop."

"I did."

"But he didn't meet Anastasia."

"No, he didn't."

"So what was he doing?"

"Sneaking something off the boat," she said. She picked up her burger. It was huge and a detachable snake jaw was required to eat it. She took a big bite and munched on it with a smile. I loved watching her eat. Not toast or cauliflower, but something big and messy and bad for you like a burger. She attacked it with a zeal I thought most people reserved for sex, but when I looked around the world, I suspected most people really didn't have that much zeal for anything at all anymore.

"What, though?"

"My first thought was it might be the missing rings."

"I thought that too. But he went through the metal detector. His bag was searched."

Danielle wiped her mouth with a napkin. "Yeah, I was thinking about that. Maybe he was receiving something."

"Only to bring it back on board?"

"Doesn't fit, does it?"

"But here's the thing. I can connect him to Anastasia. Frederick took a photo of the guy coming out of his house. What if he was right about the link but wrong about the reason?"

"How?"

"What if Anastasia and Guy X aren't having an affair at all? What if they were conspiring to steal the rings."

Danielle took another bite and thought it through. "Doesn't mean they aren't having an affair."

"No, you're right, it doesn't. But whether or not they are romantically involved is secondary to whether they are in cahoots to steal the rings."

"Cahoots?"

"I watched *Bonanza* when I was a kid."

She shook her head.

I sipped my wine. It was nice but it wasn't hitting the spot. I wondered if I had gotten a touch dehydrated on the beach, so I poured myself some water. "But why try to kill Frederick?"

"There's motive either way. An affair is a motive, so is theft. All it suggests is that either way, Frederick was superfluous to the plans."

I thought about that. I didn't feel good about it. I had no idea what was going on, but I was fairly certain that Danielle was right. It wasn't a good ending for old Frederick. Danielle sat back with her wine and we looked at the ocean as the ship turned and began to pick up speed. We dropped into silence, together with our own thoughts.

"Can I say something?" Danielle said, putting down her wine.

"That never goes well for me, but okay."

"I've been thinking."

"About the case?"

"No. Something else."

"Double down on the not good for me."

"Will you shut up for a second?"

I nodded and put my water glass to my mouth.

"What I mean is, last night. I thought I'd lost you. Twice."

I wasn't sure if I was supposed to respond but I went with the *shut up*.

"Once when you jumped off the deck, and once when we found you in the water. I can't tell you how that feels."

"I know how that feels." I put my hand over my mouth. "Sorry. I'll stop talking."

"No, go on. When did you feel that?"

"When you got shot that time."

She nodded. "Yeah, okay. I can see that. How did that feel?"

"Not great. Unimaginable, really. I can't see this life without you in it. I'm not sure I'd want a life like that."

She nodded again. "But there's more. The confusing part."

She sipped her wine and continued. "I thought I'd lost you, and that feeling was the worst feeling I've ever had. And then I found Chief Mahoney and he radioed it in and then we went down to the rescue tender. As soon as we were on the water, I felt better, like I was doing something. And as soon as I was doing something, I knew I'd find you. I just knew."

"And you did."

"We did. I saw Mr. Connors. I didn't see you until we pulled alongside. I thought he was the one kicking." She stopped and took a deep breath. "I thought you were dead."

"But I wasn't."

"No, but that didn't help the feeling of losing you. I don't want to feel that way, MJ."

"Me, either."

"And that's the confusing part. I want to tell you to stop it. To stop doing that sort of thing, putting yourself in danger like that. To save me from that feeling. But I can't ask you that."

"Why?"

"Because of the other feeling."

"Which is?"

"Pride. You literally jumped off a ship into the ocean to save a guy, who, yes, might be a client, but is really someone you don't know at all. He doesn't mean any more to you than any other person on the planet. And you jumped off a ship because you knew he couldn't swim and he was going to die if you didn't."

I shrugged. I had no words.

"So I can't ask you to stop it, can I?"

I shook my head. "No, you can't. Anymore than I can ask you."

"I didn't jump off a ship, MJ."

"Not today. But you're a cop. You do that sort of thing every day. You save people and risk yourself every single day. And you don't go looking for a parade because of it. You just do it. And every day when you go out the door, I get that little knot in my guts."

"I didn't know that."

"Well, trust me. I know what you're feeling because I feel it, too. When you got shot, I was worried and sad and angry. But I was also proud. You weren't going to let the bad guys win. That's not who you are."

"We're a hell of a pair."

"Just think how many people we're saving by not having to be in a relationship with either of us."

"Making a lot of people happy and they don't even know it."

"Right on."

We sipped our drinks and nibbled at our fries. They were cold.

"So what is the deal with Fred and Ana?" Danielle asked.

"Let me correct you there. They are definitely not Fred and Ana. It's Frederick and Anastasia, all the way."

"They are, aren't they? But what's their deal? Do they seem happy to you?"

"One of them is paying me to spy on the other's affair, and

we think the other may have tried to have the first killed. So no, I don't think they're too happy."

"But they must have been once, surely? I just can't see it."

"You need some old photographs."

"Of what?"

"Of Frederick and Anastasia. They're an odd pair, I'll give you that. But they aren't what they were. None of us are. When people get older, everyone assumes they were always old. But let me tell you a story. About a young guy who gets a bad knee and has to give up his Saturday pickup basketball game, and he puts on some weight, and then he can't keep up with his kid anymore. So he tells himself he doesn't do that roustabout stuff now, he's an adult, not a child. And he drifts away from all his basketball buddies, and his bad knee turns into hip pain, and then he's taking drugs to soften the wear, and then stepping down the front steps hurts, and he's forgotten what it felt like to be pain-free. Like all that stuff before had been someone else's life. And the pain just wears him down, and no one knows because it's all on the inside. He's on edge, and he's always irritable, and he knows it and hates it, but that just makes it worse. And then he loses his wife to cancer, and he can't see any damned point to it anymore. He's just unhappy all the time, except when he drinks the pain away. And the neighbor kids all think he's the local grouch, because he's always so mean and grumpy. Don't throw your baseball on his lawn. You'll never get it back from the mean old man. But that mean old man would love nothing more than to be able to throw a ball with a kid, like he had years ago. If you saw an old photograph you'd know. You'd see this young man and the love of his life, arm in arm, laughing. And you probably wouldn't believe it was him. Because it all happens so slowly, and so quickly at the same time."

I sipped my water. I had no idea where that had come from.

It had been one hell of a trip and I was no longer responsible for my rambling brain. That was my story and I was sticking with it.

Danielle just looked at me. Or through me, or maybe inside me. I couldn't tell. Law enforcement types have those kinds of eyes. They can look like Santa one second and your high school principal the next.

"MJ," was all she said. She reached across the table and took my hands, which meant I couldn't pick up my wine, which I suddenly wanted.

"You know what I think?" she said.

"Tell me."

"I think we should grow old disgracefully."

"That's been my plan since high school."

"Law-abiding, mind you."

"To a point. But sure."

She smiled, and then she lost it.

"Tell me," I said.

"You just made me think of my dad."

"I didn't want to press," I said. "Tell me when you want to tell me."

"You kind of just described him."

"I just described a lot of people. How is he?"

"He's not himself, MJ. And he knows it. And he hates it. That's why he didn't want me to come. He doesn't want me to see him."

"He's still your dad."

"Of course he is. I don't care. I mean I care, but what the ALS is doing to his body doesn't mean I don't want to see him."

"Is that it?"

"What do you mean?"

"Is that the thing that makes him not want you to see him? His body?"

"He's in a chair. He can't walk anymore. He's incontinent. He's embarrassed."

I said nothing.

"What?" she asked. "Tell me what you're thinking."

"I've never met the man. But you've told me plenty. And I'm sure losing his physical abilities is part of it. But you've always described a different guy. The young guy in the old photo that I see? He's a book guy. He's going to be an English professor. He loves the theater and reading and all that discourse stuff that they love at college. He's a man of ideas and thoughts."

"But the doctors say the ALS isn't affecting his mind."

"I'm no doctor, but I call baloney on that. The ALS might not be causing memory loss, but it sure as hell is messing with his mind. The way he thinks, the way he sees himself. The way he thinks others see him."

"But you say he's a thinking guy. He's still got all his thoughts. It's his body that's failing him."

"I'm gonna go all philosophical on you now, but what is an idea if that idea cannot be expressed?"

She took a deep breath. The ship sounded its horn. It was loud.

"You're saying he can't express what he's thinking and that's what's making him withdraw?"

"It's a theory."

"I didn't see it that way."

"I never had an English teacher who didn't love to jabber on about language, quote Shakespeare or Whitman."

"My dad loved Keats. He used to read it to me."

I nodded.

Danielle finished her wine. "Thanks, MJ."

"Back at ya."

"I don't know what to do about it but I'm sure there's something."

"Stephen Hawking wrote physics papers, for crying out loud."

"I'm sure he had all kinds of expensive equipment. Like you say, Dad was an English professor. And I'm a special agent. We're not exactly flush."

"I know a lot of people. We'll find a way."

"A legal way."

"Absolutely. One hundred percent, guaranteed, almost certainly legal."

She smiled like she had indeed just looked at an old photograph, and I captured the smile for later. Much, much later.

I felt the breeze on my face as the ship gained speed. I was done. I had no more coherent thoughts to share on anything, and my body was ready to fall into a week-long coma.

Then my pocket vibrated. I pulled out the comms device. There was a message. It was from Lucas.

*There's action on the beach.*

# CHAPTER TWENTY-FOUR

I told Danielle what it said.

"Maybe Guy X dropped the bag for someone else to collect," she said.

"Two drops sounds convoluted."

"What are you going to tell him?"

"I told him we're back on the boat."

"Is he on the beach?"

"I don't know."

"It might be dangerous. He should back off."

"Lucas can handle himself."

"Even so."

The device pinged with another message.

*I know. Heard foghorn.*

I repeated the message to Danielle. Then I heard the ringing from inside the suite. I jumped up and went in and found my phone on the bar.

"Lucas," I said. I walked back to the balcony and put it on speaker so Danielle could hear.

"Mate, you were right."

"Why? What's going on?"

"I'm sitting out here filleting some fish and I hear another boat."

"Another boat?"

"Yeah. A speedboat. Twin 75 Mercuries, I reckon. Coming in from the south."

"Not a delivery?"

"No chance. Wrong boat, wrong time. You don't do deliveries at night on the banks, and you especially don't do them without running lights."

"They're running dark?"

"They are. So they slow down as they get off the east side of the island."

"Are they there now?"

"No, mate."

"Where'd they go?"

"To the light."

"What light?"

"Will you stop yabbering for five minutes and I'll tell ya? A light came on, a signal from the beach."

"Like a spotlight?"

"Kind of. Probably a high-powered flashlight, if I had to say. But it signaled the boat for sure, because the engines started up again and they motored nice and easy into the beach."

"They're on the back beach?"

"No."

"No? Where are they?"

"They've just left the beach. They're headed back to the south."

"What's down there?"

"Not much. Eventually you'll hit something. Maybe Chub Cay."

"Is that inhabited?"

"It is."

"Ferries?"

"Yep. And an airstrip."

"We need to call the cops."

"This ain't Miami, Miami. It's the Berry Islands. At best it'll be *a* cop, singular, and he or she might be anywhere. And these guys might bank around to the north of the cay and head for Great Harbour Cay. Hell, if they've got twin Mercuries, they could head for Florida."

"Then we have to stop that boat."

"That's why I'm calling. I'll pick you up."

"Lucas, the ship's left already. We're at sea."

"Yeah, I know. Get off."

I looked at Danielle. She shook her head.

"I can't get off a moving ship."

"Sure you can. Put on a life jacket and get in the drink. I'll come get you."

Danielle shook her head again.

"It's dark out."

"Take a flashlight. And you've got your locator beacon, right? I can track that. I'll be there in five."

He hung up. I stared at the phone for moment. I couldn't believe that I was actually contemplating jumping off a moving cruise ship for the second time in two days. It was becoming a thing.

Danielle didn't look happy.

"You can't be serious, MJ."

"What's the other option? Leave it to Lucas? It's not his case. He's not being paid to do this."

"*You're* not being paid to do this. Not to jump off a cruise ship. Look, what I said before, about being proud. I wasn't proud that you jumped off. I was proud you did it to save a person. Jumping off is just dumb."

"The coast guard does it all the time. Out of helicopters."

"To save people, MJ. Not to chase a boat that could very well have no connection to anything."

"Oh, it's connected all right. You know it is."

"And what if it is? What are you going to do if you catch them? Ram them?"

"I hadn't gotten that far."

"And just because you didn't get hurt last time doesn't mean the jump alone won't kill you."

"I don't plan on jumping this time. Come on, let's go."

I dashed into the suite and called the security control office and told them to find Chief Mahoney and to get him to meet me. Then I handed Danielle my phone.

"I'll keep this one," I said, holding up the comms unit.

We jogged to the stairs and ran down them. There was a line on every deck for the elevator. Dinner was in full swing. We kept going. Down and down. To the deck I had noted before. The stairs didn't deliver us exactly where I wanted to be. Instead, we came out on the crew deck and hit the I-95. The corridor was as busy as its namesake. Crew were rushing in both directions. It was organized chaos. I took Danielle's hand and dropped into a gap in the traffic and dashed toward the bow of the ship. When I saw the door I wanted, I cut in front of a guy pushing a cart of unbaked bread rolls and pulled to the side of the rush. The guy gave me a dirty look and kept going. It really was like the freeway.

Army arrived shortly after us. The traffic seemed to move around him. He had the other security officer, Porter, with him.

"What do you think you're going to do?" he asked.

"I need to get off."

"Listen, Mr. Jones. I can overlook the fact you jumped off my ship last night because you saved another passenger. But don't mistake that for consent. I could just as easily have you charged and banned from the cruise line."

"You could, and I would get that. But let's look at it this way. Think of the PR that would come with banning me, a person who saved someone who got pushed overboard. That's attempted murder, right? It wouldn't be a good look for you. And it wouldn't be that much better if the story got out that you allowed three million dollars in jewelry to zoom away on a speedboat that is right outside that door." I pointed to the closed hatch where the crew had been unloading goods that morning. I liked that it was at dock level and therefore close to the water. Not three high-dive platforms in the air.

"We can launch a tender," said Army.

"A, that will take too long. You have to slow the ship to do that, right? And then B, a tender isn't going to catch a speedboat. No chance."

"What are you going to do? Run on water?" he asked.

"I had a buddy watching the cay. He saw the boat approach the uninhabited side and collect someone. Now's it's headed away at knots and he's just off the ship waiting for me. He'll pick me up."

Army shook his head. He shouldn't do it. It was lose–lose for him. The rings had been stolen and that story was going to get out. Even if I got them back, that part was fact. So his upside was zero. But allowing me to jump off the boat again? There was plenty of downside to that. If I drowned, he'd never work in the cruise industry again. Hell, he'd probably be found guilty of some kind of criminal negligence and do time. His only hope was the fuzzy legal jurisdiction that went with being at sea.

"I'm sorry, Miami. I can't allow it."

"They're getting away," I said, although I had no idea who they were, or if they even had the rings. It was just a gut feel.

"Can't do it," he said. He walked over to a cupboard that hung on the wall. "I'll tell you why." He pulled a life preserver out of the cupboard. "This PFD is not rated for jumping from a moving vessel. It might come off unless it was tied very well, between a person's legs. Second, this hatch. It is not supposed to be opened at sea. It's only about five feet from sea level. Besides, if you turned this wheel and then pulled down on this lever, an alarm would sound in the security room and security personnel would arrive within minutes."

Army stepped to me. "Do you have the comms device I gave you?"

I took it out of my pocket.

"See? You put it in your pocket like that, it can fall out and you'd be done for. A smart man would tie it to his wrist." Army tied the device to me.

"It's water-activated anyway, isn't it?" I asked.

"It is, but you wouldn't want anyone looking in the wrong place. Besides, if you hit this button and hold it, it will activate anyway."

He turned to Porter. "Flashlight?"

She handed him a flashlight that was attached to her belt and he passed it to me.

"Now, you see my point? I can't allow it. So don't do anything stupid. Porter."

Army marched away and Porter followed.

"What just happened?" Danielle asked.

"Nothing. Nothing at all."

I moved to the hatch and turned the wheel. It took some doing. Then I put my hand on the lever. I looked at Danielle.

"Lucas is right out there."

"I know."

"I can swim back to Paradise Cay if I have to."

"I know."

I slipped the life preserver over my head and ran the straps between my legs and tied them tight. Then I pulled the lever on the door down and waited for the alarm. There wasn't one. I assumed that Army hadn't lied. It was probably sounding all kinds of trouble in the security control room. I pushed the door open. It didn't open like a regular door. It was more like something I had seen on an aircraft. It pushed out and then the hinges pulled it back along the side of the ship.

The water broke white below me. I took a breath. For a moment I agreed with Danielle and Army. Jumping would be a decidedly dumb thing to do. But Lucas was out there, and I had more confidence in him than I had in myself. I pressed and held the button on the locator beacon and a light began flashing red. I looked at Danielle.

Hers was the last face I ever wanted to see. I knew that more than I had ever known anything in my life. But I also knew I wanted to see it again tomorrow. So I was coming back. I was almost certain of that.

Danielle grabbed me by the life preserver and pulled me in and kissed me deeply.

"Call me," she said.

I nodded, and then for the second time in two days, I jumped off a perfectly good cruise ship.

## CHAPTER TWENTY-FIVE

This time, I didn't have as much time to think on the way down. I just pushed out to get as far from the hull as I could, and hit the water like I was entering a pool from the deck. Not hard at all. I didn't even go all the way under. The life preserver did its job, although it very nearly neutered me in the process. I saw Army's point.

Like last night, the water was cold. I'd thought before that feeling had been a result of fear or maybe adrenaline, but now I figured it was because it was dark and I was being pushed back and away by the ship's wake. Once the major buffeting stopped, I turned on the flashlight.

I saw no evidence of Lucas. Not the sound of an engine, not running lights on a bow. I spun slow circles, turning my flashlight around like a lighthouse. I slowed a little each time I faced the ship, which was moving away, getting smaller.

As I circled I checked the locator beacon. It was still attached to me and the light still flashed red. I hoped that meant something. I preferred having a life preserver around me to having Frederick Connors around me. And I resolved never to go swimming in a tuxedo again. Shorts and a shirt made the going much easier. I watched the ship slip away and wondered if Lucas had broken down. I circled again.

Then I heard it. The steady throb of a powerful engine being held back from its full potential. More boom, boom, boom, than putt, putt, putt. I pointed the flashlight in the direction of the sound, and soon my light was mirrored by a light pointed at me.

The torpedo-like hull of a speedboat burst from the darkness. The engine dropped to an idle and the boat pulled alongside, and Lucas's smiling face appeared. He directed the boat past me and then threw down his hand to grip mine as I reached the low point at the stern. He pulled up with an uncommon strength. This wasn't the kind of power you hear about, like when people pick cars up off their trapped loved ones. This was more the result of years of pulling in really big fish.

He yanked me into the boat and let me drop unceremoniously onto the floor. I saw fishing tackle arranged along the side and I used a large ice chest to lever myself into a sitting position. Lucas smiled.

"Fancy meeting you here." He turned the drivers seat around and put one knee on it and then pushed down hard on the throttle. I was driven back into the ice chest as the propeller bit and the rear of the boat dropped low in the water and the boat took off like a rocket.

Getting up while wearing a life preserver wasn't easy. I grabbed the other seat and hoisted myself up, then turned it and mimicked Lucas, a knee on the seat and a foot planted on the floor. I held onto the windshield.

My hair was dry inside of thirty seconds. We were going that fast. I saw the lights of the Canaveral Star making its way toward Florida, while we cut away to the south.

"Nice jacket," Lucas yelled.

I nodded. I wasn't sure if he was making fun of me or not.

He delivered most comments in a drawl that sounded like sarcasm.

"Thanks for picking me up."

"No worries."

"You find me okay?"

He nodded. "Trawled behind the ship, figured I'd come upon you sooner or later."

"The beacon helped I'm sure."

"The what?"

I held up the comms unit-cum-locator beacon. It was still flashing red.

"Oh that. Yeah, I can't track that."

"You said you could."

"You wouldn't have jumped in if I hadn't."

"You might have missed me."

"I told ya, I was behind the ship. I saw the hatch open. Where were you going to go?"

I shook my head. I wasn't going to win, so I let it go.

"Where are they?" I asked.

He nodded ahead. "They went this way."

"Can we find them?"

"If we go fast enough."

"What if they cut back to the north?"

He smiled. "Then we'll lose 'em."

We kept going at pace. The ocean was calm and the speedboat skimmed across the surface like a hydrofoil. I untied the beacon and sent a message to the ship that I was safe on board with Lucas. I really didn't want Danielle to have that feeling. Then I set the device in a cubby in the console of the boat. I left the life preserver on.

Suddenly Lucas pulled back on the throttle and the boat lurched forward and came to a stop. The engine cut out and the boat floated forward.

"What's wrong?" I asked.

"Shhhh," he said. He put his finger to his lip for effect.

I kept quiet. My ears were still ringing from the sound of the engines. It was like walking from a light room into a dark one. At first you see nothing, and then come shapes, which grow more precise as your eyes adjust. My hearing got used to the silence around us. Water lapped gently against the hull. Then I heard it. The distant growl of a marine engine. Another speedboat. I wasn't sure which direction it was coming from.

Lucas knew. He hit the throttle and we took off again. As we gained speed he flicked off the running lights. We were going fast. I couldn't tell how fast. The dark ocean offered no visual cues. But it was fast. Fast enough that if we hit something in the water, we would be toast. At least the locator beacon would tell authorities where to find the wreckage and our dead bodies.

We went hard for another few minutes and then Lucas pulled back a little on the throttle. Not like before. We didn't come to a full stop. He just slowed down, like he could see in the darkness or had sonar. He broke hard to starboard and then straightened up.

We were running west now. I could see the moon glow across the water like a reverse Bat-Signal. Up ahead, running in the trail of moonlight, was another boat.

I pointed. Lucas nodded. He knew. He kept our heading off the other boat's rear quarter, so that whoever was ahead wouldn't see us in the moonlight if they chanced to look back. It didn't take long to gain on them. They weren't going anywhere near as fast as us. They were running without lights, too, but clearly weren't feeling anywhere near as reckless. Lucas pulled up on their rear starboard quarter and backed off the throttle so we wouldn't pass them. We could see the outlines of two men.

"What now?" I asked. I'd told Danielle the truth. I really

hadn't thought that far ahead. I wasn't sure how we could stop them. We couldn't shoot out their tires, and ramming them felt like a really poor option.

"I'll pull alongside and you jump over," Lucas said.

"Jump over? Are you nuts?"

"I'll get close."

"I'm not jumping from one speeding boat into another speeding boat."

"Why?"

"Physics?"

He shook his head. "Physics. Seriously." He yanked the wheel to bring us just behind and then pushed the throttle down again and we moved alongside. Our boats were inches apart. If everything was stationary I could have easily stepped from one to the other. I licked my lips and looked at the men. Even if I jumped and somehow didn't smash my head and drop into the water and drown, I would pretty certainly hit the floor hard. And I had no reason to believe these men didn't have guns. I heard Danielle's voice in my head.

*Save me from that feeling.*

Lucas tapped my shoulder.

"Take the wheel," he said.

I didn't have time to discuss it. He put one foot onto the gunwale and pushed up and thrust his other foot out over the water. Then he strode casually from one boat to the other. Most people looked less confident stepping over the gap into a stationary train car. I grabbed the wheel with one hand and once I was sure he was across, edged away from the other boat so we wouldn't collide.

Lucas got his balance in the other boat. The two guys were still standing up the same way we had been, eyes forward. They had no idea he was there. Like a nautical ninja, Lucas moved toward them, and I watched as he tapped the outline of the guy in the passenger's position. The guy appeared to turn around and Lucas may have punched him in the solar plexus. I couldn't have said for sure. It was possible he knew how to do that *Star Trek* Vulcan thing. I put nothing past Lucas.

All I knew for sure was that the guy collapsed back in his seat. Lucas turned to the driver, who must have got the message, because he instantly slowed. This caught me by surprise, and I sped right past them into the night. I pulled back on the throttle and did a wide turn. but couldn't see the other boat.

Then their running lights came on and they cut the engine. I pulled slowly alongside, putting the throttle into neutral so we touched nice and gentle, and I grabbed the side of the other boat to keep us that way.

Lucas was having words with the driver. My ears took a moment to rid themselves of the ringing. The driver was speaking. He appeared to apologizing. Or maybe pleading. He had a distinct Bahamian accent.

"I'm sorry, man, I didn't know."

"Dumb, just dumb," said Lucas.

"You can't tell him, man. You can't."

I grabbed ahold of the other boat's windshield frame. "What's the deal?"

Lucas turned me. "Miami, meet Ridley."

The driver was nothing but eyes and teeth in the darkness. He said nothing.

"You know each other?" I asked.

"Ridley's dad owns a fishing charter on Chub. And he's going to be mightily pissed that Ridley has been zooming around after hours without running lights."

"Lucas, man. Don't tell him, please. I didn't know."

"Didn't know what, mate? How to turn your running lights on? Or who you were driving?" Lucas bent over the guy in the passenger's seat, who was doubled over and breathing hard.

"And who exactly do we have here?" Lucas pulled the guy up by the lapels and looked at him close. He shook his head and looked at me.

"You know this plonker?"

In the dark and from the back, I couldn't tell, so Lucas dumped the guy in the seat and I flicked on the flashlight.

And saw the deep set features of Guy X.

# CHAPTER TWENTY-SIX

Lucas asked Ridley if he had a gun. The answer was an unequivocal and somewhat frightened no. He asked about Guy X and Ridley said he didn't know. Given he had come from a cruise ship it seemed unlikely, but Lucas wasn't about to take any chances. He patted the guy down with prejudice and then dumped him back in the chair. Then Lucas had me toss him some rope, and he lashed the two boats together. I turned on our running lights, too.

"So what are you boys doing out here in the dark?" asked Lucas.

"I'm just picking up this guy, Lucas, I promise you," said Ridley. With some light on him, I noticed he was younger than I'd thought. He couldn't have been more than sixteen.

"But why?" asked Lucas. "Rid, do you understand that if this guy is carrying drugs you'll get charged with drug trafficking, too?"

"Are you serious? The guy just paid for a ride. He said he needed to get away from his nagging wife for a while."

"Keep your mouth shut, kid," said Guy X. It was the first

time I had heard him speak. He was all New York, despite the loud shirt. Lucas kicked him in the guts.

"You keep quiet, you'll get your turn." Lucas turned back to Ridley. "So you're saying this scumbag's got nothing with him?"

Ridley shook his head. "Just his little bag."

"Where?"

Ridley nodded toward the stowage space in the bow. Lucas reached in and pulled out a familiar blue travel bag with the cruise line logo. The same bag Guy X had carried to the bar, except I was sure it *wasn't* the same bag. It just looked the same.

Lucas unzipped the bag.

"This is an illegal search," said Guy X.

Lucas smiled. "We ain't cops, champ." He pulled the bag open and removed a black box, which he handed across to me.

I put the box on the seat and opened it. A collection of Super Bowl rings gleamed at me in the muted moonlight. I had no idea if they were real or real fakes or fakes fakes, but I knew one thing: They were in the correct order. Green Bay was first.

"There's another box in here," said Lucas.

"You stole the rings," I said to Guy X.

"Those aren't mine. They belong to the kid."

Lucas moved to face Guy X. "So who exactly are you?" Lucas asked.

Guy X said nothing.

"His name is Francis Martelli."

Martelli shot me a look that suggested we wouldn't be golfing together anytime soon. I wasn't sure if he was disturbed by me knowing his name or by me calling him Francis.

"What do they call you?" I asked. "Frankie?"

"Yeah. What of it?"

I knew he was a Frankie. "I know who you are."

"You don't know squat."

"I know you're in possession of stolen property. I know we have video of you attempting to commit murder."

He frowned but said nothing.

"So why don't you tell me how you did it? How did you steal the rings?"

"What rings? I just picked up the wrong bag."

"You did. And a Florida law enforcement officer saw you do it."

"We're not in Florida, hotshot."

"You going to take the fall for this are you? You happy to do time in a Bahamian jail?"

"The ship lives in America."

"You're right about that. Jurisdiction on the ship is kind of fuzzy, I agree. But not on the island. The island is The Bahamas, one hundred percent."

"You've got nothing."

I looked at Lucas. I really was getting nowhere.

Lucas said, "You're not being very helpful." He pulled Martelli up out of his seat and dragged him to the side of the boat and sat him on the edge. Martelli gave Lucas a smug look. So Lucas pushed him overboard.

But not all the way overboard. As Martelli's back hit the water, Lucas grabbed his legs as they flipped up. Martelli's knees bent and he hung upside down, and flapped and spluttered to pull his head up out of the ocean. It wasn't easy to do. It takes a lot of core strength to do an upside-down ab crunch like that. And Frankie Martelli wasn't built for ab crunches. He flailed like a fish out of water. Lucas held him there for longer than was necessary and then offered him a hand and dragged him back into the boat.

He dumped Martelli on the floor.

"Now, you want to answer my friend's questions, or you wanna go swimming again?"

Martelli spat water onto the floor.

"Go to hell."

Lucas nodded. "Tough guy."

"Help yourself out," I said. I figured I'd start with something softer. "Tell me about Ana."

Martelli spat more saltwater. "Who?"

"Come on, Frankie. Anastasia Connors. Who cooked up the scheme? You or her? Or did you come up with it together, since you were having an affair?"

"An affair?"

"Yes, Frankie. We have photos. You and Anastasia."

"You think I'm having an affair with the old lady?"

"Aren't you?"

"Come on, bro. You think I'm gonna sleep with that?"

"You're not?"

"I'd rather eat my own arm."

I took this in. I believed him. So he wasn't having an affair with Anastasia Connors. I doubted the news would come as any kind of comfort to my client.

"So you're just in it for the money?"

Martelli said nothing, but he gave me his best defiant face.

"Whose idea was it? Yours or hers?"

Still nothing.

Lucas dunked him all over again, and Martelli spat more seawater on the floor. Then I repeated my questions. The defiant face got more defiant.

"You're gonna do time," I said. "Unless you help us out."

"You the district attorney?" he said smugly.

"No. But he's a personal friend. And he's gonna love you."

The truth was the state attorney in West Palm wasn't a personal friend. He was Danielle's ex-husband, and he didn't think much of me. But that didn't feel like the kind of information that was going to help. As it was, nothing did.

Lucas sat on the gunwale between the two boats and twisted around so he was back in the boat with me.

"I really don't think he going to fess up," he whispered.

"Doesn't look like it."

"He's more afraid of whoever he's working for than anything I'll do to him. Even jail time."

I nodded. Martelli was a proving a tough nut to crack. So I thought about my options. In the end, I had done my job. I had the information my client had asked for. Although I didn't have conclusive photos, I was sure enough that Frederick's wife was not having an affair. Of course, it wasn't all good news. The rub was that she was working with some kind of gangster to steal her own jewels. I suspected an insurance scam, but the involvement of Francis Martelli suggested there was a plan to fence the rings.

My friend Sal Mondavi ran a pawnshop that occasionally saw such items. And he knew a lot of people like Frankie from his native New York. He probably even knew Frankie's people. And Sal had told me many times that such organizations preferred the path of least resistance. They didn't go looking for problems. They knew that what they did was hard enough. So moving such famous rings, even genuine fakes, was going to be tough. They were too well known. But Sal would have said there's still one way to on-sell a well-known stolen car: in pieces.

The fact that the fakes were genuine fakes made all the difference. If you couldn't move the rings, then you could certainly sell the gemstones in them. And these things were covered in gems. Diamonds were a favorite. And Anastasia had told me herself she had used the real things. If the rings were worth around three million dollars, then the gemstones alone, plus the gold and whatever else the rings were made from, had to be worth half that. One and a half million in parts, plus three million in insurance.

A worthwhile payday.

What Frederick Connors had stumbled onto wasn't an affair but the planning of a heist. And his decision to come on the cruise at the last moment had probably caused last minute consternation. I couldn't see how, though. So I did what I asked clients to do. I started at the end.

Frankie had the rings. He hired Ridley to get him off the island. He got the rings from a bag drop at the tiki bar. He hadn't brought them through the metal detector because he knew he couldn't. They had come off via someone who didn't go through the metal detector.

The barman. He had swapped the bags. And up until that point, Frankie hadn't taken possession. Which meant someone else took the rings initially. Maybe that was Anastasia's role. But I still couldn't see how.

Then I got an idea.

"We need to get back to the ship."

"You sure?" asked Lucas.

"I'm sure."

"All righty." Lucas picked up Martelli and sat him between the two boats. Martelli wasn't talking but he wasn't stupid. He scrambled around to put both feet firmly in the boat with me, and then with a nod Lucas directed him to sit on the floor.

"Keep your eye on him," Lucas said, so I did.

Then Lucas sent Ridley on his way.

"You get home now. Do not pass go, do not collect two hundred dollars. And if I hear of you doing something this stupid again, not only will I tell your father, I'll hold you down while he tears you a new one. Do I make myself clear?"

"Yes, Lucas. I'm sorry, man. I'm really sorry."

"Get home."

Lucas untied the two boats and Ridley motored away at a circumspect speed. I wasn't so sure about sending a teenager away into the darkness in the middle of the ocean, but Lucas seemed to think Ridley knew his way home.

I sat with my chair turned toward the rear, watching Martelli, aka Guy X. He said nothing and I said nothing.

Lucas fired up the engine and headed off fast, but not quite so fast as before. I assumed he knew where he was going, so I grabbed the comms device from the cubby and typed a message to Army. Then I sat back and watched Frankie Martelli say nothing at all.

# CHAPTER TWENTY-SEVEN



"Coming up on them now," Lucas called.

I didn't glance around. I wasn't taking my eyes off Frankie Martelli. He didn't look like he was going to try anything. He looked wet and tired and resigned. But I wasn't taking any chances.

Lucas pulled the speedboat up over the wake of the ship so we could get in close, and moved in alongside. The hull towered above us, and the decks further above that. It struck me again how truly remarkable it was that this thing floated at all.

As we crept along, I saw the open hatch, a rectangle of light in the dark hull. Army was standing on one side of it. He wasn't permitted to assist someone jumping off, but I figured it was certainly in his job description to help them back on.

Danielle stood on the other side of the hatch. She looked serious. They had dropped a net made of orange nylon ribbon, and Lucas got in close. Too close for my liking. The curve of the hull meant I couldn't see even the lowest deck anymore. It felt like we were poking a dinosaur with a stick.

Lucas didn't seem too fussed by it all. He angled alongside so the net fell right by the side of the boat.

"All right, let's get that donkey off this boat."

I directed Martelli to get up. At first he didn't move, so I got down near him.

"It's up the net or in the water. And we're not coming back. You won't be missed."

He growled and pushed himself up. I think his knees were stiff, because he edged around the side of the speedboat to where the net hung.

"Don't jump," said Lucas. "Grab ahold with your hands, then step your feet over."

Martelli nodded. He was a low-level gangster, so he knew how to take orders. He leaned out and grabbed the net with both hands. Fortunately, the sea wasn't too rough, because Martelli was a bonafide landlubber. He tried to step out with one foot just as the speedboat dipped, and he found himself hanging in midair. He kicked with both feet, looking for a toehold. I'd seen four-year-olds make a better job of it down at the local playground.

Eventually he got lucky and one of his feet looped into the net. Then bit by bit, he laboriously climbed the five feet to the hatch. Once his arms got to the bottom of the hatch, Army and another officer grabbed him and dragged him in.

I was next. I'm no ballerina. *Grace* has never been a word associated with me. But I hoped to get up the damned net in better style than Martelli. I looped the travel bag around my arm and then moved into position.

"I owe you one," I told Lucas. It wasn't true. I owed him many.

"No sweat. I got enough fish for a month." He grinned and his eyes shone in the light from the hatch.

"Where you going now?" I asked.

"I'll stop in at Chub Cay Marina, cook up some wahoo."

I nodded and turned back to the net. I reached out and

grabbed it with both hands. Then I did as Lucas had said and I picked a spot to land my foot. I hit the wide net first try and then pushed away from the speedboat with my other foot. I confirmed my grip and then climbed up. When I got to the hatch I gripped the side of the opening and used the net to step up rather than being dragged in by my arms.

I turned around on my backside to see the running lights from the speedboat heading off into the distant darkness. Then I dropped the bag and stood.

Army, Porter and another male officer I didn't know were watching me. I looked to Danielle.

"You okay?" she asked.

"Good now. You?"

"Good now."

I hugged her before asking Army, "Where's Martelli?"

"Who?"

"Guy X."

"Right. He's in the brig."

"I thought you didn't have a brig?"

"We don't. We just call it that. Sounds better than being in crew quarters behind a locked door."

I nodded. It did sound better.

Porter and the other officer moved me out of the way so they could close the hatch, and then they went through a little cross-check process to make sure everything was squared away.

"What did you find," said Army. "Other than a missing passenger?"

I picked up the blue travel bag.

"What's that?" he asked.

I smiled.

"No way," said Danielle.

"Yep," I said.

Porter said, "The rings?"

"Three millions bucks worth. Assuming they're the real ones."

"What did he say?" asked Danielle. "Martelli?"

"Not a lot. He's answering to someone back home who values silence and knows how to get it."

"You know, jurisdiction can be problematic in these things. Technically this is probably a Bahamas crime," said Army.

"Yeah, I know."

"And as soon as we get back to Palm Beach, they'll have to extradite him, which they probably won't do, since the problem has gone away."

"Yeah, I know."

"So he's going to get away with it?" asked Danielle. She didn't look happy. She really didn't like the bad guys getting away with it.

"Oh, I didn't say that."

Army said, "What do you need?"

"A shopkeeper, a barman and a favor or two."

Army nodded. "What first?"

"Is Martelli secure?"

"We'll hand him to the FBI when we get back in. They'll have to let him go, but he won't see daylight until then."

"Okay, so the fact that he's on board and in the brig, that stays between us."

"The captain will have to be informed," Army said.

"Is he at dinner now?"

"Yes. The captain's dinner."

"Don't go disturbing him," I said. "Tell him later."

"I will. What now?"

"Let's go to your control room. We need to find someone."

# CHAPTER TWENTY-EIGHT



THE SECURITY CONTROL ROOM WAS QUIETER THAN I'D thought it would be.

"We've got a lot of people out on the floor. It's a busy night," said Army. "Who are we looking for?"

"You got a jewelry store on board, right?" I asked Porter. She was the one who seemed to know her way around the system.

"Of course."

"Is it run by sales staff or is there an actual jeweler?"

"Both. We have a jeweler, because we get a lot marriage proposals."

I nodded and thought of Ron and Cassandra, though they'd gotten their ring back in Palm Beach.

"Can you track the jeweler down?"

"He's probably at dinner."

"The captain's dinner?"

"No, in the staff cafeteria. But I would expect him to be at the auction. He knows about those sorts of things."

"Find him. Get him here."

"Can I ask why?" said Army.

"I want to make sure the rings I got from Martelli are the

real deal. And I don't want to use the auctioneer. He's not in the clear yet, and he's too close to Anastasia."

"You're not planning on telling her you found them?"

"Oh, I'm planning on telling her all right. But I want to be sure of what I have first."

Porter had taken a seat at the computer console and she put out a call for the jeweler. Within thirty seconds she got a reply. He was at dinner. She asked him to come to the security control office immediately.

"Second, we need to find another crew member. Guy X—Martelli—got a bag drop on the island. He didn't take these rings off the ship. They came off with a crew member."

"Are you sure?" asked Army.

"I'm sure. And with some help, we can prove it. The drop was done at the tiki bar on the beach. Who worked there today?"

Porter tapped away and then leaned back in her chair so I could see the screen. "Two staff. Martin Perkins and Shelley Roebuck."

"The guy, not the woman."

"How do you know it's not the woman?" asked Porter. She said it like she was a little ticked off, like I had made an assumption that a woman could not be party to such a crime. Clearly she was forgetting that I was looking to link Martelli with Anastasia Connors. When it came to crime, I was equal opportunity. Women were capable of as much scumbaggery as men. Sometimes.

"Because we couldn't figure out how Martelli got back onto the ship from the island," I said.

"He didn't," said Danielle. "You just nailed him now."

"I did. But when I followed him, Ron ran back to the dock. The security guy there reported that the system said Martelli was already back on board." I looked at Army. "How could that happen?"

"It couldn't," he said.

"It did."

"I don't know."

"The system just records what?"

Porter said, "The passenger's ship pass is scanned as they embark."

"Exactly."

"So you're saying his pass was scanned but he didn't get on?" asked Army. "You think one of my security team is in on this?"

"No, I don't. I think someone was wearing Martelli's ship pass, pretending to be him."

"Doesn't work," said Porter. "The passenger count would be out."

"If it was a passenger."

Porter frowned and then said, "You think it's the bartender, Perkins."

"I do."

"But the security at embarkation would check the ID of the passenger against the photo the scan puts on the screen. Plus, he would be missed at his station. They had to close up the bar, do inventory, all that."

"It's only a theory, but how's this? Perkins does the drop. Martelli is at the bar wearing a horrible shirt and a ball cap. He has black hair. Then Perkins goes on a break. He puts on a horrible shirt and a ball cap. He has dark hair. He takes Martelli's ship pass off the bar. He uses it to get on board. Remember, your guys aren't passport control. They know they're on a private island. All they're really concerned with, as Porter just said, is that the numbers add up. If a thousand people got off, a thousand have to get back on. They'll scan the ID, look at the photo and see a guy in a loud shirt with a ball cap on over dark hair. Close enough, move on."

"But now you're saying Perkins is on board. He would have been missed during clean up at the tiki bar," said Army.

"How hard is it to return to his cabin, dump the shirt and the hat and then cut back out the supply hatch? It would be open to allow for the on boarding of stock. He's in uniform, he has his crew ID. He's packing up, putting away. He skips off and returns to the bar."

"I don't like it," said Army.

"You don't have to like it for it to be true," I said.

He frowned. We all knew there was a breach in security, and that was his house of cards. He'd have to learn from it and deal with it. In my experience that took proud guys like him a little while to process.

"Where does this Perkins work, Porter?" he asked.

She didn't tap her keyboard. She was way ahead of him, so she just pointed to the screen.

"Sporting lounge. He's on dinner break and then he's rostered on tonight."

We stood in silence for a while. A lot was going on in Army's mind. He was retelling the story, looking for holes, not finding many.

Then there was a knock at the door. An old man in a gray suit and blue tie stepped in.

"I got a call?" he said.

"Mr. Gold?" said Porter.

"Yes. Is there a problem?"

Porter looked at me. I looked at her. I had no idea what she wanted from me.

"This is the jeweler," she said, clearly holding back an eye roll. I resolved to work on my ESP capabilities.

"Your name is Gold?"

He nodded and smiled a resigned smirk like he had heard all the lines.

"Yes," he said.

I could have had some fun with it but I had more important things to do. I pulled a ring from my pocket. I had removed it from the box of rings I had taken from Martelli. I didn't need the jeweler to see them all. I just needed one. I handed it to him.

"I need to know if this is real."

Gold frowned and took the ring. He looked it over, letting the light sparkle off and through the diamonds. Then he took a monocular out of his jacket pocket. Jewelers were like spies. They liked to carry the tools of their trade with them. You never knew when you were going to have to verify how many carats something had.

He inspected the ring and then looked at me. The monocular on his head made him look like a cyborg on a fixed income.

"You want to know if this is real?" he asked.

"Yes."

"No."

"No, it's not real?"

"That is correct."

"It's a fake?"

"I would call it a reproduction."

"How do you know it's not real?" asked Army.

"It's a Super Bowl ring," he said. "Not to my taste, but there you have it. If this ring was real, it would have been made by Jostens of Minneapolis. They would have put their mark on the ring, inside the band. There is no such mark, ergo it is not their work."

I realized my error. "Okay, it's not original. It's a reproduction."

"As I said."

"But is it a real reproduction?"

"What would a real reproduction be?"

"The diamonds. Are they real? Is the gold real?"

"Oh, I see your meaning. Yes, sir. The diamonds are real. The gold? I don't know. Do you have a magnet?"

Army turned and pulled a magnet off a whiteboard on the wall. The jeweler held the base of the magnet against the ring. It didn't stick.

"I'd say the gold is real," he said, and returned the magnet to Army.

"Thanks, Mr. Gold," I said. I took the ring back and Gold bid us a good evening. He didn't ask any more questions about the ring. A real but not real Super Bowl ring. I would have had questions, but I suspected that discretion was a fine quality in a jeweler. Some people thought that about a PI.

I returned the ring to its box and looked at Army. I wanted to know if he had finished his ruminating. He looked at me with a set jaw.

"What do you need?"

"From you, a favor." Then I looked at Danielle.

"And I'll need one from you, too."

# CHAPTER TWENTY-NINE

I GOT IN THE ELEVATOR WITH DANIELLE AND PORTER. Porter carried a blue travel bag with the cruise line logo on it. I got off the elevator first, on the floor for our suite. As I got to our room, I wondered if other people spent as little time in their cabins as I had. I realized that not everyone was running around trying to catch an adulteress or a thief. But passengers did seem to be in the bars and restaurants and the casino and the pool and the spa and wherever else instead of their cabins. Which made me wonder why people sprang for such expensive digs when all they did was sleep there. Then I remembered why. Because they could.

I walked past our suite and stopped two doors down. Then I knocked. I waited longer than was necessary. Then the door opened a crack, revealing the nose of a Russian princess.

"Mr. Jones, what do you want?"

"I caught him," I said.

"Caught who?"

"The man who took your rings."

The door snapped open.

"You found my rings?"

"Would you like to talk about this in the hallway?"

She thought about that more than I'd thought she would, then held the door open. I stepped into their suite. It was the same as ours. Exactly. Even the art. Frederick Connors was lounging on the sofa in a pair of khakis and a pressed blue button-up shirt. He dressed better for lounging than most people did for church. He sat opposite the television but it wasn't turned on. Maybe they turned it off when someone knocked at the door. People did that on sitcoms. I never really understood why.

"Mr. Connors," I nodded.

"Mr. Jones."

"So, you found my rings?" interjected Anastasia.

"Unfortunately, no. Not yet."

"What's this?" asked Frederick.

Anastasia ignored him. "What do you mean *not yet?*"

"We have the man responsible. He didn't have rings on his person, just one of the cruise line's travel bags. But we're confident."

"How do you know it's him?" she asked.

"He confessed."

"He confessed?"

She didn't sound convinced. She clearly knew Martelli. He wasn't the confessing kind.

"Yes," I lied. "I just wanted you to know that we're working hard to recover your property."

"Not hard enough," she said. "I'll still miss the auction."

"Probably," I said. "You didn't go to the captain's dinner?"

She looked at her husband. "Frederick didn't feel up to going out."

I glanced at Frederick. He looked better. Not good, but better. He frowned. It wasn't a great look on him. I turned back and found his wife standing by the open door.

"Goodbye, Mr. Jones."

I nodded and stepped out into the corridor. I turned to say goodnight or something equally witty but the door closed in my face. Polite people really know how to be rude.

I took the crew elevator back up using a card Army had loaned me. I knocked and he let me into his office.

"How we doing?" I asked.

"Porter and Ms. Castle are doing their thing," said Army. "You?"

"I let the cat out. We'll see how the pigeons react."

"You have a very interesting turn of phrase."

I shrugged. I didn't think about it and I didn't know what to say. I was no poet. I was a ballplayer. Once upon a time. Now I was just a guy. A guy whose internal dialogue included phrases like *once upon a time*. I wondered if that was what he meant.

"What's your story, Army?"

"What do you mean?"

"You said you were in the army."

"Yes."

"Twenty-two years."

"You have a good memory, Mr. Jones."

"I memorized a lot of playbooks. You said how you ended up on a ship was a long story."

"I did."

"You got something better do to?"

"I have a lot of better things to do, Mr. Jones."

I gave him my *I'm not buying it* face.

He pushed back on his office chair and rolled out from his desk. Then he opened the drawer and pulled out two small glasses. He set them on his desk and then pulled out a bottle of single malt scotch and poured us each a couple of fingers, handing one to me.

I smelled it. I do that. Wine people do it. I've been told it's not really a scotch thing, but I don't care. I like the smell. It's clubby and peaty and it makes me think of large men in kilts.

I sipped my drink. It was smooth and fierce all at the same time and I felt myself warm from the inside.

Army sipped his and then looked at the glass like he was inspecting it for cracks or fingerprints.

"You were a ballplayer, I understand."

"I was. How did you know that?"

"Porter looked you up online."

"I'm online?"

"More than you know. So you understand something about career changes."

"As much as anyone, I guess. Is that what this is? A career change?"

"Something like that." He sipped his drink again. "Why did you become a private investigator?"

"How do most people become something? A door opened and I went through it."

Army nodded softly.

"I was at college in Miami. I met a guy. He became a kind of mentor. Maybe more. Like a father, if your father let you stay up late and took you out drinking. I went off to play ball after college and I didn't think about what I would do after. But the universe brought us back together and I stayed."

"Was that Ron?"

"No. Ron and I were both moons in the orbit of Lenny."

"You work with him, this Lenny?"

I took some more scotch. "No. Lenny died."

Army nodded again. He didn't say sorry or commiserate. I figured army folks knew more about death than most of us.

"This isn't your story, though," I said.

"No." He swirled his drink around. "Twenty-two years I

was in. Joined out of college. Gulf War, first time around. They were good years, apart from the war."

"Were you married?"

He nodded. "Just before my first deployment in Iraq. It was hard on her. Hard on all of us. But I did my duty and she did hers. She moved a lot and raised two wonderful kids mostly by herself. So when the second—our daughter, Kaylie—went to college, I called time. Took my leave. My Meredith wanted to live the island life. She loved it down here. Kayaking the mangroves, visiting the manatees, watching that summer rain that could knock people off their feet."

He stopped and swirled his drink again. He looked at it like he wanted to drink it but knew if he did it would be gone and he wouldn't be able to look at it anymore.

"She got breast cancer, second year here. She fought, like she fought everything. But the enemy was relentless. Too much for her. We lost her, Thanksgiving four years ago."

I wanted to say how sorry I was but I took his lead and kept quiet.

"I can't tell you how much I wanted to go with her. I can't tell you. But a father has to be strong for his kids. See them on their way."

I nodded but I didn't know. I knew the other story. The loss of a wife and mother, and a father who wanted to go with her so bad he forgot about his son and took the path that Army had forgone.

"If it wasn't for them, I don't know, Miami. Maybe I wouldn't be here. But I didn't want to go kayaking in the mangroves anymore. My son's in Atlanta, so I thought about going there. But Meredith wanted this so bad, and I wanted it for her. Then a guy I knew at the veteran's hall tells me the cruise line is looking for a chief security officer. I was an MP so it wasn't completely out of my wheelhouse. It let me get away but not go away. So here I am."

"An army officer floating the high seas."

"Army, retired."

"Well, I'm glad they've got you."

"I'm not sure they'll share your sentiment."

"Why?"

"On my watch three million in jewels were stolen and moved off my boat past my security team. A passenger was pushed overboard. And you. You went overboard, twice."

"You can't stop crime, Army. You can try, you can minimize it, but you can't stop it. And as for the rings, a smart guy like you doesn't sit around crying about his mistakes. He learns from them. Am I right? And as for me going over . . ." I shook my head. "I'm not planning on cruising again anytime soon."

"That's a shame, Miami. These voyages are usually so boring."

I smiled. I was almost certain he did too.

Then there was a knock at the door and Porter stepped in.

"Chief, we got some action here."

# CHAPTER THIRTY

We followed Porter back into the security control room, where Danielle was watching a screen.

"How were Fred and Ana? They have plans for the evening?" she asked me.

"Ana said they were staying in. Fred wasn't himself," I said.

"Well, he must be feeling better because they both just left their suite."

I saw Anastasia and Frederick on the video feed, waiting for an elevator to arrive.

"Where do you suppose they're off to? Captain's dinner?" Danielle asked.

"The dinner's nearly over," said Porter. "I think they're serving dessert."

"I know where they're going," I said.

We watched them get off the elevator and walk down the corridor.

"Not the captain's dinner," said Porter. "Wrong deck."

"No," I said. "It's the right deck."

They entered a bar. Porter changed the camera and we got an angle that looked across a clubby space with leather chairs and paintings of men in red jackets on horseback and dogs hunting foxes. At the opposite end of the space was a bar with leather-topped stools.

"Is this the right place?" I asked.

"The sporting lounge," said Porter.

"I've been in the sports bar. There were big screen televisions."

"That was the sports bar. This is the sporting lounge."

"It doesn't look sporty."

"I think it's about the sporting class of dogs, as in hunting," said Porter.

I looked at her. "Whose idea was it to have an English hunting motif on a tropical cruise ship?"

Porter shrugged. "We cater to many tastes."

"Or none at all," I said.

"Either way, this doesn't seem like Anastasia's type of place," said Danielle.

She was right about that. I could see Anastasia in a clubby space. I was sure that plenty of her Palm Beach clientele spent time in such places. What I didn't see was the hunting. Dogs baying for the blood of foxes was as aristocratic as rounded vowels, but it didn't feel very Anastasia.

But then, neither did palm trees and beaches, and she lived in South Florida. On the screen, Anastasia went over to the bar while Frederick searched for and found a table with wing-backed chairs.

Anastasia was talking to the bartender. It was another move that I didn't associate with her. She didn't strike me as an *order at the bar* type of gal. She liked to be served. But she was at the bar, and I had good hunch why. The bartender opened a bottle of champagne and poured two flutes. That was a drink I associated with her. I liked champagne, but it wasn't an everyday kind of drink for me. Beer filled that role. Not so much Anastasia Connors.

Anastasia carried the glasses of bubbles across to the table. She placed the flutes down and then looked around the room. Perhaps she wanted to see if there were any faces she knew. Perhaps she wanted to make sure there were no faces that knew her. Maybe she just thought Frederick had chosen a poor table.

Either way she eventually sat down. She sat ramrod straight in a club chair built for a decent slouch, and she and Frederick held their drinks up in some kind of toast. It wasn't any kind of toast I knew. When I toasted I looked the other person in the eye as our glasses touched. Lenny had been big on that. He flat out didn't trust a person who didn't look you in the eye during a toast. Some things rubbed off.

It was an interesting study watching the jeweler and her husband on camera. There was no audio so we had no idea what they were saying to each other, but that was no great loss since they barely spoke two words. They sipped their drinks and Frederick looked around the room. At one point I thought Anastasia might have dropped into a trance. They were just old enough to have avoided the addiction of staring at a phone screens in the company of others. I've always found that behavior mind-bogglingly rude, but if this was the other option then maybe I was wrong.

I was watching the couple but Porter was not. She was watching someone else. She reported that there was nothing out of the ordinary happening.

"He's not doing anything?" I asked.

"Pouring drinks, cracking jokes."

After about fifteen minutes, Frederick stood. He brushed off his trousers like he had been sleeping in them and then collected the two flutes. He carried them over to the bar. The bartender came over with a towel across his shoulder. He nodded at Frederick and they spoke. I got the sense Frederick was ordering something complex, like a cocktail the bartender didn't know, because he frowned. But he poured two more champagnes and watched Frederick carry them back to his table. I noted Anastasia. She watched him the whole way.

They did their eyeless toast again and then resumed their positions doing nothing at all. I didn't see the point. Why not stay in your room if all you were going to do was sit and stare at the walls? The art really wasn't that good. I could forgive being on an outside deck, looking at the stars. Terrestrial bodies were tailor-made for contemplating one's tiny existence in the greater scheme of things, and such contemplation was best done in silence. But bars were meant for drinks and friends and laughs. Even when they weren't—those times they were for sitting alone and crying in your pretzels—those were solitary moments. If I was going to sit in silence with Danielle and stare at the walls, I'd do it at home where my beers costs pennies on the dollar.

Porter pulled me from my meandering thoughts.

"We got movement," she said.

It wasn't on my screen, so I looked at hers. We all did.

The bartender had thrown his towel down on the bar and slapped his colleague's back in the time-honored way of telling someone you were taking a quick nature break. Perhaps he said he was getting some more bubbles from the cellar, or wherever the bubbles were kept on a ship. Whatever he said, he slipped out of shot and through a door behind the bar.

"Where's that go?" I asked.

"It's a galley," said Porter. "A small one for the bar menu. Fried food, mainly."

Man can't live on bread alone.

"You got video?"

"Not in the galley," she said. "But . . ." Porter changed the view to a corridor. We saw a plain white door open and the bartender stepped out and walked away from us, and then stopped and stood at what seemed to be a wall.

"Crew elevator," said Porter.

From our angle, the bartender appeared to step into the wall and was gone. Then Porter switched to another camera. I knew this one. People strode busily along it in both directions. It was the main crew corridor. I-95, named after the freeway that runs from the Canadian border with Maine all the way down the East Coast to Miami. We saw the bartender come out of an elevator and slip into the traffic on I-95. He fit in, just another crew member going about his work on a busy night. He walked toward the stern of the ship and then took a set of fire stairs behind another plain white door.

The next shot Porter brought up reminded me of the corridor to our original cabin. Maybe we had been in crew quarters. If so, I pitied the crew. The bartender came into shot and stopped at a cabin door. He looked around to see if he was alone, and then opened the door and stepped inside.

I looked at Danielle, who nodded. Then we waited. There were no cameras in the cabins. It didn't take long, though. After all, the rooms were tiny and there were only so many places a person could hide something.

The door opened again and then bartender returned the corridor, carrying a blue travel bag with the cruise line logo. He looked around once more, and then pulled the door shut and strode away.

Army said, "Let's go."

# CHAPTER THIRTY-ONE

WE BEAT THE BARTENDER TO THE GALLEY BEHIND THE sporting bar. Army stood tall like he was readying himself for battle. I had a good idea of what was going through his mind and suspected he was taking the whole thing personally. This was his team, his people. Although he wasn't responsible for the service staff, and he didn't hire them and they didn't report to him, he still saw them as part of the unit that he oversaw. He wasn't the captain of the ship. He knew that. It was worse for him. He was the captain's minder. He made sure nothing bad happened on the captain's ship. But bad things were happening. And now that Army knew who was behind it, he looked none too happy.

When Martin Perkins stepped into the galley carrying the blue bag, his life flashed before his eyes. Of course, I couldn't say that for sure, but the way his eyes went wide, he certainly knew the jig was up.

"Do you know who I am?" said Army.

Perkins stumbled for the power of speech. "No," he said.

It was a big ship. There were thousands of passengers and almost as many crew. Not everyone knew everyone. So maybe

Perkins didn't know *who* Army was. But he knew *what* he was. The uniform and the square jaw and the *don't mess with me* tone got the message across just fine.

"I am Chief Mahoney. Head of shipboard security."

Perkins gulped. I hadn't been sure before, but now I knew. My plan was going to work. To get to the big dog you had to break the chain. Some chains were hard to break. Some chains were made of strong links like Francis Martelli. He wasn't giving anything away. But as I watched Perkins gulp, I knew he was no kind of hero. And unlike Martelli, he had been chosen to do a job because he was a weak link. Now that was going to come back and bite the big dog on the backside.

"You've been a bad boy," Army said. "You've been smuggling things off the ship."

The word smuggling hung in the air, dripping with its multitude of meanings.

Perkins shook his head. "No," he said. "No, it's a mistake."

Army looked at me and I took the baton.

"Let me tell you what we know," I said.

Perkins frowned and looked me up and down. In my palm tree print shirt and khaki shorts I wasn't quite as imposing as Army in his whites.

"Who are you?" asked Perkins.

"Miami Jones. I'm an investigator." That didn't seem to put the fear in him that I had hoped, so I nodded toward Danielle.

"And this is Special Agent Castle from the Florida Department of Law Enforcement."

That was a little better. He gulped again.

"So let me start again," I said. "We know you impersonated a passenger to make it look like he got back on board when he didn't."

Perkins shook his head but said nothing.

"And the person you impersonated is being held for attempted murder."

Now his face dropped.

"Special Agent Castle, would that be considered accessory to attempted homicide?"

"I think the state attorney could make a case that he committed the actual crime itself. He dressed up like the perp we have on video."

"No, no, no," said Perkins. "I don't know anything about that."

Army stepped forward. "At the very least it's a dismissible offense," he said.

He certainly could deliver that drill sergeant voice, but I didn't see how being dismissed from his job was adding to the pain of being accused of attempted murder.

I nodded at the bag in Perkins's hand.

"What's in your bag there?"

"Nothing."

"Why would you carry a bag with nothing in it? And why would you go and retrieve an empty bag in the middle of a shift?"

"No reason."

"No reason? Can I see inside?"

"No."

"No? You want to do it the hard way?"

"You need a warrant."

I smiled. "Martin—it is Martin, right? Let me explain where we are right now. You're in a world of hurt. You've done some dumb things. You know what they are, and so do we. You don't want to do any more. Because right now, you're not in US waters. We don't need a warrant. We can throw you to the ground and rip the bag from your hands. Right, Chief?"

"We're a Bahamian-registered vessel. US law doesn't apply.

And even if we were in US waters, we'd just call the coast guard. They can search any boat they like, for any reason. There are no Fourth Amendment protections against search and seizure while on a boat."

I looked at Army. "Is that true? The Fourth doesn't apply at sea?"

"Doesn't apply to any boat in the US. At sea or tied up to a dock behind your house in Fort Lauderdale. Coast guard has wide powers to board any vessel for safety inspection or any other reason."

"I gotta remember that." I looked back at Perkins. "Either way, Martin, you're done."

"I didn't do anything. Well, nothing major."

"Martin."

"Look, I just thought it was some spirits or something that he shouldn't have had on board."

"You're not that stupid."

"I swear. I was just supposed to take the bag and leave it at the tiki bar. But the guy must've took the wrong bag."

"That so?"

"I don't know." He glanced at the bag in his hand. "The bag I took back on board wasn't so heavy. I don't get it."

He didn't get it because the bag in his hand wasn't the bag he had brought back on board. It was a bag full of rings. Danielle and Porter had switched the two bags in the bartender's cabin earlier. Now, even I knew that in a court that would be considered planting evidence. But that was only if we planned on prosecuting Perkins. Which I certainly didn't. Army certainly had a long list of reasons to dismiss the guy from employment, but I just wanted him as bait.

"So you just received the bag, and then took it onto the island."

He nodded.

"And who arranged this?"

"The guy at the tiki bar."

Army pulled out a sheet of paper with Francis Martelli's passenger photo on it.

"This guy?" I asked.

"Yeah, that's him."

"And he was at the tiki bar?"

"Yes."

"And you pretended to be him getting back onto the ship?"

"Hey, he said he was just playing a prank on his wife."

"Sure. That's sounds like a hoot. You got his ID?"

Perkins pulled a ship pass from his pocket and handed it to Army.

Army took it and said, "Why?"

I watched the guy for a moment. He was young and impressionable. He was at that age where young men think they are immortal. That was a good feeling. I no longer felt it, but I still remembered it. It had served me well at times, and not so well at others. It hadn't served Perkins well. It made him susceptible to doing dumb things. It made a lot of young men susceptible to doing dumb things. If they made it through, they often wised up with the passing of the years. Often, but not always.

"You know how much I make?" asked Perkins, rhetorically. "I'd do better at Walmart."

"They won't hire you," said Army. "Not if they call me for a reference."

"There's a way out, Martin," I said.

He frowned. "What way?"

"I need you to do something for me."

"I'm not doing nothing with that guy," he said, nodding at the picture of Francis Martelli.

"No, not that guy."

"And then I'm good? I keep my job?"

"No, Martin. I'm pretty sure you're done on the *Canaveral Star*. But you do this thing and maybe you won't go to jail."

He frowned again. I waited. He was either going to try and negotiate, or his brain was going to collapse like a black hole under the weight of all the thinking going on in his head. He might realize that offering no jail time wasn't my offer to make. I was neither the cruise line nor law enforcement. But I did know that the cruise line would want to see the back of Martin Perkins and they would want to sweep the whole sorry thing under the rug. And as for law enforcement, there really was no telling whose job it was to give a damn. We were on a Bahamian registered ship in Bahamian waters, dealing with a US citizen who would be back in the US before anyone called any kind of cop. It was going to fall into the *too hard* basket. I was confident of that.

"No jail?" Perkins asked.

"No."

"And what do I have to do?"

"One very simple thing. I want to you pick up that travel bag, and I want you to give it back to the person who gave it to you."

# CHAPTER THIRTY-TWO

PERKINS TOOK THE DEAL. HE DIDN'T HAVE A LOT OF options, not that he could see. He picked up the bag and he wandered into the bar. At the end of the counter there was a section where the bar could be folded over itself to let people through. He didn't fold it over. He just ducked under. And then he shrugged his shoulders like he was readying himself for battle, and he started across the lounge.

We watched from the galley doorway. A waiter wanted through, so I slipped out behind the bar. I kept my eyes on Anastasia Connors. She wasn't going to see me. She was looking straight ahead, into a space between spaces, another dimension, maybe another time. Maybe she was looking at old photographs in her mind.

Frederick Connors was still looking around the room. His eyes would stop at a painting of a group of men on horseback, hunting dogs at their feet, horn at one man's lips, declaring the hunt was on. There were no foxes in that painting. They were running for their lives off-canvas. I didn't see the point of it all. The activity or the art. Did anyone even eat fox? They seemed all sinew and bone to me. Surely there was more utility in raising a herd of sheep. And as a piece of art it really didn't give me the sense of wonder that great art was supposed to. I just wondered about the poor fox, and he wasn't even in the picture.

Maybe Frederick had similar thoughts. I wasn't sure. We were both men, and that was where the similarities ended. But he tossed some thoughts around and then moved his eyes to the next thing in the room, maybe another cluster of chairs. Maybe he was looking at the people sitting in them, wondering who they were, what they did for a living, the way folks do when they are people watching. Maybe he was wondering what they were talking about and why he couldn't think of a single thing to say to his own wife.

Or maybe his mind was blank. I really had no idea. Anastasia sipped her drink. Her movement prompted Frederick to do the same. As he put his drink down he saw the bartender coming toward him. It gave him something to look at, something to do. Watch the approaching person. Then out of her peripheral vision, Anastasia must have caught the movement because she dropped back into the time and space the rest of us occupied and she looked at Perkins and frowned.

Perkins walked slowly. I figured he was uncertain. He stepped up to the couple, who both looked up at him the way people do in a bar, with that look that says, *I didn't order anything, did you order something?*

For a moment Perkins stood before them. Anastasia's wonderment about a potential order changed to her more normal frown, as if this idiot of a bar boy was harshing her mellow by interrupting her daydreaming. I had been on the end of that face. Then Perkins handed over the bag.

To Frederick Connors.

Frederick took it like it was his dinner and Perkins had warned him the plate was hot. Two hands, at the bottom. He looked surprised. I knew the look. I was pretty sure I was wearing it. I didn't know what Perkins was up to.

I heard Perkins say, "We found your bag, sir."

Frederick said nothing.

Anastasia said, "His bag? Where did you find his bag?"

"On Paradise Cay," said Perkins, then he offered a small nod and retreated. He walked away much quicker than he had approached. Anastasia turned her frown on her husband. I got the feeling he knew that look better than I did.

"How did your bag get on the island?"

Frederick just pulled the bag into his lap, nice and tight. Then he glanced inside and recoiled like it contained a human head. Anastasia looked at the bag, and then at Frederick. And then at the bag again.

"I don't know what is going on with you," she said. "Carrying that bag everywhere you go."

He wasn't alone. Lots of people were carrying that exact bag around. For a moment I wondered if Frederick had indeed lost his bag. Then I wondered how he might have lost it on the island when he never got off the boat. Then I realized my entire line of thought was wrong.

Anastasia took a long pull on her champagne and then turned her eye back to Frederick.

"Are you quite all right?" she asked.

Perkins stepped back under the bar, and I edged past him and slipped under and out into the lounge.

Anastasia said, "Frederick, I asked if you are all right?" She turned up her lip. "You're sweating."

He was. As I moved closer I could see the hair on his temples glistening. Rivulets had begun running down the side of his head, around his ears and along his chin. He looked like he had been feasting on a spicy vindaloo. He didn't say anything to Anastasia. He looked hard at the men on the horses and the excited dogs at their feet.

Then he looked at me. He wasn't a confident guy. He dressed well and presented just fine, but I got the feeling that a lifetime of not quite measuring up to his wife's expectations had worn him down. It had taken some effort to come to my office to hire me, but it wasn't an effort born of confidence. Yet he had looked polished doing it. The nice clothes and the pocket squares and the well-tended beard. It was all a mask, hiding the tumult below.

Now that the mask had fallen, he no longer looked polished. He looked like a guy who didn't know what the hell was going on around him. He wore the eyes of a quarterback about to be sacked, crushed by a three-hundred-pound lineman. A dash of fear and a good dose of *how did this happen?*

I ambled toward him. I wasn't completely sure what the hell was going on, either. But I wanted to find out why the rings were sitting in Frederick's lap.

Then the look on his face changed. Like the quarterback had just seen an out, a way to avoid the sack. Maybe. If he moved fast. Frederick jumped up. He didn't look at his wife. He didn't look at me. He didn't look around. He already had. His bored face had perused every inch of the room. So he knew just where he wanted to go.

He ran.

# CHAPTER THIRTY-THREE

I didn't chase him. Not at first. It took longer than was necessary for me to figure out what he was doing. Running? He was on a ship, in the middle of the ocean. And we had well and truly established the fact that he couldn't swim. There was nowhere to go.

I still didn't move. I was paralyzed by the action. Like when a runner at base forgets to run because he's watching a humdinger of a hit go over the fence. He still has to complete the run around the bases, but he's too busy watching this amazing thing. And it was amazing. Frederick Connors running was a sight to behold. Just not in a good way. He was slightly on the tubby side, for sure, but he wasn't massively overweight. But he held the travel bag against his belly and it put his center of gravity all off. His legs were thick but they stumbled like a baby giraffe's.

All my life I have been in sports. I had thrown balled-up socks to my dad before I was old enough to remember. I once saw the old photographs. I didn't have them anymore, but I did see them. We tossed a football on the field at Yale when I was in elementary school. I played soccer and then Pop Warner and then baseball in New Haven. I ran track in high school and I got football and baseball scholarships to college. I played pro-baseball for six years and since then I have run along City Beach with Danielle on a regular basis. I wouldn't say that sports were my life but they have certainly been a big part of it.

So it took me a moment to comprehend what I was looking at. It was something I couldn't recall ever having seen before. I was watching a man who had never learned to run. As if he literally had missed every single PE class for thirteen years of school. A man who had never taken up a bat or kicked a ball or even rushed to catch a bus.

Some people aren't sporty. I get that. I can't program a computer or write a sonnet. Don't ask me how cold air and hot air get produced from the same air-conditioning unit. But most people have done at least some athletics. They once slogged their way around a high school field in baggy shorts wishing they were anywhere else. They curled up like roly-polies to defend themselves in dodgeball. They whacked a ball against a wall or did a run-up to leap inside a double-dutch jump rope. Plenty of people still have nightmares about their sports escapades. But they have been there and done that.

Frederick Connors had never run before. It was obvious to everyone in the lounge. I wasn't the only one watching. Mouths were dropping all throughout the bar as Frederick made his way across. I couldn't help thinking that it would have been quicker to just walk. His knees went up and his feet came down but he really didn't really get anywhere. There was no stride to his stride. He sort of bounced across the carpet with splayed legs like a newborn colt. But foals picked up the whole running thing within an hour. Frederick wasn't going to have any such luck. I watched him go until Danielle appeared at my shoulder.

"What is he doing?" she asked.

"I'm not sure. I think he's running away."

"To where? We're still on a ship."

We watched him head toward a set of concertina glass doors, which had been pushed aside to allow access to a deck where party lights hung in subtle clusters.

"You don't think he'll jump, do you?" she asked.

"I am not going in again." I wasn't. If Frederick wanted to go over he was on his own.

"We should get him," said Danielle.

I nodded and started walking. Nothing more was required. It was a slow-motion chase. I ambled across the lounge. Fredrick hit the outside deck about five feet in front of me. He kept going. I could have reached out and grabbed him but I didn't see much point. If he made to go over the edge I was going to kick his feet out from under him. Otherwise he was running himself into a corner.

He reached the gunwale and put one hand against it. I could hear him breathing heavily. All that herky-jerky motion would take it out of anyone. Frederick stumbled like he might collapse, but he caught himself and thrust his body forward at the gunwale.

And then he flung the blue travel bag out into the air like a discus. He couldn't run but he could throw. The bag spun and spun, the handles reaching out as if they wanted to be caught. Then the bag dropped away into the night. I didn't hear the splash over the sound of the ship cutting through the ocean.

Frederick put both his hands on the gunwale and collected his breath, and then he turned around and leaned against the edge and looked back at me.

I stayed where I was just outside the doors. Danielle and Army joined me. Then Anastasia arrived. She wasn't a fast mover, but she didn't need to be. She walked like she had rollers on her feet, drifting like a ghost. She got to the doors but she didn't step out.

"Frederick, have you lost your mind?"

We looked at Frederick for an answer but he didn't give one. He just stood in glow of the colored party lights.

"He hasn't lost his mind," I said, "but he did steal your rings."

# CHAPTER THIRTY-FOUR

Anastasia gave me the look. At this point, a different facial expression would have been a surprise. She could never have been an actor. Her facial expressions for mad, confused, contrite, exasperated, disappointed and plain disgusted were all exactly the same.

Frederick, however, had found a new expression. Smug. Maybe he'd taken it from his wife when he took her rings. The thought of which made a whole lot of things become clear. In my mind, I watched the bag flying out over the water one more time and it was like filling in that one word in the crossword that makes all the other words apparent. Not that I did a lot of crosswords. But I understood the concept.

Anastasia looked from her husband to me. Then her face did change. Like a penny was dropping.

"Why did you throw that bag overboard, Frederick?" she asked.

"What bag?" said Frederick.

"My rings were in there? In that bag?"

"What rings?"

"You threw my rings into the sea?"

I looked at Frederick, all smug and sweaty. Then I turned back to his wife.

"No," I said. "He didn't throw your rings overboard."

The smugness dropped a little from Frederick's face. He had looked inside the bag and seen the rings, and I saw the first hint of confusion.

"He just tossed the fakes overboard," I said.

"I've told you before," said Anastasia, "they are not fakes."

"Not your reproductions, Mrs. Connors. I'm talking about the fake fakes that Mr. Connors brought on board with him."

"I did no such thing," said Frederick.

"Yeah, you did. And you switched them for your wife's rings."

"Oh, really? I'm a cat burglar now?"

"Not the way you run. And I have to admit, I didn't get it until now. It was pretty slick. How do you get valuable rings out of a locked room? There's video, there were guards. No one went in. No one. So how could it happen?"

"I have no idea," Frederick said.

"You didn't, I'm sure. But your partners did."

"Oh, I have partners now."

"You do. See, I think you had this idea about stealing the rings but you had a couple problems. The first was how do you actually steal them? You're many things, Mr. Connors, but as we just agreed, you're no cat burglar. So you needed someone to help plan this thing. And then there was your second problem. How do you sell them? You needed some help there, too."

Frederick said nothing.

"Now that I'm thinking it through, how do you find a person like that? I know how I would do it. I'd ask my friend Sal. He knows people like that. But they don't advertise. So how does a guy like you find them? Answer. You don't. They find you. You told me you ran a chain of fast-food outlets."

"Fast-casual restaurants," said Frederick.

"They're donut shops," said Anastasia.

"They're fast-casual restaurants!"

I looked between the couple. It was clearly a sore point.

"Whatever you call them, what they are is cash intensive. Lots of currency passes through restaurants, especially fast-food ones. And cash-intensive businesses attract the attention of people like the ones my friend Sal knows. They call it protection. The FBI calls it racketeering. I bet you pay off some guys like that. That's how you know them. So you go to them and you make a proposal. There are these rings, worth three million bucks. And they come up with the plan."

"It's genius, Mr. Jones. I'm sure you even know the plan."

"I didn't. I got it just now, when you threw that bag overboard. You solved it for me. How do you get rings out of a locked room? Easy. You do it before the room gets locked."

"What are you talking about, Mr. Jones?" asked Anastasia. "I locked them in the safe. You were there. We were all there when the room got locked."

"Yeah, we were. That was the clever part, and not a little bold. Because the theft happened right before my eyes."

"Before your eyes?" said Danielle.

I nodded. "Yep. Before yours, too. I had no idea, until I just remembered something I had said to Mrs. Connors. Maybe deep down I knew. Maybe not. I said there was some David Copperfield stuff going on."

"I remember," said Anastasia.

"I meant it like you had to be a magician to get something out of a locked room."

"I understood the reference," she said.

"But I was wrong. David Copperfield isn't just a magician. He calls himself an illusionist. And what's the key ingredient of the illusion?"

Everyone shook their head. No one knew.

"The art of misdirection."

I got a lot of confused faces.

"We were all in the auction room. The auctioneer inspected the rings and confirmed they were the real fakes."

"Reproductions!" said Anastasia.

"Whatever. The real ones. And then what happened?"

"I went with Arnold to sign the auction agreement."

"Right. And our attention was on you doing that. It was then that Frederick put the rings into the safe."

"Exactly," said Anastasia. "In the safe. Which, as I just said, I locked."

"Right. The second part of the misdirection, or a second misdirection. I don't know, I'm not a magician. But first he put the rings in the safe. Only he didn't. He had the fakes—"

"Reproductions, Mr. Jones!"

"No, Mrs. Connors, this time I mean the fakes. The eBay knockoff fakes. He had them in his little blue travel bag. That bit was clever. Everyone had one of those bags. You could take it anywhere, and he did. Someone might question a different kind of bag, but not that one. They're everywhere. So he slipped behind the display cabinet and opened the safe and took his fakes out of the bag and slipped them inside the safe, and put your rings in his bag. Then he let you lock the safe, so you were the last person to see your rings. But you didn't really see them. You saw two boxes of fakes."

Anastasia frowned and shook her head.

"It's not possible." She said it, but she didn't sound convinced.

"Good luck proving any of this," said Frederick.

"Yeah, it's all pulled tight, your plan," I said. "Except for that one weak link."

Frederick said nothing.

"You had to get them off the ship," I said. "That was the tough part, really. There's security and passport control and everything. But your partners had a plan for all that, didn't they? Only something went wrong."

"Something went wrong?" Danielle asked.

"Yeah. You remember when we were in the casino last night? The opening cocktails thing? There was a bit of a disturbance. Someone accused someone of cheating or something. Security was called."

Danielle said, "I remember."

"So fine, no big deal. But then Army came in and told me there had been a fight in the Hall of Fame room. Again, it's a cruise, people are drinking, things happen. But they happened at the same time. Dumb luck as much as anything. But it made all the vendors skittish about their stuff. So we all trooped down to the auction room. It was then we found out the rings were fakes."

"We know all this, Mr. Jones," said Anastasia. "You can be quite tedious."

"Tedious or not, we now knew about the theft. But imagine we didn't. Imagine that disturbance didn't happen in the casino, no fight in the Hall of Fame. We didn't bother to check the rings."

"We wouldn't have known it happened," said Danielle.

"Exactly."

"Of course we would have," said Anastasia. "Buyers would have verified their purchase at the auction. It has to be done to validate the certificate of authenticity."

"Sure. But that would happen when? A couple hours from now. After the auction tonight. So we wouldn't have known until then."

"And the rings would have walked off the ship on Paradise Cay," said Danielle.

"Exactly. We wouldn't have even started looking for them until way too late."

Everyone stood silent for a moment to think it through. I did the same thing. After all, I hadn't been sitting around for the past two days with the plan in my head. Things only came to me once I realized Frederick was the one behind it. But I waited for the question I knew would come.

"You're saying they got off the boat?" asked Anastasia. "How?"

"It was a good plan and it might have worked if we hadn't known about the theft as early as we did. Frederick couldn't do it. Passengers are often security checked on and off the ship. Bags can be searched. But crew, they have more freedom of movement. So Frederick gave the bag to Martin Perkins."

"Who on earth is Martin Perkins?" asked Anastasia. She was rapidly losing her composure. I could understand why.

"The bartender who just handed Frederick the bag."

"Him? What has he got to do with anything?"

"Nothing. He's just a guy who would carry a bag onto the cay and give it to another guy, and then pretend to be that second guy getting back on board so the passenger numbers would add up."

"He gave the bag to whom?" asked Anastasia.

"Frankie Martelli," I said.

Anastasia leaned against the glass panels of the folded door and put her hand to her head. "Mr. Jones, you will be the very end of me. Who on earth is this Martelli person?"

"I'm willing to bet he works for the people your husband approached to do this job."

We all looked at Frederick. He sort of shrugged, like he didn't care. I had a good idea why. He knew who he had gotten in with. He knew they were serious people. The sort of serious people whose people didn't turn on them. That was a death sentence. Or life in the witness protection program, living in Des Moines, which for those guys was the same thing.

I said, "Mr. Connors knows that his partner's people won't turn on them. They're those kind of guys."

Connors smiled, just a little.

"But the bartender isn't one their guys. He's not dumb, though. He won't roll over on them. But he will roll over on you, Fred."

Frederick dropped the smile. Maybe it was because I used the short form of his name but I didn't think so.

"He's got plenty to say. Like how he received stolen property from you, and was asked to pass it on to an organized crime figure, who, he says, he cannot identify."

I watched Frederick. He hadn't looked his polished self since getting fished out of the Atlantic Ocean. His look wasn't improving. I wasn't sure why he had done what he had done, but I figured things were not all they could be in his life, and they had clearly just gotten a good deal worse.

His eyes drifted to his wife. They were sad eyes. Sad because of what he had lost or sad because he had been caught out, I couldn't say. But I followed his look and turned to Anastasia. Her look was not one of sorrow. Or even anger. If I were pushed, I would have called it a look of resignation. Of an expectation that Frederick would one day disappoint her to a level that put all other disappointments to shame. Her eyes bored into him for an uncomfortable amount of time. Then she turned her eyes to me.

"Mr. Jones, does this story end with you telling me where my pieces are?"

I nodded. "It does."

Army stepped forward. "Mrs. Connors, I have your items in the safe in my office."

"So we can still partake in the auction."

"Well, yes. I suppose. It will have started already, but I guess they could slip your items in. I'm not sure that the buyers will be able to take their items home, though. The authorities in Palm Beach may want to hold the rings as evidence."

"I understand," she said. "But that will only increase their value. You'll get them for me?"

"I will."

"Thank you." Anastasia turned to leave.

"Mrs. Connors," I said. "What about your husband?"

She spun around to looked at me. She didn't look at him.

"You can throw him overboard if you wish. I have to get dressed."

# CHAPTER THIRTY-FIVE

I didn't watch Anastasia and Army leave. I kept my eye on Frederick. I wasn't worried about him getting away. He couldn't swim and he couldn't run, so unless a helicopter dropped a rope ladder from the sky he was out of options. And I didn't even like his chances of making it up a rope ladder.

He wasn't quite so smug anymore. Rather, he looked annoyed. The muscles at the edge of his mouth twitched like he wanted to snarl, but he either didn't know how or he had suppressed the urge to do it to his wife for so many years his muscles had forgotten the process.

"If you think you're getting paid now . . ."

I shrugged. "Why not? You hired me to find out if your wife is having an affair. And I did. By the way, she's not."

"You haven't proven anything. About her or about me."

"Freddy, my boy, you really are a card."

"My name is not Freddy."

"I'll let your fellow inmates come up with your new name."

"You have nothing."

"Wrong, Fred. I would have had nothing. I would have

come back with no definitive proof of anything. We owe our thanks to one person."

"Who?"

"You, Fred. You were the architect of your own demise."

I liked that line and had been wanting to deliver it for some time.

"You think so, do you?"

"I do, Fred. I figure it like this. You're unhappy in your marriage, or something like that. Maybe it's midlife crisis time. I can't read your mind, so I don't know why you did it exactly. Maybe you were sick of Ana talking down your business. Maybe your restaurants were in financial trouble. I don't know and I don't care. But I see it going down like I said. You pay some bad hombres protection money. You figure they know about things like jewel heists. You take the idea to them. Three million in rings. Specially designed for this weekend and best of all, being moved out of the relative security of your wife's store and onto a relatively unsecured ship."

"It's a fine story, Mr. Jones."

"Nah, it's a terrible story. Because I don't like sad endings. I've been around my fair share of them. Some through my own actions and some despite me. And I'll tell you now, Fred. You don't know these people like I know these people."

"You do, do you?"

I nodded. "I do. And I know this about them. They're like pirates. Plan A is always to take it all whenever they can. There really is no honor among thieves. They always want it all. So after you laid out the job, the first thing they did was look at all the ways they could do this thing without you."

Frederick frowned and said nothing. But I could tell I had his attention.

"I'm sure they checked out the store, did a wander through, maybe two, pretending to be customers. They would have checked out any other weak points. Maybe your house or other places your wife goes. Maybe they canvassed the idea of kidnapping her and forcing her back to the store. But there's a lot of risk in that. And considering what these guys do for a living, they're generally more risk-averse than you'd think. But they were a bit sloppy. They were careful not to get made by the mark—Mrs. C —but they forgot about you. You spotted them."

"I did no such thing."

"But you did, Fred. You spotted a man repeatedly in places with your wife. The store, The Breakers, at your house."

"What?" he whispered.

"Yeah, what a pain, hey? The crooks you went to had one of their guys check into doing the job without you and you spotted him and thought he was having an affair with your wife. That's tough luck, right there."

"That's not true." He said it but he didn't mean it. It lacked any kind of conviction.

"So you came to me. Had you not, you would have gotten away with it."

He shook his head as he thought it through.

"Of course," I said, "on the flip side, you'd be dead."

"Dead?"

"Dead, Fred. Dead. See, they couldn't come up with a plan A. So they went to plan B. You were never supposed to be on the ship. I bet you made that clear from the beginning. You don't cruise. They would have to do the job at sea, which is harder than it sounds. But they didn't like those odds. So they came back to you with another plan."

I looked at Danielle. "Why does a guy who doesn't cruise, who doesn't like boats, who can't swim, change his mind at the last minute to go cruising?"

Danielle said, "Someone puts the idea in his head."

"Exactly. With prejudice, I'll bet. They said there was no

other way, didn't they? You needed to take the rings before the room got locked up, that was the weak point. And then, they said they would handle getting them off the ship. Right?"

Frederick seemed to have lost his voice.

"But here's something else you didn't know about these guys. Plan A is always they keep everything for themselves. Plan B is pretty much the same thing. So once you took the rings and passed them on to the bartender as instructed, you weren't required anymore. In fact, you were a loose end."

Frederick's face dropped as he processed what I was saying. It wasn't great news, even in a bulletin full of not-so-great news for him.

"So they instructed their guy on board—Guy X—to get rid of you. The bartender had given Guy X a stolen crew pass, and I bet he had been instructed to scope out where the cameras were along the route via the crew passageway out to the forward deck. So Guy X snuck up there and pushed you overboard."

Frederick dropped against the side of the deck as if he might faint. He wasn't going overboard this time; the sides were designed nice and high for a reason. But he looked like he might collapse.

"Tell me, Fred. Why were you on that deck last night? You must have hated it."

"I had to make a phone call."

"Let me guess. Your partners told you to call once the handoff was made."

His eyes glazed over like he was drifting away to another universe.

"Who told you the best reception was on the forward deck?"

Frederick gazed away. "The bartender."

"That's what I figured. You were set up. They wanted you dead. And if I hadn't been there, right now you'd be chum."

He frowned. "I don't . . . it doesn't . . . why *were* you there?"

"Your guys got cute. They tried to set Anastasia up for your death. They called her with a story about the rings and told her to go to the bathroom near the forward deck. They wanted her in the area to cast suspicion on her. And it would have worked too, except that we were on board. I was doing what you hired me to do—watching your wife. I saw her go forward and then lost her. But I found you."

It was too much for old Frederick. His knees finally gave way and he slid like a flattened cartoon character down the edge of the deck until he was sitting on the polished boards. His shirt was all rumpled and for the first time I noted a hair sticking out of his beard at an odd angle. It reaffirmed my belief that facial hair was too much work.

"So here's my client debrief, Fred. Your wife isn't having an affair. She doesn't even know Guy X. He belongs to your organized crime buddies. We have means and opportunity for you to steal the rings, and we've got testimony from the bartender that you handed him a bag containing said rings." I looked at Danielle. "Do you think the state attorney could make something of that?"

Danielle shook her head. "The state attorney won't get the chance. Crimes involving US citizens at sea fall under the jurisdiction of the FBI. What Mr. Connors did was a federal crime."

I liked the way she said *federal crime*. I liked the way all law enforcement types said it. It was like a federal crime was another ring or two closer to the fires of hell. Like going to the federal pen was somehow worse than any other kind of jail. In my book, doing time was doing time. None of it was fun. But the way she said *federal crime* made Frederick cry.

Or maybe he realized he was done. Maybe it was the release of decades of churning in his guts. I didn't know. What I did know was that he cried ugly. First a tear ran down his cheek and was absorbed by his beard, and then the floodgates opened. He coughed and spluttered and gagged for air. It was quite the display. Danielle and Porter and I waited him out, glancing at each other uncomfortably. I didn't think any of us were of the opinion that Frederick was an out-and-out bad guy. He hadn't hurt a child or masterminded a murder. He took some stuff that, when all was said and done, no one but his wife would miss. But Danielle would argue that it wasn't his to take and though I thought that point could be debated, since Ana's property could be considered marital property and therefore also Frederick's, I'd leave that train of thought for his lawyers.

We waited for the tears to stop and the breathing to return to something resembling a sprinter at the end of the hundred-yard dash. I stepped toward him and he looked up at me through puffy eyes. I squatted down so I was face to face with him.

I was going to ask him why, but I didn't. We shared a look and that was all that was required.

"You don't understand," he said.

I shook my head.

"No one could."

"But you were successful," I said. "Well-known and well-liked in Palm Beach society. Some folks would give their left arm for that."

"I hate Palm Beach. I hate the society. Thirty years we've been there. Thirty years of getting dressed up and pretending to like those people. As if we were like them. But we weren't like them. You could see it in their eyes. They looked at Anastasia like she was the help. A shopkeeper. Sure, she was a jeweler, something they liked, but she wasn't really one of them. And me? I didn't even do business there. They looked down on my business like it was loose change in their pockets. Thirty years of sinking every penny into keeping up the pretense. The Palm

Beach house, the nice cars, the clothes. I would have been happy wearing what you wear."

I took it as the compliment I was sure it wasn't meant to be.

"Every Sunday doing brunch with people I despised just to sell a few pearls. I would have preferred to stay home and watch football."

I nodded and reconsidered my earlier theory. Maybe deep inside, under all those layers of Frederick, there really was a Fred, bursting to get out.

"Drastic move, though," I said.

"I was done. I did my time. I wanted to find an island and lie back by the pool. I'd earned it. But Anastasia wouldn't leave. She actually believes this is her home, these are her people. But I couldn't do it anymore. I put every penny into keeping up the house, the cars. Not Anastasia. I never saw a red cent from her business. She thought it was my job to give her the life she wanted. And I wanted to do it. But did she have to put it down so much? Never a word of thanks. That business paid for everything we had and she spoke of it like it was prostitution or something."

"You wanted what was yours?"

"I wanted my life back. You were right. My business started failing. Between the Mafia leeches and the anti-sugar Nazis, I was getting squeezed. I told Anastasia it was time to get out before the market moved beyond us, and she said she always knew I'd fail. That was all she said about it. I told her I wanted to go away, to relax for a change. But she's like a clock. If she's not moving constantly she'll die. So I realized I had to do it myself. She never gave anything from her business, so I decided to take something. Put it away for later. After the divorce."

"You were divorcing her?"

He shook his head. "I might have. I would have. But when I saw the guy at our house I thought I wouldn't have to. I thought if she was having an affair then she'd divorce me. But I knew she'd hire the best lawyers and keep all her business for herself. So I hired you to get some proof of infidelity. And I went ahead and took something for myself. I earned it."

"But there wasn't any infidelity."

He shook his head again and took a long slow breath. "No. Not that it changes anything. She might not have been with him, but she wasn't with me, either." He looked up at me, his eyes red and watery. "She never said thank you. Not once. Not ever. Once would have done it. I could have held onto it if I had just heard it once."

Army returned and directed Porter to take Frederick below. She stepped forward and together she and I helped Frederick to his feet.

"If you ladies wouldn't mind finding Mr. Connors suitable quarters," said Army.

Porter and Danielle moved to take him away. Army put his hand on my arm to hold me from following. I frowned but I let them go. I wondered how many spare crew cabins with backward locks they had. Perhaps Frederick and Guy X would have to bunk together.

"Is there a problem?" I asked.

"Just wanted you to see something."

I followed Army up the crew elevator and into the security control room. He brought up some video. It was a shot of the forward deck at night, from above where Frederick had been standing before he went overboard.

"I think I've seen this more than enough," I said.

"Give it a minute, son," said Army.

We saw me come out onto the deck, with Danielle right behind. The Cleveland boys appeared. Words we couldn't hear. Then I did what I did, across the deck and out of shot. Into the big blue. Danielle was left standing on the deck. She took a step toward where I had disappeared. Then she spun. The Cleveland boys each took a step forward as if to surround her. The leader, the guy with the sick grandad, said something.

Then Danielle punched him in the nose. I didn't know what he said, but I imagined it was a proposition to which she was not inclined to acquiesce. She gave it a good solid step and the full follow-through. The guy went down hard, holding his snout. His buddies decided discretion was the better part of valor and backed away, and Danielle made off through the hole they left, looking for Army, and a rescue boat.

Army hit a button to stop the video.

"Is he making a complaint?" I asked.

"No."

"So why did you show me that?"

"Because I thought you should see it."

"Why?"

"Because she's a keeper."

I had to agree. I thanked Army and told him I needed some downtime. He called Porter on the radio to tell Danielle that I was going to our suite.

I didn't even turn the lights on. I walked through the suite to the balcony and leaned on the gunwale and stared out at the dark ocean. Danielle arrived and, leaving the light off, came to stand by me. We watched the silver ripples on the wake, splashing and pulsing like they were alive and full of intent, and then they fell away and got smaller and dimmer until they weren't there at all anymore.

# CHAPTER THIRTY-SIX

WE DIDN'T GO TO THE AUCTION. I DIDN'T WANT TO SEE gaudy real-fake rings go under the hammer for the kind of money that the average family made in a year. We didn't head for the pool bar. It was too lively and too loud and the people were having too much fun.

Instead, we found Ron and Cassandra. They had slipped out of the auction after Anastasia had arrived and told them that her rings had been recovered but she had nothing further to say on the matter.

I gave them the brief version of events and then Ron led us to another bar that I hadn't seen before. It was dark and clubby and a quartet played jazz on a small stage. Folks were dancing to the easy rhythms. Ron ordered drinks but we didn't toast. Then Ron asked Danielle if she would like to dance, which was like asking Einstein if he liked math.

I didn't much feel like it but I asked Cassandra if she would join me on the dance floor. She gave me her soft, thin hand. The music wasn't slow but it was easy, and it allowed couples to dance as close as they wanted. Cassandra took a position like she was a ballroom dancer, one hand high and the other on my shoulder.

"I can't believe it was Frederick," she said.

"Yeah."

"I have to say, Anastasia didn't appear as sad about it as I would have thought."

"Folks have different ways of processing things. She wore her attitude like a suit of armor. Maybe there was a reason for it."

"You're right. Still, I feel for them."

"Me too."

"Do you think he'll go to jail?"

"Danielle doesn't think so. There's really only the say-so of the bartender. And if Fred's attorney has half a brain he'll claim it was a mix-up with the bags. Those things all look the same. Plus, there are still jurisdictional issues. If it goes to trial it'll be messy, and I don't think anyone wants messy. Not the cruise line, not Anastasia. Not Fred."

"I suppose the end of a marriage is bad enough."

"And he almost drowned."

"Yes, horrible. He has a lot to thank you for."

"Not sure he sees it that way. He thought an affair was the worst of it."

Cassandra stopped dancing and frowned. She did so by tilting her head to the side rather than pinching her eyes together. Fewer lines that way.

"Anastasia was having an affair?"

I gulped. "Well, no, not as it turned out."

She nodded and began dancing again. I figured she was leading, because she made me start again as well.

"That's why you were hired," she said. "By Frederick. He suspected an affair."

"Yes. But it was my case. Not Ron's."

"How could that be? You didn't know Frederick. Ron did."

I wanted to stop talking. The more I said the worse it got for Ron. He knew about the suspected affair and he hadn't told Cassandra what her friend was doing, or what we were doing by following her.

"Look, this isn't Ron's fault. I told him he couldn't say anything to you. I told him he'd be fired if he did."

"You said you'd fire him?"

"I did."

"Oh, Miami, really. How many people have you fired, ever?"

"I don't know."

"Would the number be close to zero?"

"It might."

And you don't have to make up stories to cover for Ron. He's a big boy. Why would he tell me anyway?"

"I thought you and Anastasia were friends."

"We are."

"So you don't care that he didn't tell you?"

"Miami, I care. I care that my friend might have been going through something like that."

"Ron didn't participate in the case, if it helps. He kind of recused himself."

"Of course he did. Because that's Ron."

"You can trust him."

"Miami, you don't need to sell me on Ron. I love him. And I trust him."

"You do? Good."

She smiled. "When you get to my age you learn a thing or two. You learn that trust isn't about telling your partner everything. It's about knowing that when they don't tell you something, there's a darn good reason for it. And if you are really supposed to be together, that reason is good enough for the both of you."

I said nothing. I just danced. Then Cassandra dropped her hand from my shoulder.

"I'd like some champagne," she said.

"Sounds like a plan."

She led me off the floor and we took a small table. I ordered a champagne and a beer, and we watched Danielle and Ron. They were both smiling, as if dancing was the best thing in the world. They weren't talking. It reminded me of a father-daughter dance at a wedding. I'd seen that once or twice. The happiest and saddest thing I ever saw. A little girl that a father loved was leaving him to be loved by another.

"Will she be okay? Anastasia?" I asked.

"If I know her, she'll put on a face, throw herself into her work. But no. I don't see how she'll be okay. Not for a long time. I've lost a husband. Not to divorce, but maybe that's worse. I don't know. People handle these things in their own way. I wasn't right for the longest time, maybe not until I met Ronnie. Maybe I'm still not completely right, even now. But we soldier on."

I nodded and sipped my beer.

"It does feel wrong, though," she said.

"What does?"

"Knowing that she must feel heartbroken, in her own way, and at the same time I feel so happy."

"It's okay to be both."

She nodded.

"What about you, Miami?"

"What about me?"

"Are you happy?"

I looked at Danielle, dancing on. "I am."

"Hold onto that. If I've learned anything apart from trust,

it's how fleeting these things are. Hold onto the good things. The days are long and the years are short and it's all gone before you know it."

I swirled my beer. In it I saw the face of my friend and mentor, Lenny Cox. He had seemed timeless when he was alive but he was taken before I ever had a chance to consider a life without him in it.

Cassandra set down her flute and rose and offered me her hand.

"May I have one more dance? Then I should go and see after Anastasia."

I stood. "It would be my honor."

We took the floor again, and Danielle and Ron nodded at us and swirled away. Ron dipped Danielle and she kicked her leg high.

"We don't need to do that." Cassandra smiled.

I agreed.

"You know what we do need?"

She shook her head. "What?"

"We need a wedding."

# CHAPTER THIRTY-SEVEN

The amphitheater was packed to the rafters and there weren't even any rafters. It was Pro Bowl Sunday and many of the passengers were tucked into bars and in the main theater where they were showing the game. But maybe it said something about the crowd on this cruise because most of the passengers were dressed up for a wedding.

Flowers rimmed the stage and the backdrop. Where they had come from I had no idea. Perhaps they kept a stock of flowers in the cool room for emergencies. Captain Sterling looked stunning in his white uniform. It was blinding and sharp and nearly stole the thunder from the bride.

Nearly but not quite. The bride wore a cream-colored dress that had come from one of the boutiques on board. She held a bouquet of carnations, and she was beaming. There's something about a woman's skin that has the capability to do that. It's more than makeup. It comes from within. I'd seen men gushing with pride as their bride came down the aisle and they sure looked happy, but they didn't radiate the way a woman did.

At least, not the way this woman did. She was radiant. The

afternoon was getting on and the sun was ahead of us as we made our way back to Florida, so the ocean glowed a deep blue backdrop behind the stage. I lifted my chin and took a deep breath. I looked good in my new tuxedo, courtesy of the cruise line. Their tailor did good work. It did what a fine tux should do. It made me both look good and fade into the background, all at the same time. I took another breath. I didn't want to mess up. I really didn't want to mess up.

There was no aisle, but there were a lot of stairs. From the back of the amphitheater looking down the steps it looked like the view a ski jumper has at the top of the run.

A brass ensemble was set up on the side of the stage, and they hit the first notes of the *Bridal Chorus*. I wondered how Wagner felt about saxophones and trumpets. I offered my arm and the bride wrapped hers around it and we took our first careful step. I wasn't sure if it qualified as a congregation when it was in an amphitheater big enough to hold the orca show at Sea World, but every head turned to us. It was the biggest crowd I had stood in front of since my final game of baseball.

All eyes tracked us as we made our way down the steps. We dropped into a time so that we stepped together, and I provided support, since I wasn't reckless enough to risk wearing high heels like the bride.

I thought for a moment the music might finish before we even got halfway down, but someone had thought ahead. The band took a collective breath, more for effect than anything and then broke into *Signed, Sealed, Delivered (I'm Yours)*. A cat in a sparkling blue jacket jumped up and hit the lyrics. He didn't look much like like Stevie Wonder but he sure could belt out that tune. I arched an eyebrow at the bride. She winked.

By the time we got to the bottom of the amphitheater, the crowd was clapping to the beat, bopping in place like it was a

Paul Simon concert. We made our way up to the stage as the band hit the final notes. I nodded to the captain. He smiled like a priest, which I knew he wasn't. When I had approached him the previous evening with my idea, he had been more receptive than expected. But it seemed I had done enough for him and his cruise line that he was willing to repay the favor. Plus I got the distinct impression he was an old romantic.

He had warned me that the old wives' tale about ship's captains being able to marry people at sea was just that, a tale. That had put a crinkle in my plan until he informed me that he was also a civil celebrant, and as such could perform the ceremony once we reached US waters and as long as the official documents were signed upon returning to dock in Palm Beach.

Captain Sterling nodded. I led the bride forward so she could drop my arm and take Ron's. She offered me another beaming smile. I nodded to Ron. He was beaming as well, but his radiance didn't come from within. Too many Florida summers had given him a permanent crimson tinge, but he sure did look happy with himself.

The captain stepped to the mic and gave the audience a moment to settle.

"Ladies and gentlemen, we are gathered on this fine vessel today to witness the marriage of Cassandra and Ronald. Who gives this woman to be married?"

It was a terribly old-fashioned thing to ask, especially, but not limited to the fact, that the Lady Cassandra sure as hell wasn't mine to give away. But she and Ron had asked it to be so, and I figured it was just a tradition that they weren't over.

"I do," I said.

The captain turned to Ron's side.

"And who gives this man to be married?"

The traditionalists were turning over in their graves now,

but I kind of liked it. If the woman was given away, why not the man?

Danielle looked breathtaking. She was wearing a long dress the color of the ocean as it moves from the reef to the deep, a regal blue that she and Cassandra had selected and that took my breath away. She smiled that half smile and looked at me.

"I do," she said.

I almost lost motor control of my legs, but I managed to back away and leave the bride and groom to their business.

The captain said some nice words. I think. I was watching Danielle. She was watching Cassandra and wiping tears from her eyes. Then the captain asked Danielle if she had hers, and me if I had mine.

We both stepped forward and handed over the symbols of a commitment to a life to be lived. It was a good start. There would be bad times. Life was no kind of perfect game. There were runs and hits and groundouts. Good and bad. Smiles and tears. But I hoped the smiles would outweigh the tears. I glanced down at the audience and saw Anastasia Connors. She sat rigid, chin held high. A Russian aristocrat. She might have just lost her husband or won the lottery. I couldn't say from her demeanor. I hoped she found a smile somewhere, even if it was only on the inside.

Danielle and I stepped back and our eyes connected. Hers were filled with tears of joy. I had no such tears. I was sure I was capable of them, but I rarely reacted to happiness that way.

"Ronald, do you take Cassandra to be yours, to cherish and hold from this moment, and for all moments to come?"

For a second I thought he wasn't going to be able to answer. Unlike me, Ron was a cryer. I could see a lump in his throat the size of a baseball. He nodded fervently but I didn't think that satisfied the legal side of the proceedings.

"I do," he managed to say. He took the silver necklace with

the small claw of a stone crab at the end of it and placed it around Cassandra's neck. They both already wore wedding rings that neither of them cared to remove. The memories held within those rings were neither sad nor to be forgotten. They both had pasts and both were just fine with that. Plus we'd all had enough of rings for a while. No one else they knew had stone crab claws.

"And, Cassandra, do you take Ronald to be yours, to cherish and hold from this moment, and for all moments to come?"

"I do." She hung the necklace around Ron's neck and lingered there for a moment.

I could see tears in the corners of her eyes too, but she was a different model of vehicle from Ron. They didn't seem to make her kind anymore. Stiff upper lip and all that. Having known her for a while, I couldn't help but think the world was poorer for it.

"Then I have the joyful responsibility to tell you that by the power vested in me by the great state of Florida, I pronounce you husband and wife."

The captain glanced at Cassandra and grinned.

"You may kiss the groom."

The band wasted no time in kicking up again. They broke into *Only You* by the Platters, which set the crowd off swaying and clapping as the happy couple wasted no time and got straight into their first dance. They had the spotlight for a verse and then the singer invited everyone to join in.

I took Danielle's hand and we hit the floor, joined by a number of other couples, friends of the newlyweds, offering congratulations. Other people just danced in the aisles. Crew brought around trays of champagne. I was confident that the free drinks weren't going to last all night, but I was happy to wait for later and pay for my own. Right at that moment, I had business to take care of, and I wasn't letting her go for all the bubbles in France.

We danced for an hour. The sun fell low and the champagne flowed and I didn't have any of it. I was intoxicated by something else. Life, perhaps. One of the good days. The ones you capture in photographs and keep in a drawer and then pull out one day when you're searching for socks or a passport or lip balm, and you look at it and you sit on your bed for an hour reliving every damned moment of it. It was one of those days.

And then BJ Baker ruined it.

I was off to the side watching Danielle dance with some guy who may have come over on the *Mayflower*. His back was as crooked as a mobster, but he was on his feet and giving it a red-hot go, so I had nothing further to say. BJ drifted over with a scotch in hand. As I watched him, I thought about how unfair life could be. BJ was as healthy as a Grand National winner while Adrian Pascal's brain was exiting out the back door. Same game. Same hits.

"Jones."

"What do you want, BJ?"

"Nice ceremony."

It had been a nice ceremony, and I supposed that was the kind of small talk people made at weddings. But there were a thousand people within a football field's worth of space. Why couldn't he small-talk with them?

"I heard you organized all this."

"A lot of people helped organize this."

For a moment we said nothing.

"You know, Jones, you get in my craw."

"There is a God."

"But I have to admit, you do know how to look after your people."

"They're called friends, BJ. It's what we do for each other."

"Whatever, Jones. Listen, that kid you were talking about yesterday. The one with the granddaddy in Pittsburgh."

"Yeah."

"You know his name?"

I did know his name. Army had told me.

"Why?"

"Just curious."

"Wagner," I said.

BJ turned from me and took out his cell phone and hit a contact.

"You might want to watch those ship-to-shore calls," I said. "They cost a bomb."

BJ shrugged. "Fox Sports gets the bill."

He connected the call and practically shouted down the phone.

"Milt. No, still here. Listen, I need you to fix something. We were supposed to do a cross to a hospital during the last Pittsburgh game. Yeah, the whiteout game. You know what hospital that was? No? Find out. I want to do a piece this week, for the Super Bowl coverage. Yeah, that's it. Human interest thing. There's an old guy in the hospital, he's a huge football fan, sick as a dog. His name?"

BJ glanced at me.

"Wagner."

"Yeah, Milt. Wagner. Set it up. I wanna meet the old guy, do some on-camera. I'll fly up tomorrow. Gotta be back for the game, Milt. Good. You'll make it happen? Good man. I'll see you tomorrow."

BJ hung up and put his phone away and then turned and looked at me.

"What do you think just happened?"

I shrugged. "You called your manager to set up a doctor's

appointment? I don't know, I wasn't really listening. None of my business."

"Damned right, none of your business."

"You okay, BJ? You look pale."

"I can still take you, Jones."

"I don't doubt it."

"Remember that," he said, and he turned and strode away.

"I'll remember, BJ," I said to myself. "You're still hard as nails. A real tough guy."

I watched the captain dancing with the bride, who he twirled into the groom's waiting arms. Then the captain retreated to his perch above us all. He also had business to attend to. Like docking a big ship without crashing the damned thing. And as his name implied, he did a sterling job of it. The music was still going when the lines were cast and the gangway dropped onto the dock.

The passengers and crew lined the decks as the newlyweds disembarked first. Rice rained down as if a tornado had hit a paddy field. The gulls swooped in. Ron and Cassandra waved to the cheering friends and strangers.

Then, a pair of US customs and border patrol officers strode up to the happy couple. Even in the midst of a wedding, they had a job to do. I thought they could give it a pass, but they generally weren't as carefree about these things as I was. To their credit though, once they gave the passports a stern look, both officers gave the bride a kiss, and one gave Ron a peck on the cheek for good measure.

The happy couple's chariot awaited. I had called Sal Mondavi. He knew a lot of people with a lot of fingers in a lot of pies. I had asked if he could rustle up a limo. He had said he could. He had lied. What he had rustled up was a horse-drawn carriage. Two white ponies nibbled at hay being offered by Muriel, who had clearly left the bar at Longboard Kelly's unattended. I figured she would be safe. All her best customers were here. She gave both Ron and Cassandra a big smooch. Mick stood beside her, furtively glancing at the border patrol like they were his sworn enemy, and offered hearty handshakes to the newlyweds.

The driver helped Ron and Cassandra up into the carriage and they waved like the king and queen of Florida as they rode away into what was now, quite literally, the sunset.

## CHAPTER THIRTY-EIGHT

THE HOUSE WAS QUIET. NO HAMMERING, NO SAWING. IT seemed Paco had packed up and gone home for the day. The place looked clean and new and smelled vaguely of sawdust. I dropped my bag in the living room and then went back out to retrieve Ron and Cassandra's luggage from the SUV. When I got there, I remembered that not everyone traveled as light as I did, so I left their cases in the back of the Cadillac. I'd drive them over tomorrow.

As I closed the door I heard Danielle say, "Um, MJ."

"Yep."

She was standing in the kitchen, looking at a piece of paper.

"What is it?"

"It's a note. From the contractor, Danny Rucci."

"What needs fixing now?"

"Nothing. He says Paco's done."

I stopped and looked around. Nothing looked different. But then, to my eye it had looked done for weeks.

"So what's next?"

"Nothing." She looked up from the note. "They're done. Finished. Completed."

"The house is done?"

Danielle smiled and nodded. She picked up the keys that Danny had left on the counter. I gave her my impressed face, and then turned in place. The house looked brand new, like a show home, as if a hurricane had never even contemplated roaring through. The recessed lights shone down on the wood-look tile. The white beadboard kitchen gleamed. It looked like a beautiful home.

It didn't look like my place at all.

"Danny says the last job to do is in the refrigerator."

"The fridge? Is it broken?"

Danielle opened the fridge and then turned around with a smile.

"What?"

She stood up, holding a cold bottle of champagne.

"He's a class act, that Danny," I said.

"Grab some glasses," she said. "Let's take it outside."

"Nothing to sit on, remember? The loungers got moved back into the garage while they did the patio."

"We'll sit on the grass then."

I said nothing. At such times I find it best just to do what I'm told. I grabbed two flutes from the kitchen and stepped out onto the patio.

Danielle stood looking at the two loungers and the small table between them. A card sat on one of them. Danielle picked it up.

"Welcome home, love Sal."

That was Sal. Danielle handed me the champagne bottle to uncork.

"You do know some very unusual people," she said.

I nodded as I tore the foil.

"But they sure do care about you."

"Us," I said, and I let the cork fly with a pop.

I poured two glasses, and we sat down on the loungers. They were pointed across the darkened Intracoastal waters, and the lights of Riviera Beach beyond. I handed Danielle a flute and held up mine. She looked into my eyes.

"What shall we toast?" I asked.

"Happy endings, and happy beginnings."

We touched glasses.

"You did good work today," she said. "You might have a future as a wedding planner."

"I had a lot of help. Porter knows everything that happens on that ship."

"You know when we were up on the stage with Ron and Cassandra? I thought for a second you might pull something."

"Pull something? Like a hamstring?"

"No, like a stunt. Like pulling out a ring and making it a double wedding."

"Are you sorry I didn't?"

"No. It was Ron and Cassandra's day. It's just the kind of thing you would do."

"Well, if it makes you feel any better, the thought did cross my mind."

"But it was Ron and Cassandra's moment."

I shrugged. "It was. But it wasn't really that."

She frowned, the little line appearing between her eyebrows. "What else?"

"I thought about how I was giving away Cassandra and you were giving away Ron."

"I liked that."

"I did too. But you have someone who should do that."

She sighed. "My dad?"

"Sure."

"He won't travel, or can't travel. I told you that."

"I know. But we can."

Her face went blank. I couldn't read it. It was one of those law enforcement faces that says they could lock you up for a thousand years or let you go, they wouldn't care either way.

"Are you—"

Her phone rang. She pulled it from her pocket and looked at the screen and then looked back at me. The blank face was gone. Now she wore every expression at once. She put the phone to her ear.

"Special Agent Castle," she said. It was maybe the third time I had heard her say it, and I liked the sound of it more every time.

Danielle listened. Then she nodded. Then she listened some more.

"Yes, sir," she said. "Thank you, sir. I'll see you tomorrow."

She hung up and placed the phone on the table between us, and then took a sip of her drink. I waited. She might have been pausing for effect but I didn't think so. That wasn't really her style. She was thinking. About what she had heard or what she was going to say, I couldn't be sure.

"That was the FDLE," she said.

I nodded. I had gotten that far all by myself.

"I've been assigned."

"Which office?"

She watched me as she spoke.

"The regional operations center in Miami."

I smiled.

"What?" she said.

"See, I told you. It doesn't matter what you do. You just can't get away from old Miami."

# READERS' CREW

Sign up to AJ Stewart's readers' crew for exclusive discounts, reads and occasional updates on new books. Visit ajstewartbooks.com/cc-reader.

**Danielle Castle Mysteries**

Little Packages

**Lenny & Lucas Adventures**

Temple of Gold

# IF YOU ENJOYED THIS BOOK

One of the most powerful things a reader can do is recommend a writer's work to a friend. So if you have friends you think will enjoy the capers of Miami Jones and his buddies, please tell them.

Your honest reviews help other readers discover Miami and his friends, so if you enjoyed this book and would like to spread the word, just take one minute to leave a short review. I'd be eternally grateful, and I hope new readers will be too.

## ACKNOWLEDGMENTS

Thanks to Constance Renfrew for the fabulous editorial advice. Wayne Leininger for the insight into cruising, and a whole lot more. Bob, James, Mike, and Carole for your feedback. All the betas.

All errors are mine, up to and including sneaking a bottle of scotch onto a cruise ship. That's trouble, right there.

# ABOUT THE AUTHOR

A.J. Stewart is the USA Today bestselling author of more than 20 novels, including the Miami Jones Florida mystery series and the John Flynn thriller series.

He currently resides in Los Angeles with his two favorite people, his wife and son.

AJ is working on a screenplay that he never plans to produce, but it gives him something to talk about at parties in LA.

*You can find AJ online at*
www.ajstewartbooks.com